WHITE NIGHTS
AND
THE GAMBLER

ROYAL

CLASSICS

White Nights and The Gambler
Dostoevsky, Fyodor 1821 – 1881
White Nights
First published in Russian in 1848
Translated by Constance Garnett
Garnett, Constance 1861 – 1946
Published by Macmillan in 1918
The Gambler
First published in Russian in 1866
Translated by Charles James Hogarth
Hogarth, Charles James 1869 – 1945
Published by J. M. Dent & Sons in 1915

Cover design by: A.R. Roumanis

Text set in Minion Pro. Chapter headings set in News Gothic Standard.

ISBN: 978-1-77878-432-3

FIRST EDITION / FIRST PRINTING

Many classics were originally published with inconsistent spellings of the same word, spelling errors, and printer errors. The text of our titles have been edited to give readers the best possible reading experience. Sometimes we can make mistakes, which is why we post "first edition" in all of our titles. This is a standard notice that is historically used by publishers. The above edition notice refers to our edition of this title. If changes are made to correct an error in the text, we will change the wording to "second edition." If we change printers but the text remains the same, the wording will change to "second printing."

LIBRARY AND ARCHIVES CANADA CATALOGUING IN PUBLICATION

Title: White nights ; and, The gambler / Fyodor Dostoevsky.
Other titles: Prose works. Selections. English | Gambler
Names: Dostoyevsky, Fyodor, 1821-1881, author. | Garnett, Constance, 1861-1946, translator. | Hogarth, C. J., translator. | Container of (expression): Dostoyevsky, Fyodor, 1821-1881. Belye nochi. English. | Container of (expression): Dostoyevsky, Fyodor, 1821-1881. Igrok. English.
Description: First edition. | Translations of: Belye nochi and Igrok. | "White Nights first published in Russian in 1848; translated by Constance Garnett; published by Macmillan in 1918"--Copyright page. | "The Gambler first published in Russian in 1866; translated by Charles James Hogarth; published by J.M. Dent & Sons in 1915"--Copyright page.
Identifiers: Canadiana 20240346262 | ISBN 9781778784323 (hardcover)
Subjects: LCGFT: Short stories. | LCGFT: Novels.
Classification: LCC PG3326 .A2 2024B | DDC 891.73/3—DC23

WHITE NIGHTS
AND
THE GAMBLER

FYODOR DOSTOEVSKY

VANCOUVER:
ROYAL CLASSICS
2024

CONTENTS

WHITE NIGHTS

A SENTIMENTAL STORY FROM THE DIARY OF A DREAMER

FIRST NIGHT

It was a wonderful night, such a night as is only possible when we are young, dear reader. The sky was so starry, so bright that, looking at it, one could not help asking oneself whether ill-humoured and capricious people could live under such a sky. That is a youthful question too, dear reader, very youthful, but may the Lord put it more frequently into your heart!... Speaking of capricious and ill-humoured people, I cannot help recalling my moral condition all that day. From early morning I had been oppressed by a strange despondency. It suddenly seemed to me that I was lonely, that every one was forsaking me and going away from me. Of course, any one is entitled to ask who "every one" was. For though I had been living almost eight years in Petersburg I had hardly an acquaintance. But what did I want with acquaintances? I was acquainted with all Petersburg as it was; that was why I felt as though they were all deserting me when all Petersburg packed up and went to its summer villa. I felt afraid of being left alone, and for three whole days I wandered about the town in profound dejection, not knowing what to do with myself. Whether I walked in the Nevsky, went to the Gardens or sauntered on the embankment, there was not one face of those I had been accustomed to meet at the same time and place all the year. They, of course, do not know me, but I know them. I know them intimately, I have almost made a study of their faces, and am delighted when they are gay, and downcast when they are under a cloud. I have almost struck up a friendship with one old man whom I meet every blessed day, at the same hour in Fontanka. Such a grave, pensive countenance; he is always whispering to himself and brandishing his left arm, while in his right hand he holds a long gnarled stick with a gold knob. He even notices me and takes a warm interest in me. If I happen not to be at a certain time in the saSme spot in Fontanka, I am certain he feels disappointed. That is how it is that we almost bow to each other, especially when we are both in good humour. The other day, when we had not seen each other for two days and met on the third, we were actually touching our hats, but, realizing in time, dropped our hands and passed each other with a look of interest.

I know the houses too. As I walk along they seem to run forward in the streets to look out at me from every window, and almost to say: "Good-morning! How do you do? I am quite well, thank God, and I am to have a new storey in May," or, "How are you? I am being redecorated to-morrow;" or, "I was almost burnt down and had such a fright," and so on. I have my favourites among them, some are dear friends; one of them intends to be treated by the architect this summer. I shall go every day on purpose to see that the operation is not a failure. God forbid! But I shall never forget an incident with a very pretty little house of a light pink colour. It was such a charming little brick house, it looked so hospitably at me, and so proudly at its ungainly neighbours, that my heart rejoiced whenever I happened to pass it. Suddenly last week I walked along the street, and when I looked at my friend I heard a plaintive, "They are painting me yellow!" The villains! The barbarians! They had spared nothing, neither columns, nor cornices, and my poor little friend was as yellow as a canary. It almost made me bilious. And to this day I have not had the courage to visit my poor disfigured friend, painted the colour of the Celestial Empire.

So now you understand, reader, in what sense I am acquainted with all Petersburg.

I have mentioned already that I had felt worried for three whole days before I guessed the cause of my uneasiness. And I felt ill at ease in the street – this one had gone and that one had gone, and what had become of the other? – and at home I did not feel like myself either. For two evenings I was puzzling my brains to think what was amiss in my corner; why I felt so uncomfortable in it. And in perplexity I scanned my grimy green walls, my ceiling covered with a spider's web, the growth of which Matrona has so successfully encouraged. I looked over all my furniture, examined every chair, wondering whether the trouble lay there (for if one chair is not standing in the same position as it stood the day before, I am not myself). I looked at the window, but it was all in vain ... I was not a bit the better for it! I even bethought me to send for Matrona, and was giving her some fatherly admonitions in regard to the spider's web and sluttishness in general; but she simply stared at me in amazement and went away without saying a word, so that the spider's web is comfortably hanging in its place to this day. I only at last this morning realized what was wrong. Aie! Why, they are giving me the slip and making off to their summer villas! Forgive the triviality of the expression, but I am in no mood for fine language ... for everything that had been in Petersburg had gone or was going away for the holidays; for every respectable gentleman of dignified appearance who took a cab was at once transformed, in my eyes, into a respectable head of a household who after his daily duties were over, was making his way to the bosom of his family, to the summer villa; for all the passers-by had now quite a peculiar air which seemed to say to every one they met: "We are only here for the moment, gentlemen, and in another two hours we shall be going off to the summer villa." If a window opened after delicate fingers, white as snow, had tapped upon the pane, and the head of a pretty girl was thrust out, calling to a street-seller with pots of flowers – at once on the spot I fancied that those flowers were being bought not simply in order to enjoy the flowers and the spring in stuffy town lodgings, but because they would all be very soon moving into the country and could take the flowers with them. What is more, I made such progress in my new peculiar sort of investigation that I could distinguish correctly from the mere air of each in what summer villa he was living. The inhabitants of Kamenny and Aptekarsky Islands or of the Peterhof Road were marked by the studied elegance of their manner, their fashionable summer suits, and the fine carriages in which they drove to town. Visitors to Pargolovo and places further away impressed one at first sight by their reasonable and dignified air; the tripper to Krestovsky Island could be recognized by his look of irrepressible gaiety. If I chanced to meet a long procession of waggoners walking lazily with the reins in their hands beside waggons loaded with regular mountains of furniture, tables, chairs, ottomans and sofas and domestic utensils of all sorts, frequently with a decrepit cook sitting on the top of it all, guarding her master's property as though it were the apple of her eye; or if I saw boats heavily loaded with household goods crawling along the Neva or Fontanka to the Black River or the Islands – the waggons and the boats were multiplied tenfold, a hundredfold, in my eyes. I fancied that everything was astir and moving, everything was going in regular caravans to the summer villas. It seemed as though Petersburg threatened to become a wilderness, so that at last I felt ashamed, mortified and sad that I had nowhere to go for the holidays and no reason to go away. I was ready to go away with every waggon, to drive off with every gentleman of respectable appearance who took a cab; but no one – absolutely no one – invited me; it seemed they had forgotten me, as though really I were a stranger to them!

I took long walks, succeeding, as I usually did, in quite forgetting where I was, when I suddenly found myself at the city gates. Instantly I felt lighthearted, and I passed the barrier and walked between cultivated fields and meadows, unconscious of fatigue, and feeling only all over as though a burden were falling off my soul. All the passers-by gave me such friendly looks that they seemed almost greeting me, they all seemed so pleased at something. They were all smoking cigars, every one of them. And I felt pleased as I never had before. It was as though I had suddenly found myself in Italy – so strong was the effect of nature upon a half-sick townsman like me, almost stifling between city walls.

There is something inexpressibly touching in nature round Petersburg, when at the approach of spring she puts forth all her might, all the powers bestowed on her by Heaven, when she breaks into leaf, decks herself out and spangles herself with flowers.... Somehow I cannot help being reminded of a frail, consumptive girl, at whom one sometimes looks with compassion, sometimes with sympathetic love, whom sometimes one simply does not notice; though suddenly in one instant she becomes, as though by chance, inexplicably lovely and exquisite, and, impressed and intoxicated, one cannot help asking oneself what power made those sad, pensive eyes flash with such fire? What summoned the blood to those pale, wan cheeks? What bathed with passion those soft features? What set that bosom heaving? What so suddenly called strength, life and beauty into the poor girl's face, making it gleam with such a smile, kindle with such bright, sparkling laughter? You look round, you seek for some one, you conjecture.... But the moment passes, and next day you meet, maybe, the same pensive and preoccupied look as before, the same pale face, the same meek and timid movements, and even signs of remorse, traces of a mortal anguish and regret for the fleeting distraction.... And you grieve that the momentary beauty has faded so soon never to return, that it flashed upon you so treacherously, so vainly, grieve because you had not even time to love her....

And yet my night was better than my day! This was how it happened.

I came back to the town very late, and it had struck ten as I was going towards my lodgings. My way lay along the canal embankment, where at that hour you never meet a soul. It is true that I live in a very remote part of the town. I walked along singing, for when I am happy I am always humming to myself like every happy man who has no friend or acquaintance with whom to share his joy. Suddenly I had a most unexpected adventure.

Leaning on the canal railing stood a woman with her elbows on the rail, she was apparently looking with great attention at the muddy water of the canal. She was wearing a very charming yellow hat and a jaunty little black mantle. "She's a girl, and I am sure she is dark," I thought. She did not seem to hear my footsteps, and did not even stir when I passed by with bated breath and loudly throbbing heart.

"Strange," I thought; "she must be deeply absorbed in something," and all at once I stopped as though petrified. I heard a muffled sob. Yes! I was not mistaken, the girl was crying, and a minute later I heard sob after sob. Good Heavens! My heart sank. And timid as I was with women, yet this was such a moment!... I turned, took a step towards her, and should certainly have pronounced the word "Madam!" if I had not known that that exclamation has been uttered a thousand times in every Russian society novel. It was only that reflection stopped me. But while I was seeking for a word, the girl came to herself, looked round, started, cast down her eyes and slipped by me along the embankment. I at once followed her; but she, divining this, left the embankment, crossed the road and walked along the pavement. I dared not cross the street after her. My heart was fluttering like a captured bird. All at once a chance came to my aid.

Along the same side of the pavement there suddenly came into sight, not far from the girl, a gentleman in evening dress, of dignified years, though by no means of dignified carriage; he was staggering and cautiously leaning against the wall. The girl flew straight as an arrow, with the timid haste one sees in all girls who do not want any one to volunteer to accompany them home at night, and no doubt the staggering gentleman would not have pursued her, if my good luck had not prompted him.

Suddenly, without a word to any one, the gentleman set off and flew full speed in pursuit of my unknown lady. She was racing like the wind, but the staggering gentleman was overtaking – overtook her. The girl uttered a shriek, and ... I bless my luck for the excellent knotted stick, which happened on that occasion to be in my right hand. In a flash I was on the other side of the street; in a flash the obtrusive gentleman had taken in the position, had grasped the irresistible argument, fallen back without a word, and only when we were very far away protested against my action in rather vigorous language. But his words hardly reached us.

"Give me your arm," I said to the girl. "And he won't dare to annoy us further."

She took my arm without a word, still trembling with excitement and terror. Oh, obtrusive gentleman! How I blessed you at that moment! I stole a glance at her, she was very charming and dark – I had guessed right.

On her black eyelashes there still glistened a tear – from her recent terror or her former grief – I don't know. But there was already a gleam of a smile on her lips. She too stole a glance at me, faintly blushed and looked down.

"There, you see; why did you drive me away? If I had been here, nothing would have happened...."

"But I did not know you; I thought that you too...."

"Why, do you know me now?"

"A little! Here, for instance, why are you trembling?"

"Oh, you are right at the first guess!" I answered, delighted that my girl had intelligence; that is never out of place in company with beauty. "Yes, from the first glance you have guessed the sort of man you have to do with. Precisely; I am shy with women, I am agitated, I don't deny it, as much so as you were a minute ago when that gentleman alarmed you. I am in some alarm now. It's like a dream, and I never guessed even in my sleep that I should ever talk with any woman."

"What? Really?..."

"Yes; if my arm trembles, it is because it has never been held by a pretty little hand like yours. I am a complete stranger to women; that is, I have never been used to them. You see, I am alone.... I don't even know how to talk to them. Here, I don't know now whether I have not said something silly to you! Tell me frankly; I assure you beforehand that I am not quick to take offence?..."

"No, nothing, nothing, quite the contrary. And if you insist on my speaking frankly, I will tell you that women like such timidity; and if you want to know more, I like it too, and I won't drive you away till I get home."

"You will make me," I said, breathless with delight, "lose my timidity, and then farewell to all my chances...."

"Chances! What chances – of what? That's not so nice."

"I beg your pardon, I am sorry, it was a slip of the tongue; but how can you expect one at such a moment to have no desire...."

"To be liked, eh?"

"Well, yes; but do, for goodness' sake, be kind. Think what I am! Here, I am twenty-six and I have never seen any one. How can I speak well, tactfully, and to the point? It will seem better to you when I have told you everything openly.... I don't know how to be silent when my heart is speaking. Well, never mind.... Believe me, not one woman, never, never! No acquaintance of any sort! And I do nothing but dream every day that at last I shall meet some one. Oh, if only you knew how often I have been in love in that way...."

"How? With whom?..."

"Why, with no one, with an ideal, with the one I dream of in my sleep. I make up regular romances in my dreams. Ah, you don't know me! It's true, of course, I have met two or three women, but what sort of women were they? They were all landladies, that.... But I shall make you laugh if I tell you that I have several times thought of speaking, just simply speaking, to some aristocratic lady in the street, when she is alone, I need hardly say; speaking to her, of course, timidly, respectfully, passionately; telling her that I am perishing in solitude, begging her not to send me away; saying that I have no chance of making the acquaintance of any woman; impressing upon her that it is a positive duty for a woman not to repulse so timid a prayer from such a luckless man as me. That, in fact, all I ask is, that she should say two or three sisterly words with sympathy, should not repulse me at first sight; should take me on trust and listen to what I say; should laugh at me if she likes, encourage me, say two words to me, only two words, even though we never meet again afterwards!... But you are laughing; however, that is why I am telling you...."

"Don't be vexed; I am only laughing at your being your own enemy, and if you had tried you would have succeeded, perhaps, even though it had been in the street; the simpler the better.... No kind-hearted woman, unless she were stupid or, still more, vexed about something at the moment, could bring herself to send you away without those two words which you ask for so timidly.... But what am I saying? Of course she would take you for a madman. I was judging by myself; I know a good deal about other people's lives."

"Oh, thank you," I cried; "you don't know what you have done for me now!"

"I am glad! I am glad! But tell me how did you find out that I was the sort of woman with whom ... well, whom you think worthy ... of attention and friendship ... in fact, not a landlady as you say? What made you decide to come up to me?"

"What made me?... But you were alone; that gentleman was too insolent; it's night. You must admit that it was a duty...."

"No, no; I mean before, on the other side – you know you meant to come up to me."

"On the other side? Really I don't know how to answer; I am afraid to.... Do you know I have been happy to-day? I walked along singing; I went out into the country; I have never had such happy moments. You ... perhaps it was my fancy.... Forgive me for referring to it; I fancied you were crying, and I ... could not bear to hear it ... it made my heart ache.... Oh, my goodness! Surely I might be troubled about you? Surely there was no harm in feeling brotherly compassion for you.... I beg your pardon, I said compassion.... Well, in short, surely you would not be offended at my involuntary impulse to go up to you?..."

"Stop, that's enough, don't talk of it," said the girl, looking down, and pressing my hand. "It's my fault for having spoken of it; but I am glad I was not mistaken in you.... But here I am home; I must go down this turning, it's two steps from here.... Good-bye, thank you!..."

"Surely ... surely you don't mean ... that we shall never see each other again?... Surely this is not to be the end?"

"You see," said the girl, laughing, "at first you only wanted two words, and now.... However, I won't say anything ... perhaps we shall meet...."

"I shall come here to-morrow," I said. "Oh, forgive me, I am already making demands...."

"Yes, you are not very patient ... you are almost insisting."

"Listen, listen!" I interrupted her. "Forgive me if I tell you something else.... I tell you what, I can't help coming here to-morrow, I am a dreamer; I have so little real life that I look upon such moments as this now, as so rare, that I cannot help going over such moments again in my dreams. I shall be dreaming of you all night, a whole week, a whole year. I shall certainly come here to-morrow, just here to this place, just at the same hour, and I shall be happy remembering to-day. This place is dear to me already. I have already two or three such places in Petersburg. I once shed tears over memories ... like you.... Who knows, perhaps you were weeping ten minutes ago over some memory.... But, forgive me, I have forgotten myself again; perhaps you have once been particularly happy here...."

"Very good," said the girl, "perhaps I will come here to-morrow, too, at ten o'clock. I see that I can't forbid you.... The fact is, I have to be here; don't imagine that I am making an appointment with you; I tell you beforehand that I have to be here on my own account. But ... well, I tell you straight out, I don't mind if you do come. To begin with, something unpleasant might happen as it did to-day, but never mind that.... In short, I should simply like to see you ... to say two words to you. Only, mind, you must not think the worse of me now! Don't think I make appointments so lightly.... I shouldn't make it except that.... But let that be my secret! Only a compact beforehand...."

"A compact! Speak, tell me, tell me all beforehand; I agree to anything, I am ready for anything," I cried delighted. "I answer for myself, I will be obedient, respectful ... you know me...."

"It's just because I do know you that I ask you to come to-morrow," said the girl, laughing. "I know you perfectly. But mind you will come on the condition, in the first place (only be good, do what I ask – you see, I speak frankly), you won't fall in love with me.... That's impossible, I assure you. I am ready for friendship; here's my hand.... But you mustn't fall in love with me, I beg you!"

"I swear," I cried, gripping her hand....

"Hush, don't swear, I know you are ready to flare up like gunpowder. Don't think ill of me for saying so. If only you knew.... I, too, have no one to whom I can say a word, whose advice I can ask. Of course, one does not look for an adviser in the street; but you are an exception. I know you as though we had been friends for twenty years.... You won't deceive me, will you?..."

"You will see ... the only thing is, I don't know how I am going to survive the next twenty-four hours."

"Sleep soundly. Good-night, and remember that I have trusted you already. But you exclaimed so nicely just now, 'Surely one can't be held responsible for every feeling, even for brotherly sympathy!' Do you know, that was so nicely said, that the idea struck me at once, that I might confide in you?"

"For God's sake do; but about what? What is it?"

"Wait till to-morrow. Meanwhile, let that be a secret. So much the better for you; it will give it a faint flavour of romance. Perhaps I will tell you to-morrow, and perhaps not.... I will talk to you a little more beforehand; we will get to know each other better...."

"Oh yes, I will tell you all about myself to-morrow! But what has happened? It is as though a miracle had befallen me.... My God, where am I? Come, tell me aren't you glad that you were not angry and did not drive me away at the first moment, as any other woman would have done? In two minutes you have made me happy for ever. Yes, happy; who knows, perhaps, you have reconciled me with myself, solved my doubts!... Perhaps such moments come upon me.... But there I will tell you all about it to-morrow, you shall know everything, everything...."

"Very well, I consent; you shall begin...."

"Agreed."

"Good-bye till to-morrow!"

"Till to-morrow!"

And we parted. I walked about all night; I could not make up my mind to go home. I was so happy.... To-morrow!

SECOND NIGHT

"Well, so you have survived!" she said, pressing both my hands.

"I've been here for the last two hours; you don't know what a state I have been in all day."

"I know, I know. But to business. Do you know why I have come? Not to talk nonsense, as I did yesterday. I tell you what, we must behave more sensibly in future. I thought a great deal about it last night."

"In what way – in what must we be more sensible? I am ready for my part; but, really, nothing more sensible has happened to me in my life than this, now."

"Really? In the first place, I beg you not to squeeze my hands so; secondly, I must tell you that I spent a long time thinking about you and feeling doubtful to-day."

"And how did it end?"

"How did it end? The upshot of it is that we must begin all over again, because the conclusion I reached to-day was that I don't know you at all; that I behaved like a baby last night, like a little girl; and, of course, the fact of it is, that it's my soft heart that is to blame – that is, I sang my own praises, as one always does in the end when one analyses one's conduct. And therefore to correct my mistake, I've made up my mind to find out all about you minutely. But as I have no one from whom I can find out anything, you must tell me everything fully yourself. Well, what sort of man are you? Come, make haste – begin – tell me your whole history."

"My history!" I cried in alarm. "My history! But who has told you I have a history? I have no history...."

"Then how have you lived, if you have no history?" she interrupted, laughing.

"Absolutely without any history! I have lived, as they say, keeping myself to myself, that is, utterly alone – alone, entirely alone. Do you know what it means to be alone?"

"But how alone? Do you mean you never saw any one?"

"Oh no, I see people, of course; but still I am alone."

"Why, do you never talk to any one?"

"Strictly speaking, with no one."

"Who are you then? Explain yourself! Stay, I guess: most likely, like me you have a grandmother. She is blind and will never let me go anywhere, so that I have almost forgotten how to talk; and when I played some pranks two years ago, and she saw there was no holding me in, she called me up and pinned my dress to hers, and ever since we sit like that for days together; she knits a stocking, though she's blind, and I sit beside her, sew or read aloud to her – it's such a queer habit, here for two years I've been pinned to her...."

"Good Heavens! what misery! But no, I haven't a grandmother like that."

"Well, if you haven't why do you sit at home?..."

"Listen, do you want to know the sort of man I am?"

"Yes, yes!"

"In the strict sense of the word?"

"In the very strictest sense of the word."

"Very well, I am a type!"

"Type, type! What sort of type?" cried the girl, laughing, as though she had not had a chance of laughing for a whole year. "Yes, it's very amusing talking to you. Look, here's a seat, let us sit down. No one is passing here, no one will hear us, and – begin your history. For it's no good your telling me, I know you have a history; only you are concealing it. To begin with, what is a type?"

"A type? A type is an original, it's an absurd person!" I said, infected by her childish laughter. "It's a character. Listen; do you know what is meant by a dreamer?"

"A dreamer! Indeed I should think I do know. I am a dreamer myself. Sometimes, as I sit by grandmother, all sorts of things come into my head. Why, when one begins dreaming one lets one's fancy run away with one – why, I marry a Chinese Prince!... Though sometimes it is a good thing to dream! But, goodness knows! Especially when one has something to think of apart from dreams," added the girl, this time rather seriously.

"Excellent! If you have been married to a Chinese Emperor, you will quite understand me. Come, listen.... But one minute, I don't know your name yet."

"At last! You have been in no hurry to think of it!"

"Oh, my goodness! It never entered my head, I felt quite happy as it was...."

"My name is Nastenka."

"Nastenka! And nothing else?"

"Nothing else! Why, is not that enough for you, you insatiable person?"

"Not enough? On the contrary, it's a great deal, a very great deal, Nastenka; you kind girl, if you are Nastenka for me from the first."

"Quite so! Well?"

"Well, listen, Nastenka, now for this absurd history."

I sat down beside her, assumed a pedantically serious attitude, and began as though reading from a manuscript: –

"There are, Nastenka, though you may not know it, strange nooks in Petersburg. It seems as though the same sun as shines for all Petersburg people does not peep into those spots, but some other different new one, bespoken expressly for those nooks, and it throws a different light on everything. In these corners, dear Nastenka, quite a different life is lived, quite unlike the life that is surging round us, but such as perhaps exists in some unknown realm, not among us in our serious, over-serious, time. Well, that life is a mixture of something purely fantastic, fervently ideal, with something (alas! Nastenka) dingily prosaic and ordinary, not to say incredibly vulgar."

"Foo! Good Heavens! What a preface! What do I hear?"

"Listen, Nastenka. (It seems to me I shall never be tired of calling you Nastenka.) Let me tell you that in these corners live strange people – dreamers. The dreamer – if you want an exact definition – is not a human being, but a creature of an intermediate sort. For the most part he settles in some inaccessible corner, as though hiding from the light of day; once he slips into his corner, he grows to it like a snail, or, anyway, he is in that respect very much like that remarkable creature, which is an animal and a house both at once, and is called a tortoise. Why do you suppose he is so fond of his four walls, which are invariably painted green, grimy, dismal and reeking unpardonably of tobacco smoke? Why is it that when this absurd gentleman is visited by one of his few acquaintances (and he ends by getting rid of all his friends), why does this absurd person meet him with such embarrassment, changing countenance and overcome with confusion, as though he had only just committed some crime within his four walls; as though he had been forging counterfeit notes, or as though he were writing verses to be sent to a journal with an anonymous letter, in which he states that the real poet is dead, and that his friend thinks it his sacred duty to publish his things? Why, tell me, Nastenka, why is it conversation is not easy between the two friends? Why is there no laughter? Why does no lively word fly from the tongue of the perplexed newcomer, who at other times may be very fond of laughter, lively words, conversation about the fair sex, and other cheerful subjects? And why does this friend, probably a new friend and on his first visit – for there will hardly be a second, and the friend will never come again – why is the friend himself so confused, so tongue-tied, in spite of his wit (if he has any), as he looks at the downcast face of his host, who in his turn becomes utterly helpless and at his wits' end after gigantic but fruitless efforts to smooth things over and enliven the conversation, to show his knowledge of polite society, to talk, too, of the fair sex, and by such humble endeavour, to please the poor man, who like a fish out of water has mistakenly come to visit him? Why does the gentleman, all at once remembering some very necessary business which never existed, suddenly seize his hat and hurriedly make off, snatching away his hand from the warm grip of his host, who was trying his utmost to show his regret and retrieve the lost position? Why does the friend chuckle as he goes out of the door, and swear never to come and see this queer creature again, though the queer creature is really a very good fellow, and at the same time he cannot refuse his imagination the little diversion of comparing the queer fellow's countenance during their conversation with the expression of an unhappy kitten treacherously captured, roughly handled, frightened and subjected to all sorts of indignities by children, till, utterly crestfallen, it hides away from them under a chair in the dark, and there must needs at its leisure bristle up, spit, and wash its insulted face with both paws, and long afterwards look angrily at life and nature, and even at the bits saved from the master's dinner for it by the sympathetic housekeeper?"

"Listen," interrupted Nastenka, who had listened to me all the time in amazement, opening her eyes and her little mouth. "Listen; I don't know in the least why it happened and why you ask me such absurd questions; all I know is, that this adventure must have happened word for word to you."

"Doubtless," I answered, with the gravest face.

"Well, since there is no doubt about it, go on," said Nastenka, "because I want very much to know how it will end."

"You want to know, Nastenka, what our hero, that is I – for the hero of the whole business was my humble self – did in his corner? You want to know why I lost my head and was upset for the whole day by the unexpected visit of a friend? You want to know why I was so startled, why I blushed when the door of my room was opened, why I was not able to entertain my visitor, and why I was crushed under the weight of my own hospitality?"

"Why, yes, yes," answered Nastenka, "that's the point. Listen. You describe it all splendidly, but couldn't you perhaps describe it a little less splendidly? You talk as though you were reading it out of a book."

"Nastenka," I answered in a stern and dignified voice, hardly able to keep from laughing, "dear Nastenka, I know I describe splendidly, but, excuse me, I don't know how else to do it. At this moment, dear Nastenka, at this moment I am like the spirit of King Solomon when, after lying a thousand years under seven seals in his urn, those seven seals were at last taken off. At this moment, Nastenka, when we have met at last after such a long separation – for I have known you for ages, Nastenka, because I have been looking for some one for ages, and that is a sign that it was you I was looking for, and it was ordained that we should meet now – at this moment a thousand valves have opened in my head, and I must let myself flow in a river of words, or I shall choke. And so I beg you not to interrupt me, Nastenka, but listen humbly and obediently, or I will be silent."

"No, no, no! Not at all. Go on! I won't say a word!"

"I will continue. There is, my friend Nastenka, one hour in my day which I like extremely. That is the hour when almost all business, work and duties are over, and every one is hurrying home to dinner, to lie down, to rest, and on the way all are cogitating on other more cheerful subjects relating to their evenings, their nights, and all the rest of their free time. At that hour our hero – for allow me, Nastenka, to tell my story in the third person, for one feels awfully ashamed to tell it in the first person – and so at that hour our hero, who had his work too, was pacing along after the others. But a strange feeling of pleasure set his pale, rather crumpled-looking face working. He looked not with indifference on the evening glow which was slowly fading on the cold Petersburg sky. When I say he looked, I am lying: he did not look at it, but saw it as it were without realizing, as though tired or preoccupied with some other more interesting subject, so that he could scarcely spare a glance for anything about him. He was pleased because till next day he was released from business irksome to him, and happy as a schoolboy let out from the class-room to his games and mischief. Take a look at him, Nastenka; you will see at once that joyful emotion has already had an effect on his weak nerves and morbidly excited fancy. You see he is thinking of something.... Of dinner, do you imagine? Of the evening? What is he looking at like that? Is it at that gentleman of dignified appearance who is bowing so picturesquely to the lady who rolls by in a carriage drawn by prancing horses? No, Nastenka; what are all those trivialities to him now! He is rich now with his *own individual* life; he has suddenly become rich, and it is not for nothing that the fading sunset sheds its farewell gleams so gaily before him, and calls forth a swarm of impressions from his warmed heart. Now he hardly notices the road, on which the tiniest details at other times would strike him. Now 'the Goddess of Fancy' (if you have read Zhukovsky, dear Nastenka) has already with fantastic hand spun her golden warp and begun weaving upon it patterns of marvellous magic life – and who knows, maybe, her fantastic hand has borne him to the seventh crystal heaven far from the excellent granite pavement on which he was walking his way? Try stopping him now, ask him suddenly where he is standing now, through what streets he is going – he will, probably remember nothing, neither where he is going nor where he is standing now, and flushing with vexation he will certainly tell some lie to save appearances. That is why he starts, almost cries out, and looks round with horror when a respectable old lady stops him politely in the middle of the pavement and asks her way. Frowning with vexation he strides on, scarcely noticing that more than one passer-by smiles and turns round to look after him, and that a little girl, moving out of his way in alarm, laughs aloud, gazing open-eyed at his broad meditative smile and gesticulations. But fancy catches up in its playful flight the old woman, the curious passers-by, and the laughing child, and the peasants spending their nights in their barges on Fontanka (our hero, let us suppose, is walking along the canal-side at that moment), and capriciously weaves every one and everything into the canvas like a fly in a spider's web. And it is only after the queer fellow has returned to his comfortable den with fresh stores for his mind to work on, has sat down and finished his dinner, that he comes to himself, when Matrona who waits upon him – always thoughtful and depressed – clears the table and gives him his pipe; he comes to himself then and recalls with surprise that he has dined, though he has absolutely no notion how it has happened. It has grown dark in the room; his soul is sad and empty; the whole kingdom of fancies drops to pieces about him, drops to pieces without a trace, without a sound, floats away like a dream, and he cannot himself remember what he was dreaming. But a vague sensation faintly stirs his heart and sets it aching, some new desire temptingly tickles and excites his fancy, and imperceptibly evokes a swarm of fresh phantoms. Stillness reigns in the little room; imagination is fostered by solitude and idleness; it is faintly smouldering, faintly simmering, like the water with which old Matrona is making her coffee as she moves quietly about in the kitchen close by. Now it breaks out spasmodically; and the book, picked up aimlessly and at random, drops from my dreamer's hand before he has reached the third page.

His imagination is again stirred and at work, and again a new world, a new fascinating life opens vistas before him. A fresh dream – fresh happiness! A fresh rush of delicate, voluptuous poison! What is real life to him! To his corrupted eyes we live, you and I, Nastenka, so torpidly, slowly, insipidly; in his eyes we are all so dissatisfied with our fate, so exhausted by our life! And, truly, see how at first sight everything is cold, morose, as though ill-humoured among us.... Poor things! thinks our dreamer. And it is no wonder that he thinks it! Look at these magic phantasms, which so enchantingly, so whimsically, so carelessly and freely group before him in such a magic, animated picture, in which the most prominent figure in the foreground is of course himself, our dreamer, in his precious person. See what varied adventures, what an endless swarm of ecstatic dreams. You ask, perhaps, what he is dreaming of. Why ask that? – why, of everything ... of the lot of the poet, first unrecognized, then crowned with laurels; of friendship with Hoffmann, St. Bartholomew's Night, of Diana Vernon, of playing the hero at the taking of Kazan by Ivan Vassilyevitch, of Clara Mowbray, of Effie Deans, of the council of the prelates and Huss before them, of the rising of the dead in 'Robert the Devil' (do you remember the music, it smells of the churchyard!), of Minna and Brenda, of the battle of Berezina, of the reading of a poem at Countess V. D.'s, of Danton, of Cleopatra *ei suoi amanti*, of a little house in Kolomna, of a little home of one's own and beside one a dear creature who listens to one on a winter's evening, opening her little mouth and eyes as you are listening to me now, my angel.... No, Nastenka, what is there, what is there for him, voluptuous sluggard, in this life, for which you and I have such a longing? He thinks that this is a poor pitiful life, not foreseeing that for him too, maybe, sometime the mournful hour may strike, when for one day of that pitiful life he would give all his years of phantasy, and would give them not only for joy and for happiness, but without caring to make distinctions in that hour of sadness, remorse and unchecked grief. But so far that threatening has not arrived – he desires nothing, because he is superior to all desire, because he has everything, because he is satiated, because he is the artist of his own life, and creates it for himself every hour to suit his latest whim. And you know this fantastic world of fairyland is so easily, so naturally created! As though it were not a delusion! Indeed, he is ready to believe at some moments that all this life is not suggested by feeling, is not mirage, not a delusion of the imagination, but that it is concrete, real, substantial! Why is it, Nastenka, why is it at such moments one holds one's breath? Why, by what sorcery, through what incomprehensible caprice, is the pulse quickened, does a tear start from the dreamer's eye, while his pale moist cheeks glow, while his whole being is suffused with an inexpressible sense of consolation? Why is it that whole sleepless nights pass like a flash in inexhaustible gladness and happiness, and when the dawn gleams rosy at the window and daybreak floods the gloomy room with uncertain, fantastic light, as in Petersburg, our dreamer, worn out and exhausted, flings himself on his bed and drops asleep with thrills of delight in his morbidly overwrought spirit, and with a weary sweet ache in his heart? Yes, Nastenka, one deceives oneself and unconsciously believes that real true passion is stirring one's soul; one unconsciously believes that there is something living, tangible in one's immaterial dreams! And is it delusion? Here love, for instance, is bound up with all its fathomless joy, all its torturing agonies in his bosom.... Only look at him, and you will be convinced! Would you believe, looking at him, dear Nastenka, that he has never known her whom he loves in his ecstatic dreams? Can it be that he has only seen her in seductive visions, and that this passion has been nothing but a dream? Surely they must have spent years hand in hand together – alone the two of them, casting off all the world and each uniting his or her life with the other's? Surely when the hour of parting came she must have lain sobbing and grieving on his bosom, heedless of the tempest raging under the sullen sky, heedless of the wind which snatches and bears away the tears from her black eyelashes? Can all of that have been a dream – and that garden, dejected, forsaken, run wild, with its little moss-grown paths, solitary, gloomy, where they used to walk so happily together, where they hoped, grieved, loved, loved each other so long, "so long and so fondly?" And that queer ancestral house where she spent so many years lonely and sad with her morose old husband, always silent and splenetic, who frightened them, while timid as children they hid their love from each other? What torments they suffered, what agonies of terror, how innocent, how pure was their love, and how (I need hardly say, Nastenka) malicious people were! And, good Heavens! surely he met her afterwards, far from their native shores, under alien skies, in the hot south in the divinely eternal city, in the dazzling splendour of the ball to the crash of music, in a *palazzo* (it must be in a *palazzo*), drowned in a sea of lights, on the balcony, wreathed in myrtle and roses, where, recognizing him, she hurriedly removes her mask and whispering, 'I am free,' flings herself trembling into his arms, and with a cry of rapture, clinging to one another, in one instant they forget their sorrow and their parting and all their agonies, and the gloomy house and the old man and the dismal garden in that distant land, and the seat on which with a last passionate kiss she tore herself away from his arms numb with anguish and despair.... Oh, Nastenka, you must admit that one would start, betray confusion, and blush like a schoolboy who has just stuffed in his pocket an apple stolen from a neighbour's garden, when your uninvited visitor, some stalwart, lanky fellow, a festive soul fond of a joke, opens your door and shouts out as though nothing were happening: 'My dear boy, I have this minute come from Pavlovsk.' My goodness! the old count is dead, unutterable happiness is close at hand – and people arrive from Pavlovsk!"

Finishing my pathetic appeal, I paused pathetically. I remembered that I had an intense desire to force myself to laugh, for I was already feeling that a malignant demon was stirring within me, that there was a lump in my throat, that my chin was beginning to twitch, and that my eyes were growing more and more moist.

I expected Nastenka, who listened to me opening her clever eyes, would break into her childish, irrepressible laugh; and I was already regretting that I had gone so far, that I had unnecessarily described what had long been simmering in my heart, about which I could speak as though from a written account of it, because I had long ago passed judgment on myself and now could not resist reading it, making my confession, without expecting to be understood; but to my surprise she was silent, waiting a little, then she faintly pressed my hand and with timid sympathy asked –

"Surely you haven't lived like that all your life?"

"All my life, Nastenka," I answered; "all my life, and it seems to me I shall go on so to the end."

"No, that won't do," she said uneasily, "that must not be; and so, maybe, I shall spend all my life beside grandmother. Do you know, it is not at all good to live like that?"

"I know, Nastenka, I know!" I cried, unable to restrain my feelings longer. "And I realize now, more than ever, that I have lost all my best years! And now I know it and feel it more painfully from recognizing that God has sent me you, my good angel, to tell me that and show it. Now that I sit beside you and talk to you it is strange for me to think of the future, for in the future – there is loneliness again, again this musty, useless life; and what shall I have to dream of when I have been so happy in reality beside you! Oh, may you be blessed, dear girl, for not having repulsed me at first, for enabling me to say that for two evenings, at least, I have lived."

"Oh, no, no!" cried Nastenka and tears glistened in her eyes. "No, it mustn't be so any more; we must not part like that! what are two evenings?"

"Oh, Nastenka, Nastenka! Do you know how far you have reconciled me to myself? Do you know now that I shall not think so ill of myself, as I have at some moments? Do you know that, maybe, I shall leave off grieving over the crime and sin of my life? for such a life is a crime and a sin. And do not imagine that I have been exaggerating anything – for goodness' sake don't think that, Nastenka: for at times such misery comes over me, such misery.... Because it begins to seem to me at such times that I am incapable of beginning a life in real life, because it has seemed to me that I have lost all touch, all instinct for the actual, the real; because at last I have cursed myself; because after my fantastic nights I have moments of returning sobriety, which are awful! Meanwhile, you hear the whirl and roar of the crowd in the vortex of life around you; you hear, you see, men living in reality; you see that life for them is not forbidden, that their life does not float away like a dream, like a vision; that their life is being eternally renewed, eternally youthful, and not one hour of it is the same as another; while fancy is so spiritless, monotonous to vulgarity and easily scared, the slave of shadows, of the idea, the slave of the first cloud that shrouds the sun, and overcasts with depression the true Petersburg heart so devoted to the sun – and what is fancy in depression! One feels that this *inexhaustible* fancy is weary at last and worn out with continual exercise, because one is growing into manhood, outgrowing one's old ideals: they are being shattered into fragments, into dust; if there is no other life one must build one up from the fragments. And meanwhile the soul longs and craves for something else! And in vain the dreamer rakes over his old dreams, as though seeking a spark among the embers, to fan them into flame, to warm his chilled heart by the rekindled fire, and to rouse up in it again all that was so sweet, that touched his heart, that set his blood boiling, drew tears from his eyes, and so luxuriously deceived him! Do you know, Nastenka, the point I have reached? Do you know that I am forced now to celebrate the anniversary of my own sensations, the anniversary of that which was once so sweet, which never existed in reality – for this anniversary is kept in memory of those same foolish, shadowy dreams – and to do this because those foolish dreams are no more, because I have nothing to earn them with; you know even dreams do not come for nothing! Do you know that I love now to recall and visit at certain dates the places where I was once happy in my own way? I love to build up my present in harmony with the irrevocable past, and I often wander like a shadow, aimless, sad and dejected, about the streets and crooked lanes of Petersburg. What memories they are! To remember, for instance, that here just a year ago, just at this time, at this hour, on this pavement,

I wandered just as lonely, just as dejected as to-day. And one remembers that then one's dreams were sad, and though the past was no better one feels as though it had somehow been better, and that life was more peaceful, that one was free from the black thoughts that haunt one now; that one was free from the gnawing of conscience – the gloomy, sullen gnawing which now gives me no rest by day or by night. And one asks oneself where are one's dreams. And one shakes one's head and says how rapidly the years fly by! And again one asks oneself what has one done with one's years. Where have you buried your best days? Have you lived or not? Look, one says to oneself, look how cold the world is growing. Some more years will pass, and after them will come gloomy solitude; then will come old age trembling on its crutch, and after it misery and desolation. Your fantastic world will grow pale, your dreams will fade and die and will fall like the yellow leaves from the trees.... Oh, Nastenka! you know it will be sad to be left alone, utterly alone, and to have not even anything to regret – nothing, absolutely nothing ... for all that you have lost, all that, all was nothing, stupid, simple nullity, there has been nothing but dreams!"

"Come, don't work on my feelings any more," said Nastenka, wiping away a tear which was trickling down her cheek. "Now it's over! Now we shall be two together. Now, whatever happens to me, we will never part. Listen; I am a simple girl, I have not had much education, though grandmother did get a teacher for me, but truly I understand you, for all that you have described I have been through myself, when grandmother pinned me to her dress. Of course, I should not have described it so well as you have; I am not educated," she added timidly, for she was still feeling a sort of respect for my pathetic eloquence and lofty style; "but I am very glad that you have been quite open with me. Now I know you thoroughly, all of you. And do you know what? I want to tell you my history too, all without concealment, and after that you must give me advice. You are a very clever man; will you promise to give me advice?"

"Ah, Nastenka," I cried, "though I have never given advice, still less sensible advice, yet I see now that if we always go on like this that it will be very sensible, and that each of us will give the other a great deal of sensible advice! Well, my pretty Nastenka, what sort of advice do you want? Tell me frankly; at this moment I am so gay and happy, so bold and sensible, that it won't be difficult for me to find words."

"No, no!" Nastenka interrupted, laughing. "I don't only want sensible advice, I want warm brotherly advice, as though you had been fond of me all your life!"

"Agreed, Nastenka, agreed!" I cried delighted; "and if I had been fond of you for twenty years, I couldn't have been fonder of you than I am now."

"Your hand," said Nastenka.

"Here it is," said I, giving her my hand.

"And so let us begin my history!"

NASTENKA'S HISTORY

"Half my story you know already – that is, you know that I have an old grandmother...."

"If the other half is as brief as that ..." I interrupted, laughing.

"Be quiet and listen. First of all you must agree not to interrupt me, or else, perhaps I shall get in a muddle! Come, listen quietly.

"I have an old grandmother. I came into her hands when I was quite a little girl, for my father and mother are dead. It must be supposed that grandmother was once richer, for now she recalls better days. She taught me French, and then got a teacher for me. When I was fifteen (and now I am seventeen) we gave up having lessons. It was at that time that I got into mischief; what I did I won't tell you; it's enough to say that it wasn't very important. But grandmother called me to her one morning and said that as she was blind she could not look after me; she took a pin and pinned my dress to hers, and said that we should sit like that for the rest of our lives if, of course, I did not become a better girl. In fact, at first it was impossible to get away from her: I had to work, to read and to study all beside grandmother. I tried to deceive her once, and persuaded Fekla to sit in my place. Fekla is our charwoman, she is deaf. Fekla sat there instead of me; grandmother was asleep in her armchair at the time, and I went off to see a friend close by. Well, it ended in trouble. Grandmother woke up while I was out, and asked some questions; she thought I was still sitting quietly in my place. Fekla saw that grandmother was asking her something, but could not tell what it was; she wondered what to do, undid the pin and ran away...."

At this point Nastenka stopped and began laughing. I laughed with her. She left off at once.

"I tell you what, don't you laugh at grandmother. I laugh because it's funny.... What can I do, since grandmother is like that; but yet I am fond of her in a way. Oh, well, I did catch it that time. I had to sit down in my place at once, and after that I was not allowed to stir.

"Oh, I forgot to tell you that our house belongs to us, that is to grandmother; it is a little wooden house with three windows as old as grandmother herself, with a little upper storey; well, there moved into our upper storey a new lodger."

"Then you had an old lodger," I observed casually.

"Yes, of course," answered Nastenka, "and one who knew how to hold his tongue better than you do. In fact, he hardly ever used his tongue at all. He was a dumb, blind, lame, dried-up little old man, so that at last he could not go on living, he died; so then we had to find a new lodger, for we could not live without a lodger – the rent, together with grandmother's pension, is almost all we have. But the new lodger, as luck would have it, was a young man, a stranger not of these parts. As he did not haggle over the rent, grandmother accepted him, and only afterwards she asked me: 'Tell me, Nastenka, what is our lodger like – is he young or old?' I did not want to lie, so I told grandmother that he wasn't exactly young and that he wasn't old.

"'And is he pleasant looking?' asked grandmother.

"Again I did not want to tell a lie: 'Yes, he is pleasant looking, grandmother,' I said. And grandmother said: 'Oh, what a nuisance, what a nuisance! I tell you this, grandchild, that you may not be looking after him. What times these are! Why a paltry lodger like this, and he must be pleasant looking too; it was very different in the old days!'"

"Grandmother was always regretting the old days – she was younger in old days, and the sun was warmer in old days, and cream did not turn so sour in old days – it was always the old days! I would sit still and hold my tongue and think to myself: why did grandmother suggest it to me? Why did she ask whether the lodger was young and good-looking? But that was all, I just thought it, began counting my stitches again, went on knitting my stocking, and forgot all about it.

"Well, one morning the lodger came in to see us; he asked about a promise to paper his rooms. One thing led to another. Grandmother was talkative, and she said: 'Go, Nastenka, into my bedroom and bring me my reckoner.' I jumped up at once; I blushed all over, I don't know why, and forgot I was sitting pinned to grandmother; instead of quietly undoing the pin, so that the lodger should not see – I jumped so that grandmother's chair moved. When I saw that the lodger knew all about me now, I blushed, stood still as though I had been shot, and suddenly began to cry – I felt so ashamed and miserable at that minute, that I didn't know where to look! Grandmother called out, 'What are you waiting for?' and

I went on worse than ever. When the lodger saw, saw that I was ashamed on his account, he bowed and went away at once!

"After that I felt ready to die at the least sound in the passage. 'It's the lodger,' I kept thinking; I stealthily undid the pin in case. But it always turned out not to be, he never came. A fortnight passed; the lodger sent word through Fyokla that he had a great number of French books, and that they were all good books that I might read, so would not grandmother like me to read them that I might not be dull? Grandmother agreed with gratitude, but kept asking if they were moral books, for if the books were immoral it would be out of the question, one would learn evil from them."

"'And what should I learn, grandmother? What is there written in them?'

"'Ah,' she said, 'what's described in them, is how young men seduce virtuous girls; how, on the excuse that they want to marry them, they carry them off from their parents' houses; how afterwards they leave these unhappy girls to their fate, and they perish in the most pitiful way. I read a great many books,' said grandmother, 'and it is all so well described that one sits up all night and reads them on the sly. So mind you don't read them, Nastenka,' said she. 'What books has he sent?'

"'They are all Walter Scott's novels, grandmother.'

"'Walter Scott's novels! But stay, isn't there some trick about it? Look, hasn't he stuck a love-letter among them?'

"'No, grandmother,' I said, 'there isn't a love-letter.'

"'But look under the binding; they sometimes stuff it under the bindings, the rascals!'

"'No, grandmother, there is nothing under the binding.'

"'Well, that's all right.'

"So we began reading Walter Scott, and in a month or so we had read almost half. Then he sent us more and more. He sent us Pushkin, too; so that at last I could not get on without a book and left off dreaming of how fine it would be to marry a Chinese Prince.

"That's how things were when I chanced one day to meet our lodger on the stairs. Grandmother had sent me to fetch something. He stopped, I blushed and he blushed; he laughed, though, said good-morning to me, asked after grandmother, and said, 'Well, have you read the books?' I answered that I had. 'Which did you like best?' he asked. I said, 'Ivanhoe, and Pushkin best of all,' and so our talk ended for that time.

"A week later I met him again on the stairs. That time grandmother had not sent me, I wanted to get something for myself. It was past two, and the lodger used to come home at that time. 'Good-afternoon,' said he. I said good-afternoon, too.

"'Aren't you dull,' he said, 'sitting all day with your grandmother?'

"When he asked that, I blushed, I don't know why; I felt ashamed, and again I felt offended – I suppose because other people had begun to ask me about that. I wanted to go away without answering, but I hadn't the strength.

"'Listen,' he said, 'you are a good girl. Excuse my speaking to you like that, but I assure you that I wish for your welfare quite as much as your grandmother. Have you no friends that you could go and visit?'

"I told him I hadn't any, that I had had no friend but Mashenka, and she had gone away to Pskov.

"'Listen,' he said, 'would you like to go to the theatre with me?'

"'To the theatre. What about grandmother?'

"'But you must go without your grandmother's knowing it,' he said.

"'No,' I said, 'I don't want to deceive grandmother. Good-bye.'

"'Well, good-bye,' he answered, and said nothing more.

"Only after dinner he came to see us; sat a long time talking to grandmother; asked her whether she ever went out anywhere, whether she had acquaintances, and suddenly said: 'I have taken a box at the opera for this evening; they are giving *The Barber of Seville*. My friends meant to go, but afterwards refused, so the ticket is left on my hands.' '*The Barber of Seville*,' cried grandmother; 'why, the same they used to act in old days?'

"'Yes, it's the same barber,' he said, and glanced at me. I saw what it meant and turned crimson, and my heart began throbbing with suspense.

"'To be sure, I know it,' said grandmother; 'why, I took the part of Rosina myself in old days, at a private performance!'

"'So wouldn't you like to go to-day?' said the lodger. 'Or my ticket will be wasted.'

"'By all means let us go,' said grandmother; why shouldn't we? And my Nastenka here has never been to the theatre.'

"My goodness, what joy! We got ready at once, put on our best clothes, and set off. Though grandmother was blind, still she wanted to hear the music; besides, she is a kind old soul, what she cared most for was to amuse me, we should never have gone of ourselves.

"What my impressions of *The Barber of Seville* were I won't tell you; but all that evening our lodger looked at me so nicely, talked so nicely, that I saw at once that he had meant to test me in the morning when he proposed that I should go with him alone. Well, it was joy! I went to bed so proud, so gay, my heart beat so that I was a little feverish, and all night I was raving about *The Barber of Seville*.

"I expected that he would come and see us more and more often after that, but it wasn't so at all. He almost entirely gave up coming. He would just come in about once a month, and then only to invite us to the theatre. We went twice again. Only I wasn't at all pleased with that; I saw that he was simply sorry for me because I was so hardly treated by grandmother, and that was all. As time went on, I grew more and more restless, I couldn't sit still, I couldn't read, I couldn't work; sometimes I laughed and did something to annoy grandmother, at another time I would cry. At last I grew thin and was very nearly ill. The opera season was over, and our lodger had quite given up coming to see us; whenever we met – always on the same staircase, of course – he would bow so silently, so gravely, as though he did not want to speak, and go down to the front door, while I went on standing in the middle of the stairs, as red as a cherry, for all the blood rushed to my head at the sight of him.

"Now the end is near. Just a year ago, in May, the lodger came to us and said to grandmother that he had finished his business here, and that he must go back to Moscow for a year. When I heard that, I sank into a chair half dead; grandmother did not notice anything; and having informed us that he should be leaving us, he bowed and went away.

"What was I to do? I thought and thought and fretted and fretted, and at last I made up my mind. Next day he was to go away, and I made up my mind to end it all that evening when grandmother went to bed. And so it happened. I made up all my clothes in a parcel – all the linen I needed – and with the parcel in my hand, more dead than alive, went upstairs to our lodger. I believe I must have stayed an hour on the staircase. When I opened his door he cried out as he looked at me. He thought I was a ghost, and rushed to give me some water, for I could hardly stand up. My heart beat so violently that my head ached, and I did not know what I was doing. When I recovered I began by laying my parcel on his bed, sat down beside it, hid my face in my hands and went into floods of tears. I think he understood it all at once, and looked at me so sadly that my heart was torn.

"'Listen,' he began, 'listen, Nastenka, I can't do anything; I am a poor man, for I have nothing, not even a decent berth. How could we live, if I were to marry you?'

"We talked a long time; but at last I got quite frantic, I said I could not go on living with grandmother, that I should run away from her, that I did not want to be pinned to her, and that I would go to Moscow if he liked, because I could not live without him. Shame and pride and love were all clamouring in me at once, and I fell on the bed almost in convulsions, I was so afraid of a refusal.

"He sat for some minutes in silence, then got up, came up to me and took me by the hand.

"'Listen, my dear good Nastenka, listen; I swear to you that if I am ever in a position to marry, you shall make my happiness. I assure you that now you are the only one who could make me happy. Listen, I am going to Moscow and shall be there just a year; I hope to establish my position. When I come back, if you still love me, I swear that we will be happy. Now it is impossible, I am not able, I have not the right to promise anything. Well, I repeat, if it is not within a year it will certainly be some time; that is, of course, if you do not prefer any one else, for I cannot and dare not bind you by any sort of promise.'

"That was what he said to me, and next day he went away. We agreed together not to say a word to grandmother: that was his wish. Well, my history is nearly finished now. Just a year has past. He has arrived; he has been here three days, and, and

"And what?" I cried, impatient to hear the end.

"And up to now has not shown himself!" answered Nastenka, as though screwing up all her courage. "There's no sign or sound of him."

Here she stopped, paused for a minute, bent her head, and covering her face with her hands broke into such sobs that it sent a pang to my heart to hear them. I had not in the least expected such a *dénouement*.

"Nastenka," I began timidly in an ingratiating voice, "Nastenka! For goodness' sake don't cry! How do you know? Perhaps he is not here yet...."

"He is, he is," Nastenka repeated. "He is here, and I know it. We *made an agreement* at the time, that evening, before he went away: when we said all that I have told you, and had come to an understanding, then we came out here for a walk on this embankment. It was ten o'clock; we sat on this seat. I was not crying then; it was sweet to me to hear what he said.... And he said that he would come to us directly he arrived, and if I did not refuse him, then we would tell grandmother about it all. Now he is here, I know it, and yet he does not come!"

And again she burst into tears.

"Good God, can I do nothing to help you in your sorrow?" I cried jumping up from the seat in utter despair. "Tell me, Nastenka, wouldn't it be possible for me to go to him?"

"Would that be possible?" she asked suddenly, raising her head.

"No, of course not," I said pulling myself up; "but I tell you what, write a letter."

"No, that's impossible, I can't do that," she answered with decision, bending her head and not looking at me.

"How impossible – why is it impossible?" I went on, clinging to my idea. "But, Nastenka, it depends what sort of letter; there are letters and letters and.... Ah, Nastenka, I am right; trust to me, trust to me, I will not give you bad advice. It can all be arranged! You took the first step – why not now?"

"I can't. I can't! It would seem as though I were forcing myself on him...."

"Ah, my good little Nastenka," I said, hardly able to conceal a smile; "no, no, you have a right to, in fact, because he made you a promise. Besides, I can see from everything that he is a man of delicate feeling; that he behaved very well," I went on, more and more carried away by the logic of my own arguments and convictions. "How did he behave? He bound himself by a promise: he said that if he married at all he would marry no one but you; he gave you full liberty to refuse him at once.... Under such circumstances you may take the first step; you have the right; you are in the privileged position – if, for instance, you wanted to free him from his promise...."

"Listen; how would you write?"

"Write what?"

"This letter."

"I tell you how I would write: 'Dear Sir.'..."

"Must I really begin like that, 'Dear Sir'?"

"You certainly must! Though, after all, I don't know, I imagine...."

"Well, well, what next?"

"'Dear Sir, – I must apologize for – – ' But, no, there's no need to apologize; the fact itself justifies everything. Write simply: –

"'I am writing to you. Forgive me my impatience; but I have been happy for a whole year in hope; am I to blame for being unable to endure a day of doubt now? Now that you have come, perhaps you have changed your mind. If so, this letter is to tell you that I do not repine, nor blame you. I do not blame you because I have no power over your heart, such is my fate!

"'You are an honourable man. You will not smile or be vexed at these impatient lines. Remember they are written by a poor girl; that she is alone; that she has no one to direct her, no one to advise her, and that she herself could never control her heart. But forgive me that a doubt has stolen – if only for one instant – into my heart. You are not capable of insulting, even in thought, her who so loved and so loves you.'"

"Yes, yes; that's exactly what I was thinking!" cried Nastenka, and her eyes beamed with delight. "Oh, you have solved my difficulties: God has sent you to me! Thank you, thank you!"

"What for? What for? For God's sending me?" I answered, looking delighted at her joyful little face. "Why, yes; for that too."

"Ah, Nastenka! Why, one thanks some people for being alive at the same time with one; I thank you for having met me, for my being able to remember you all my life!"

"Well, enough, enough! But now I tell you what, listen: we made an agreement then that as soon as he arrived he would let me know, by leaving a letter with some good simple people of my acquaintance who know nothing about it; or, if it were impossible to write a letter to me, for a letter does not always tell everything, he would be here at ten o'clock on the day he arrived, where we had arranged to meet. I know he has arrived already; but now it's the third day, and there's no sign of him and no letter. It's impossible for me to get away from grandmother in the morning. Give my letter to-morrow to those kind people I spoke to you about: they will send it on to him, and if there is an answer you bring it to-morrow at ten o'clock."

"But the letter, the letter! You see, you must write the letter first! So perhaps it must all be the day after to-morrow."

"The letter ..." said Nastenka, a little confused, "the letter ... but...."

But she did not finish. At first she turned her little face away from me, flushed like a rose, and suddenly I felt in my hand a letter which had evidently been written long before, all ready and sealed up. A familiar sweet and charming reminiscence floated through my mind.

"R, o – Ro; s, i – si; n, a – na," I began.

"Rosina!" we both hummed together; I almost embracing her with delight, while she blushed as only she could blush, and laughed through the tears which gleamed like pearls on her black eyelashes.

"Come, enough, enough! Good-bye now," she said speaking rapidly. "Here is the letter, here is the address to which you are to take it. Good-bye, till we meet again! Till to-morrow!"

She pressed both my hands warmly, nodded her head, and flew like an arrow down her side street. I stood still for a long time following her with my eyes.

"Till to-morrow! till to-morrow!" was ringing in my ears as she vanished from my sight.

THIRD NIGHT

To-day was a gloomy, rainy day without a glimmer of sunlight, like the old age before me. I am oppressed by such strange thoughts, such gloomy sensations; questions still so obscure to me are crowding into my brain – and I seem to have neither power nor will to settle them. It's not for me to settle all this!

To-day we shall not meet. Yesterday, when we said good-bye, the clouds began gathering over the sky and a mist rose. I said that to-morrow it would be a bad day; she made no answer, she did not want to speak against her wishes; for her that day was bright and clear, not one cloud should obscure her happiness.

"If it rains we shall not see each other," she said, "I shall not come."

I thought that she would not notice to-day's rain, and yet she has not come.

Yesterday was our third interview, our third white night....

But how fine joy and happiness makes any one! How brimming over with love the heart is! One seems longing to pour out one's whole heart; one wants everything to be gay, everything to be laughing. And how infectious that joy is! There was such a softness in her words, such a kindly feeling in her heart towards me yesterday.... How solicitous and friendly she was; how tenderly she tried to give me courage! Oh, the coquetry of happiness! While I ... I took it all for the genuine thing, I thought that she....

But, my God, how could I have thought it? How could I have been so blind, when everything had been taken by another already, when nothing was mine; when, in fact, her very tenderness to me, her anxiety, her love ... yes, love for me, was nothing else but joy at the thought of seeing another man so soon, desire to include me, too, in her happiness?... When he did not come, when we waited in vain, she frowned, she grew timid and discouraged. Her movements, her words, were no longer so light, so playful, so gay; and, strange to say, she redoubled her attentiveness to me, as though instinctively desiring to lavish on me what she desired for herself so anxiously, if her wishes were not accomplished. My Nastenka was so downcast, so dismayed, that I think she realized at last that I loved her, and was sorry for my poor love. So when we are unhappy we feel the unhappiness of others more; feeling is not destroyed but concentrated....

I went to meet her with a full heart, and was all impatience. I had no presentiment that I should feel as I do now, that it would not all end happily. She was beaming with pleasure; she was expecting an answer. The answer was himself. He was to come, to run at her call. She arrived a whole hour before I did. At first she giggled at everything, laughed at every word I said. I began talking, but relapsed into silence.

"Do you know why I am so glad," she said, "so glad to look at you? – why I like you so much to-day?"

"Well?" I asked, and my heart began throbbing.

"I like you because you have not fallen in love with me. You know that some men in your place would have been pestering and worrying me, would have been sighing and miserable, while you are so nice!"

Then she wrung my hand so hard that I almost cried out. She laughed.

"Goodness, what a friend you are!" she began gravely a minute later. "God sent you to me. What would have happened to me if you had not been with me now? How disinterested you are! How truly you care for me! When I am married we will be great friends, more than brother and sister; I shall care almost as I do for him...."

I felt horribly sad at that moment, yet something like laughter was stirring in my soul.

"You are very much upset," I said; "you are frightened; you think he won't come."

"Oh dear!" she answered; "if I were less happy, I believe I should cry at your lack of faith, at your reproaches. However, you have made me think and have given me a lot to think about; but I shall think later, and now I will own that you are right. Yes, I am somehow not myself; I am all suspense, and feel everything as it were too lightly. But hush! that's enough about feelings...."

At that moment we heard footsteps, and in the darkness we saw a figure coming towards us. We both started; she almost cried out; I dropped her hand and made a movement as though to walk away. But we were mistaken, it was not he.

"What are you afraid of? Why did you let go of my hand?" she said, giving it to me again. "Come, what is it? We will meet him together; I want him to see how fond we are of each other."

"How fond we are of each other!" I cried. ("Oh, Nastenka, Nastenka," I thought, "how much you have told me in that saying! Such fondness at *certain* moments makes the heart cold and the soul heavy. Your hand is cold, mine burns like fire. How blind you are, Nastenka!... Oh, how unbearable a happy person is sometimes! But I could not be angry with you!")

At last my heart was too full.

"Listen, Nastenka!" I cried. "Do you know how it has been with me all day."

"Why, how, how? Tell me quickly! Why have you said nothing all this time?"

"To begin with, Nastenka, when I had carried out all your commissions, given the letter, gone to see your good friends, then ... then I went home and went to bed."

"Is that all?" she interrupted, laughing.

"Yes, almost all," I answered restraining myself, for foolish tears were already starting into my eyes. "I woke an hour before our appointment, and yet, as it were, I had not been asleep. I don't know what happened to me. I came to tell you all about it, feeling as though time were standing still, feeling as though one sensation, one feeling must remain with me from that time for ever; feeling as though one minute must go on for all eternity, and as though all life had come to a standstill for me.... When I woke up it seemed as though some musical motive long familiar, heard somewhere in the past, forgotten and voluptuously sweet, had come back to me now. It seemed to me that it had been clamouring at my heart all my life, and only now...."

"Oh my goodness, my goodness," Nastenka interrupted, "what does all that mean? I don't understand a word."

"Ah, Nastenka, I wanted somehow to convey to you that strange impression...." I began in a plaintive voice, in which there still lay hid a hope, though a very faint one.

"Leave off. Hush!" she said, and in one instant the sly puss had guessed.

Suddenly she became extraordinarily talkative, gay, mischievous; she took my arm, laughed, wanted me to laugh too, and every confused word I uttered evoked from her prolonged ringing laughter.... I began to feel angry, she had suddenly begun flirting.

"Do you know," she began, "I feel a little vexed that you are not in love with me? There's no understanding human nature! But all the same, Mr. Unapproachable, you cannot blame me for being so simple; I tell you everything, everything, whatever foolish thought comes into my head."

"Listen! That's eleven, I believe," I said as the slow chime of a bell rang out from a distant tower. She suddenly stopped, left off laughing and began to count.

"Yes, it's eleven," she said at last in a timid, uncertain voice.

I regretted at once that I had frightened her, making her count the strokes, and I cursed myself for my spiteful impulse; I felt sorry for her, and did not know how to atone for what I had done.

I began comforting her, seeking for reasons for his not coming, advancing various arguments, proofs. No one could have been easier to deceive than she was at that moment; and, indeed, any one at such a moment listens gladly to any consolation, whatever it may be, and is overjoyed if a shadow of excuse can be found.

"And indeed it's an absurd thing," I began, warming to my task and admiring the extraordinary clearness of my argument, "why, he could not have come; you have muddled and confused me, Nastenka, so that I too, have lost count of the time.... Only think: he can scarcely have received the letter; suppose he is not able to come, suppose he is going to answer the letter, could not come before to-morrow. I will go for it as soon as it's light to-morrow and let you know at once. Consider, there are thousands of possibilities; perhaps he was not at home when the letter came, and may not have read it even now! Anything may happen, you know."

"Yes, yes!" said Nastenka. "I did not think of that. Of course anything may happen?" she went on in a tone that offered no opposition, though some other far-away thought could be heard like a vexatious discord in it. "I tell you what you must do," she said, "you go as early as possible to-morrow morning, and if you get anything let me know at once. You know where I live, don't you?"

And she began repeating her address to me.

Then she suddenly became so tender, so solicitous with me. She seemed to listen attentively to what I told her; but when I asked her some question she was silent, was confused, and turned her head away. I looked into her eyes – yes, she was crying.

"How can you? How can you? Oh, what a baby you are! what childishness!... Come, come!"

She tried to smile, to calm herself, but her chin was quivering and her bosom was still heaving.

"I was thinking about you," she said after a minute's silence. "You are so kind that I should be a stone if I did not feel it. Do you know what has occurred to me now? I was comparing you two. Why isn't he you? Why isn't he like you? He is not as good as you, though I love him more than you."

I made no answer. She seemed to expect me to say something.

"Of course, it may be that I don't understand him fully yet. You know I was always as it were afraid of him; he was always so grave, as it were so proud. Of course I know it's only that he seems like that, I know there is more tenderness in his heart than in mine.... I remember how he looked at me when I went in to him – do you remember? – with my bundle; but yet I respect him too much, and doesn't that show that we are not equals?"

"No, Nastenka, no," I answered, "it shows that you love him more than anything in the world, and far more than yourself."

"Yes, supposing that is so," answered Nastenka naïvely. "But do you know what strikes me now? Only I am not talking about him now, but speaking generally; all this came into my mind some time ago. Tell me, how is it that we can't all be like brothers together? Why is it that even the best of men always seem to hide something from other people and to keep something back? Why not say straight out what is in one's heart, when one knows that one is not speaking idly? As it is every one seems harsher than he really is, as though all were afraid of doing injustice to their feelings, by being too quick to express them."

"Oh, Nastenka, what you say is true; but there are many reasons for that," I broke in suppressing my own feelings at that moment more than ever.

"No, no!" she answered with deep feeling. "Here you, for instance, are not like other people! I really don't know how to tell you what I feel; but it seems to me that you, for instance ... at the present moment ... it seems to me that you are sacrificing something for me," she added timidly, with a fleeting glance at me. "Forgive me for saying so, I am a simple girl you know. I have seen very little of life, and I really sometimes don't know how to say things," she added in a voice that quivered with some hidden feeling, while she tried to smile; "but I only wanted to tell you that I am grateful, that I feel it all too.... Oh, may God give you happiness for it! What you told me about your dreamer is quite untrue now – that is, I mean, it's not true of you. You are recovering, you are quite a different man from what you described. If you ever fall in love with some one, God give you happiness with her! I won't wish anything for her, for she will be happy with you. I know, I am a woman myself, so you must believe me when I tell you so."

She ceased speaking, and pressed my hand warmly. I too could not speak without emotion. Some minutes passed.

"Yes, it's clear he won't come to-night," she said at last raising her head. "It's late."

"He will come to-morrow," I said in the most firm and convincing tone.

"Yes," she added with no sign of her former depression. "I see for myself now that he could not come till to-morrow. Well, good-bye, till to-morrow. If it rains perhaps I shall not come. But the day after to-morrow, I shall come. I shall come for certain, whatever happens; be sure to be here, I want to see you, I will tell you everything."

And then when we parted she gave me her hand and said, looking at me candidly: "We shall always be together, shan't we?"

Oh, Nastenka, Nastenka! If only you knew how lonely I am now!

As soon as it struck nine o'clock I could not stay indoors, but put on my things, and went out in spite of the weather. I was there, sitting on our seat. I went to her street, but I felt ashamed, and turned back without looking at their windows, when I was two steps from her door. I went home more depressed than I had ever been before. What a damp, dreary day! If it had been fine I should have walked about all night....

But to-morrow, to-morrow! To-morrow she will tell me everything. The letter has not come to-day, however. But that was to be expected. They are together by now....

FOURTH NIGHT

My God, how it has all ended! What it has all ended in! I arrived at nine o'clock. She was already there. I noticed her a good way off; she was standing as she had been that first time, with her elbows on the railing, and she did not hear me coming up to her.

"Nastenka!" I called to her, suppressing my agitation with an effort.

She turned to me quickly.

"Well?" she said. "Well? Make haste!"

I looked at her in perplexity.

"Well, where is the letter? Have you brought the letter?" she repeated clutching at the railing.

"No, there is no letter," I said at last. "Hasn't he been to you yet?" She turned fearfully pale and looked at me for a long time without moving. I had shattered her last hope.

"Well, God be with him," she said at last in a breaking voice; "God be with him if he leaves me like that."

She dropped her eyes, then tried to look at me and could not. For several minutes she was struggling with her emotion. All at once she turned away, leaning her elbows against the railing and burst into tears.

"Oh don't, don't!" I began; but looking at her I had not the heart to go on, and what was I to say to her?

"Don't try and comfort me," she said; "don't talk about him; don't tell me that he will come, that he has not cast me off so cruelly and so inhumanly as he has. What for – what for? Can there have been something in my letter, that unlucky letter?"

At that point sobs stifled her voice; my heart was torn as I looked at her.

"Oh, how inhumanly cruel it is!" she began again. "And not a line, not a line! He might at least have written that he does not want me, that he rejects me – but not a line for three days! How easy it is for him to wound, to insult a poor, defenceless girl, whose only fault is that she loves him! Oh, what I've suffered during these three days! Oh, dear! When I think that I was the first to go to him, that I humbled myself before him, cried, that I begged of him a little love!... and after that! Listen," she said, turning to me, and her black eyes flashed, "it isn't so! It can't be so; it isn't natural. Either you are mistaken or I; perhaps he has not received the letter? Perhaps he still knows nothing about it? How could any one – judge for yourself, tell me, for goodness' sake explain it to me, I can't understand it – how could any one behave with such barbarous coarseness as he has behaved to me? Not one word! Why, the lowest creature on earth is treated more compassionately. Perhaps he has heard something, perhaps some one has told him something about me," she cried, turning to me inquiringly: "What do you think?"

"Listen, Nastenka, I shall go to him to-morrow in your name."

"Yes?"

"I will question him about everything; I will tell him everything."

"Yes, yes?"

"You write a letter. Don't say no, Nastenka, don't say no! I will make him respect your action, he shall hear all about it, and if – – "

"No, my friend, no," she interrupted. "Enough! Not another word, not another line from me – enough! I don't know him; I don't love him any more. I will ... forget him."

She could not go on.

"Calm yourself, calm yourself! Sit here, Nastenka," I said, making her sit down on the seat.

"I am calm. Don't trouble. It's nothing! It's only tears, they will soon dry. Why, do you imagine I shall do away with myself, that I shall throw myself into the river?"

My heart was full: I tried to speak, but I could not.

"Listen," she said taking my hand. "Tell me: you wouldn't have behaved like this, would you? You would not have abandoned a girl who had come to you of herself, you would not have thrown into her face a shameless taunt at her weak foolish heart? You would have taken care of her? You would have realized that she was alone, that she did not know how to look after herself, that she could not guard herself from loving you, that it was not her fault, not her fault – that she had done nothing.... Oh dear, oh dear!"

"Nastenka!" I cried at last, unable to control my emotion. "Nastenka, you torture me! You wound my heart, you are killing me, Nastenka! I cannot be silent! I must speak at last, give utterance to what is surging in my heart!"

As I said this I got up from the seat. She took my hand and looked at me in surprise.

"What is the matter with you?" she said at last.

"Listen," I said resolutely. "Listen to me, Nastenka! What I am going to say to you now is all nonsense, all impossible, all stupid! I know that this can never be, but I cannot be silent. For the sake of what you are suffering now, I beg you beforehand to forgive me!"

"What is it? What is it?" she said drying her tears and looking at me intently, while a strange curiosity gleamed in her astonished eyes. "What is the matter?"

"It's impossible, but I love you, Nastenka! There it is! Now everything is told," I said with a wave of my hand. "Now you will see whether you can go on talking to me as you did just now, whether you can listen to what I am going to say to you."...

"Well, what then?" Nastenka interrupted me. "What of it? I knew you loved me long ago, only I always thought that you simply liked me very much.... Oh dear, oh dear!"

"At first it was simply liking, Nastenka, but now, now! I am just in the same position as you were when you went to him with your bundle. In a worse position than you, Nastenka, because he cared for no one else as you do."

"What are you saying to me! I don't understand you in the least. But tell me, what's this for; I don't mean what for, but why are you ... so suddenly.... Oh dear, I am talking nonsense! But you...."

And Nastenka broke off in confusion. Her cheeks flamed; she dropped her eyes.

"What's to be done, Nastenka, what am I to do? I am to blame. I have abused your.... But no, no, I am not to blame, Nastenka; I feel that, I know that, because my heart tells me I am right, for I cannot hurt you in any way, I cannot wound you! I was your friend, but I am still your friend, I have betrayed no trust. Here my tears are falling, Nastenka. Let them flow, let them flow – they don't hurt anybody. They will dry, Nastenka."

"Sit down, sit down," she said, making me sit down on the seat. "Oh, my God!"

"No, Nastenka, I won't sit down; I cannot stay here any longer, you cannot see me again; I will tell you everything and go away. I only want to say that you would never have found out that I loved you. I should have kept my secret. I would not have worried you at such a moment with my egoism. No! But I could not resist it now; you spoke of it yourself, it is your fault, your fault and not mine. You cannot drive me away from you."...

"No, no, I don't drive you away, no!" said Nastenka, concealing her confusion as best she could, poor child.

"You don't drive me away? No! But I meant to run from you myself. I will go away, but first I will tell you all, for when you were crying here I could not sit unmoved, when you wept, when you were in torture at being – at being – I will speak of it, Nastenka – at being forsaken, at your love being repulsed, I felt that in my heart there was so much love for you, Nastenka, so much love! And it seemed so bitter that I could not help you with my love, that my heart was breaking and I ... I could not be silent, I had to speak, Nastenka, I had to speak!"

"Yes, yes! tell me, talk to me," said Nastenka with an indescribable gesture. "Perhaps you think it strange that I talk to you like this, but ... speak! I will tell you afterwards! I will tell you everything."

"You are sorry for me, Nastenka, you are simply sorry for me, my dear little friend! What's done can't be mended. What is said cannot be taken back. Isn't that so? Well, now you know. That's the starting-point. Very well. Now it's all right, only listen. When you were sitting crying I thought to myself (oh, let me tell you what I was thinking!), I thought, that (of course it cannot be, Nastenka), I thought that you ... I thought that you somehow ... quite apart from me, had ceased to love him. Then – I thought that yesterday and the day before yesterday, Nastenka – then I would – I certainly would – have succeeded in making you love me; you know, you said yourself, Nastenka, that you almost loved me. Well, what next? Well, that's nearly all I wanted to tell you; all that is left to say is how it would be if you loved me, only that, nothing more! Listen, my friend – for any way you are my friend – I am, of course, a poor, humble man, of no great consequence; but that's not the point (I don't seem to be able to say what I mean, Nastenka, I am so confused), only I would love you, I would love you so, that even if you still loved him, even if you went on loving the man I don't know, you would never feel that my love was a burden to you. You would only feel every minute that at your side was beating a grateful, grateful heart, a warm heart ready for your sake.... Oh Nastenka, Nastenka! What have you done to me?"

"Don't cry; I don't want you to cry," said Nastenka getting up quickly from the seat. "Come along, get up, come with me, don't cry, don't cry," she said, drying her tears with her handkerchief; "let us go now; maybe I will tell you something.... If he has forsaken me now, if he has forgotten me, though I still love him (I do not want to deceive you) ... but listen, answer me. If I were to love you, for instance, that is, if I only.... Oh my friend, my friend! To think, to think how I wounded you, when I laughed at your love, when I praised you for not falling in love with me. Oh dear! How was it I did not foresee this, how was it I did not foresee this, how could I have been so stupid? But.... Well, I have made up my mind, I will tell you."

"Look here, Nastenka, do you know what? I'll go away, that's what I'll do. I am simply tormenting you. Here you are remorseful for having laughed at me, and I won't have you ... in addition to your sorrow.... Of course it is my fault, Nastenka, but good-bye!"

"Stay, listen to me: can you wait?"

"What for? How?"

"I love him; but I shall get over it, I must get over it, I cannot fail to get over it; I am getting over it, I feel that.... Who knows? Perhaps it will all end to-day, for I hate him, for he has been laughing at me, while you have been weeping here with me, for you have not repulsed me as he has, for you love me while he has never loved me, for in fact, I love you myself.... Yes, I love you! I love you as you love me; I have told you so before, you heard it yourself – I love you because you are better than he is, because you are nobler than he is, because, because he – – "

The poor girl's emotion was so violent that she could not say more; she laid her head upon my shoulder, then upon my bosom, and wept bitterly. I comforted her, I persuaded her, but she could not stop crying; she kept pressing my hand, and saying between her sobs: "Wait, wait, it will be over in a minute! I want to tell you ... you mustn't think that these tears – it's nothing, it's weakness, wait till it's over."... At last she left off crying, dried her eyes and we walked on again. I wanted to speak, but she still begged me to wait. We were silent.... At last she plucked up courage and began to speak.

"It's like this," she began in a weak and quivering voice, in which, however, there was a note that pierced my heart with a sweet pang; "don't think that I am so light and inconstant, don't think that I can forget and change so quickly. I have loved him for a whole year, and I swear by God that I have never, never, even in thought, been unfaithful to him.... He has despised me, he has been laughing at me – God forgive him! But he has insulted me and wounded my heart. I ... I do not love him, for I can only love what is magnanimous, what understands me, what is generous; for I am like that myself and he is not worthy of me – well, that's enough of him. He has done better than if he had deceived my expectations later, and shown me later what he was.... Well, it's over! But who knows, my dear friend," she went on pressing my hand, "who knows, perhaps my whole love was a mistaken feeling, a delusion – perhaps it began in mischief, in nonsense, because I was kept so strictly by grandmother? Perhaps I ought to love another man, not him, a different man, who would have pity on me and ... and.... But don't let us say any more about that," Nastenka broke off, breathless with emotion, "I only wanted to tell you ... I wanted to tell you that if, although I love him (no, did love him), if, in spite of this you still say.... If you feel that your love is so great that it may at last drive from my heart my old feeling – if you will have pity on me – if you do not want to leave me alone to my fate, without hope, without consolation – if you are ready to love me always as you do now – I swear to you that gratitude ... that my love will be at last worthy of your love.... Will you take my hand?"

"Nastenka!" I cried breathless with sobs. "Nastenka, oh Nastenka!"

"Enough, enough! Well, now it's quite enough," she said, hardly able to control herself. "Well, now all has been said, hasn't it! Hasn't it? You are happy – I am happy too. Not another word about it, wait; spare me ... talk of something else, for God's sake."

"Yes, Nastenka, yes! Enough about that, now I am happy. I – – Yes, Nastenka, yes, let us talk of other things, let us make haste and talk. Yes! I am ready."

And we did not know what to say: we laughed, we wept, we said thousands of things meaningless and incoherent; at one moment we walked along the pavement, then suddenly turned back and crossed the road; then we stopped and went back again to the embankment; we were like children.

"I am living alone now, Nastenka," I began, "but to-morrow! Of course you know, Nastenka, I am poor, I have only got twelve hundred roubles, but that doesn't matter."

"Of course not, and granny has her pension, so she will be no burden. We must take granny."

"Of course we must take granny. But there's Matrona."

"Yes, and we've got Fyokla too!"

"Matrona is a good woman, but she has one fault: she has no imagination, Nastenka, absolutely none; but that doesn't matter."

"That's all right – they can live together; only you must move to us to-morrow."

"To you? How so? All right, I am ready."

"Yes, hire a room from us. We have a top floor, it's empty. We had an old lady lodging there, but she has gone away; and I know granny would like to have a young man. I said to her, 'Why a young man?' And she said, 'Oh, because I am old; only don't you fancy, Nastenka, that I want him as a husband for you.' So I guessed it was with that idea."

"Oh, Nastenka!"

And we both laughed.

"Come, that's enough, that's enough. But where do you live? I've forgotten."

"Over that way, near X bridge, Barannikov's Buildings."

"It's that big house?"

"Yes, that big house."

"Oh, I know, a nice house; only you know you had better give it up and come to us as soon as possible."

"To-morrow, Nastenka, to-morrow; I owe a little for my rent there but that doesn't matter. I shall soon get my salary."

"And do you know I will perhaps give lessons; I will learn something myself and then give lessons."

"Capital! And I shall soon get a bonus."

"So by to-morrow you will be my lodger."

"And we will go to *The Barber of Seville*, for they are soon going to give it again."

"Yes, we'll go," said Nastenka, "but better see something else and not *The Barber of Seville*."

"Very well, something else. Of course that will be better, I did not think – – "

As we talked like this we walked along in a sort of delirium, a sort of intoxication, as though we did not know what was happening to us. At one moment we stopped and talked for a long time at the same place; then we went on again, and goodness knows where we went; and again tears and again laughter. All of a sudden Nastenka would want to go home, and I would not dare to detain her but would want to see her to the house; we set off, and in a quarter of an hour found ourselves at the embankment by our seat. Then she would sigh, and tears would come into her eyes again; I would turn chill with dismay.... But she would press my hand and force me to walk, to talk, to chatter as before.

"It's time I was home at last; I think it must be very late," Nastenka said at last. "We must give over being childish."

"Yes, Nastenka, only I shan't sleep to-night; I am not going home."

"I don't think I shall sleep either; only see me home."

"I should think so!"

"Only this time we really must get to the house."

"We must, we must."

"Honour bright? For you know one must go home some time!"

"Honour bright," I answered laughing.

"Well, come along!"

"Come along! Look at the sky, Nastenka. Look! To-morrow it will be a lovely day; what a blue sky, what a moon! Look; that yellow cloud is covering it now, look, look! No, it has passed by. Look, look!"

But Nastenka did not look at the cloud; she stood mute as though turned to stone; a minute later she huddled timidly close up to me. Her hand trembled in my hand; I looked at her. She pressed still more closely to me.

At that moment a young man passed by us. He suddenly stopped, looked at us intently, and then again took a few steps on. My heart began throbbing.

"Who is it, Nastenka?" I said in an undertone.

"It's he," she answered in a whisper, huddling up to me, still more closely, still more tremulously.... I could hardly stand on my feet.

"Nastenka, Nastenka! It's you!" I heard a voice behind us and at the same moment the young man took several steps towards us.

My God, how she cried out! How she started! How she tore herself out of my arms and rushed to meet him! I stood and looked at them, utterly crushed. But she had hardly given him her hand, had hardly flung herself into his arms, when she turned to me again, was beside me again in a flash, and before I knew where I was she threw both arms round my neck and gave me a warm, tender kiss. Then, without saying a word to me, she rushed back to him again, took his hand, and drew him after her.

I stood a long time looking after them. At last the two vanished from my sight.

MORNING

My night ended with the morning. It was a wet day. The rain was falling and beating disconsolately upon my window pane; it was dark in the room and grey outside. My head ached and I was giddy; fever was stealing over my limbs.

"There's a letter for you, sir; the postman brought it," Matrona said stooping over me.

"A letter? From whom?" I cried jumping up from my chair.

"I don't know, sir, better look – maybe it is written there whom it is from."

I broke the seal. It was from her!

* * * * *

"Oh, forgive me, forgive me! I beg you on my knees to forgive me! I deceived you and myself. It was a dream, a mirage.... My heart aches for you to-day; forgive me, forgive me!

"Don't blame me, for I have not changed to you in the least. I told you that I would love you, I love you now, I more than love you. Oh, my God! If only I could love you both at once! Oh, if only you were he!"

["Oh, if only he were you," echoed in my mind. I remembered your words, Nastenka!]

"God knows what I would do for you now! I know that you are sad and dreary. I have wounded you, but you know when one loves a wrong is soon forgotten. And you love me.

"Thank you, yes, thank you for that love! For it will live in my memory like a sweet dream which lingers long after awakening; for I shall remember for ever that instant when you opened your heart to me like a brother and so generously accepted the gift of my shattered heart to care for it, nurse it, and heal it.... If you forgive me, the memory of you will be exalted by a feeling of everlasting gratitude which will never be effaced from my soul.... I will treasure that memory: I will be true to it, I will not betray it, I will not betray my heart: it is too constant. It returned so quickly yesterday to him to whom it has always belonged.

"We shall meet, you will come to us, you will not leave us, you will be for ever a friend, a brother to me. And when you see me you will give me your hand ... yes? You will give it to me, you have forgiven me, haven't you? You love me *as before*?

"Oh, love me, do not forsake me, because I love you so at this moment, because I am worthy of your love, because I will deserve it ... my dear! Next week I am to be married to him. He has come back in love, he has never forgotten me. You will not be angry at my writing about him. But I want to come and see you with him; you will like him, won't you?

"Forgive me, remember and love your

"Nastenka."

* * * * *

I read that letter over and over again for a long time; tears gushed to my eyes. At last it fell from my hands and I hid my face.

"Dearie! I say, dearie – – " Matrona began.

"What is it, Matrona?"

"I have taken all the cobwebs off the ceiling; you can have a wedding or give a party."

I looked at Matrona. She was still a hearty, *youngish* old woman, but I don't know why all at once I suddenly pictured her with lustreless eyes, a wrinkled face, bent, decrepit.... I don't know why I suddenly pictured my room grown old like Matrona. The walls and the floors looked discoloured, everything seemed dingy; the spiders' webs were thicker than ever. I don't know why, but when I looked out of the window it seemed to me that the house opposite had grown old and dingy too, that the stucco on the columns was peeling off and crumbling, that the cornices were cracked and blackened, and that the walls, of a vivid deep yellow, were patchy.

Either the sunbeams suddenly peeping out from the clouds for a moment were hidden again behind a veil of rain, and everything had grown dingy again before my eyes; or perhaps the whole vista of my future flashed before me so sad and forbidding, and I saw myself just as I was now, fifteen years hence, older, in the same room, just as solitary, with the same Matrona grown no cleverer for those fifteen years.

But to imagine that I should bear you a grudge, Nastenka! That I should cast a dark cloud over your serene, untroubled happiness; that by my bitter reproaches I should cause distress to your heart, should poison it with secret remorse and should force it to throb with anguish at the moment of bliss; that I should crush a single one of those tender blossoms which you have twined in your dark tresses when you go with him to the altar.... Oh never, never! May your sky be clear, may your sweet smile be bright and untroubled, and may you be blessed for that moment of blissful happiness which you gave to another, lonely and grateful heart!

My God, a whole moment of happiness! Is that too little for the whole of a man's life?

THE GAMBLER

CHAPTER ONE

At length I returned from two weeks leave of absence to find that my patrons had arrived three days ago in Roulettenberg. I received from them a welcome quite different to that which I had expected. The General eyed me coldly, greeted me in rather haughty fashion, and dismissed me to pay my respects to his sister. It was clear that from *somewhere* money had been acquired. I thought I could even detect a certain shamefacedness in the General's glance. Maria Philipovna, too, seemed distraught, and conversed with me with an air of detachment. Nevertheless, she took the money which I handed to her, counted it, and listened to what I had to tell. To luncheon there were expected that day a Monsieur Mezentsov, a French lady, and an Englishman; for, whenever money was in hand, a banquet in Muscovite style was always given. Polina Alexandrovna, on seeing me, inquired why I had been so long away. Then, without waiting for an answer, she departed. Evidently this was not mere accident, and I felt that I must throw some light upon matters. It was high time that I did so.

I was assigned a small room on the fourth floor of the hotel (for you must know that I belonged to the General's suite). So far as I could see, the party had already gained some notoriety in the place, which had come to look upon the General as a Russian nobleman of great wealth. Indeed, even before luncheon he charged me, among other things, to get two thousand-franc notes changed for him at the hotel counter, which put us in a position to be thought millionaires at all events for a week! Later, I was about to take Mischa and Nadia for a walk when a summons reached me from the staircase that I must attend the General. He began by deigning to inquire of me where I was going to take the children; and as he did so, I could see that he failed to look me in the eyes. He *wanted* to do so, but each time was met by me with such a fixed, disrespectful stare that he desisted in confusion. In pompous language, however, which jumbled one sentence into another, and at length grew disconnected, he gave me to understand that I was to lead the children altogether away from the Casino, and out into the park. Finally his anger exploded, and he added sharply:

"I suppose you would like to take them to the Casino to play roulette? Well, excuse my speaking so plainly, but I know how addicted you are to gambling. Though I am not your mentor, nor wish to be, at least I have a right to require that you shall not actually *compromise* me."

"I have no money for gambling," I quietly replied.

"But you will soon be in receipt of some," retorted the General, reddening a little as he dived into his writing desk and applied himself to a memorandum book. From it he saw that he had 120 roubles of mine in his keeping.

"Let us calculate," he went on. "We must translate these roubles into thalers. Here – take 100 thalers, as a round sum. The rest will be safe in my hands."

In silence I took the money.

"You must not be offended at what I say," he continued. "You are too touchy about these things. What I have said I have said merely as a warning. To do so is no more than my right."

When returning home with the children before luncheon, I met a cavalcade of our party riding to view some ruins. Two splendid carriages, magnificently horsed, with Mlle. Blanche, Maria Philipovna, and Polina Alexandrovna in one of them, and the Frenchman, the Englishman, and the General in attendance on horseback! The passers-by stopped to stare at them, for the effect was splendid – the General could not have improved upon it. I calculated that, with the 4000 francs which I had brought with me, added to what my patrons seemed already to have acquired, the party must be in possession of at least 7000 or 8000 francs – though that would be none too much for Mlle. Blanche, who, with her mother and the Frenchman, was also lodging in our hotel. The latter gentleman was called by the lacqueys "Monsieur le Comte," and Mlle. Blanche's mother was dubbed "Madame la Comtesse." Perhaps in very truth they *were* "Comte et Comtesse."

I knew that "Monsieur le Comte" would take no notice of me when we met at dinner, as also that the General would not dream of introducing us, nor of recommending me to the "Comte." However, the latter had lived awhile in Russia, and knew that the person referred to as an "uchitel" is never looked upon as a bird of fine feather. Of course, strictly speaking, he *knew* me; but I was an uninvited guest at the luncheon – the General had forgotten to arrange otherwise, or I should have been dispatched to dine at the table d'hôte. Nevertheless, I presented myself in such guise that the General looked at me with a touch of approval; and, though the good Maria Philipovna was for showing me my place, the fact of my having previously met the Englishman, Mr. Astley, saved me, and thenceforward I figured as one of the company.

This strange Englishman I had met first in Prussia, where we had happened to sit *vis-à-vis* in a railway train in which I was travelling to overtake our party; while, later, I had run across him in France, and again in Switzerland – twice within the space of two weeks! To think, therefore, that I should suddenly encounter him again here, in Roulettenberg! Never in my life had I known a more retiring man, for he was shy to the pitch of imbecility, yet well aware of the fact (for he was no fool). At the same time, he was a gentle, amiable sort of an individual, and, even on our first encounter in Prussia I had contrived to draw him out, and he had told me that he had just been to the North Cape, and was now anxious to visit the fair at Nizhni Novgorod. How he had come to make the General's acquaintance I do not know, but, apparently, he was much struck with Polina. Also, he was delighted that I should sit next him at table, for he appeared to look upon me as his bosom friend.

During the meal the Frenchman was in great feather: he was discursive and pompous to every one. In Moscow too, I remembered, he had blown a great many bubbles. Interminably he discoursed on finance and Russian politics, and though, at times, the General made feints to contradict him, he did so humbly, and as though wishing not wholly to lose sight of his own dignity.

For myself, I was in a curious frame of mind. Even before luncheon was half finished I had asked myself the old, eternal question: "*Why* do I continue to dance attendance upon the General, instead of having left him and his family long ago?" Every now and then I would glance at Polina Alexandrovna, but she paid me no attention; until eventually I became so irritated that I decided to play the boor.

First of all I suddenly, and for no reason whatever, plunged loudly and gratuitously into the general conversation. Above everything I wanted to pick a quarrel with the Frenchman; and, with that end in view I turned to the General, and exclaimed in an overbearing sort of way – indeed, I think that I actually interrupted him – that that summer it had been almost impossible for a Russian to dine anywhere at tables d'hôte. The General bent upon me a glance of astonishment.

"If one is a man of self-respect," I went on, "one risks abuse by so doing, and is forced to put up with insults of every kind. Both at Paris and on the Rhine, and even in Switzerland – there are so many Poles, with their sympathisers, the French, at these tables d'hôte that one cannot get a word in edgeways if one happens only to be a Russian."

This I said in French. The General eyed me doubtfully, for he did not know whether to be angry or merely to feel surprised that I should so far forget myself.

"Of course, one always learns *something everywhere*," said the Frenchman in a careless, contemptuous sort of tone.

"In Paris, too, I had a dispute with a Pole," I continued, "and then with a French officer who supported him. After that a section of the Frenchmen present took my part. They did so as soon as I told them the story of how once I threatened to spit into Monsignor's coffee."

"To spit into it?" the General inquired with grave disapproval in his tone, and a stare, of astonishment, while the Frenchman looked at me unbelievingly.

"Just so," I replied. "You must know that, on one occasion, when, for two days, I had felt certain that at any moment I might have to depart for Rome on business, I repaired to the Embassy of the Holy See in Paris, to have my passport visaed. There I encountered a sacristan of about fifty, and a man dry and cold of mien. After listening politely, but with great reserve, to my account of myself, this sacristan asked me to wait a little. I was in a great hurry to depart, but of course I sat down, pulled out a copy of *L'Opinion Nationale*, and fell to reading an extraordinary piece of invective against Russia which it happened to contain. As I was thus engaged I heard some one enter an adjoining room and ask for Monsignor; after which I saw the sacristan make a low bow to the visitor, and then another bow as the visitor took his leave. I ventured to remind the good man of my own business also; whereupon, with an expression of, if anything, increased dryness, he again asked me to wait. Soon a third visitor arrived who, like myself, had come on business (he was an Austrian of some sort); and as soon as ever he had stated his errand he was conducted upstairs! This made me very angry. I rose, approached the sacristan, and told him that, since Monsignor was receiving callers, his lordship might just as well finish off my affair as well. Upon this the sacristan shrunk back in astonishment. It simply passed his understanding that any insignificant Russian should dare to compare himself with other visitors of Monsignor's! In a tone of the utmost effrontery, as though he were delighted to have a chance of insulting me, he looked me up and down, and then said: "Do you suppose that Monsignor is going to put aside his coffee for *you?*" But I only cried the louder: "Let me tell you that I am going to *spit* into that coffee! Yes, and if you do not get me my passport visaed this very minute, I shall take it to Monsignor myself."

"What? While he is engaged with a Cardinal?" screeched the sacristan, again shrinking back in horror. Then, rushing to the door, he spread out his arms as though he would rather die than let me enter.

Thereupon I declared that I was a heretic and a barbarian – "Je suis hérétique et barbare," I said, "and that these archbishops and cardinals and monsignors, and the rest of them, meant nothing at all to me. In a word, I showed him that I was not going to give way. He looked at me with an air of infinite resentment. Then he snatched up my passport, and departed with it upstairs. A minute later the passport had been visaed! Here it is now, if you care to see it," – and I pulled out the document, and exhibited the Roman visa.

"But – " the General began.

"What really saved you was the fact that you proclaimed yourself a heretic and a barbarian," remarked the Frenchman with a smile. "Cela n'était pas si bête."

"But is *that* how Russian subjects ought to be treated? Why, when they settle here they dare not utter even a word – they are ready even to deny the fact that they are Russians! At all events, at my hotel in Paris I received far more attention from the company after I had told them about the fracas with the sacristan. A fat Polish nobleman, who had been the most offensive of all who were present at the table d'hôte, at once went upstairs, while some of the Frenchmen were simply disgusted when I told them that two years ago I had encountered a man at whom, in 1812, a French 'hero' fired for the mere fun of discharging his musket. That man was then a boy of ten and his family are still residing in Moscow."

"Impossible!" the Frenchman spluttered. "No French soldier would fire at a child!"

"Nevertheless the incident was as I say," I replied. "A very respected ex-captain told me the story, and I myself could see the scar left on his cheek."

The Frenchman then began chattering volubly, and the General supported him; but I recommended the former to read, for example, extracts from the memoirs of General Perovski, who, in 1812, was a prisoner in the hands of the French. Finally Maria Philipovna said something to interrupt the conversation. The General was furious with me for having started the altercation with the Frenchman. On the other hand, Mr. Astley seemed to take great pleasure in my brush with Monsieur, and, rising from the table, proposed that we should go and have a drink together. The same afternoon, at four o'clock, I went to have my customary talk with Polina Alexandrovna; and, the talk soon extended to a stroll. We entered the Park, and approached the Casino, where Polina seated herself upon a bench near the fountain, and sent Nadia away to a little distance to play with some other children. Mischa also I dispatched to play by the fountain, and in this fashion we – that is to say, Polina and myself – contrived to find ourselves alone.

Of course, we began by talking on business matters. Polina seemed furious when I handed her only 700 gülden, for she had thought to receive from Paris, as the proceeds of the pledging of her diamonds, at least 2000 gülden, or even more.

"Come what may, I *must* have money," she said. "And get it somehow I will – otherwise I shall be ruined."

I asked her what had happened during my absence.

"Nothing; except that two pieces of news have reached us from St. Petersburg. In the first place, my grandmother is very ill, and unlikely to last another couple of days. We had this from Timothy Petrovitch himself, and he is a reliable person. Every moment we are expecting to receive news of the end."

"All of you are on the tiptoe of expectation?" I queried.

"Of course – all of us, and every minute of the day. For a year-and-a-half now we have been looking for this."

"Looking for it?"

"Yes, looking for it. I am not her blood relation, you know – I am merely the General's step-daughter. Yet I am certain that the old lady has remembered me in her will."

"Yes, I believe that you *will* come in for a good deal," I said with some assurance.

"Yes, for she is fond of me. But how come you to think so?"

I answered this question with another one. "That Marquis of yours," I said, " – is *he* also familiar with your family secrets?"

"And why are you yourself so interested in them?" was her retort as she eyed me with dry grimness.

"Never mind. If I am not mistaken, the General has succeeded in borrowing money of the Marquis."

"It may be so."

"Is it likely that the Marquis would have lent the money if he had not known something or other about your grandmother? Did you notice, too, that three times during luncheon, when speaking of her, he called her 'La Baboulenka'?[1] What loving, friendly behaviour, to be sure!"

1 Dear little Grandmother.

"Yes, that is true. As soon as ever he learnt that I was likely to inherit something from her he began to pay me his addresses. I thought you ought to know that."

"Then he has only just begun his courting? Why, I thought he had been doing so a long while!"

"You *know* he has not," retorted Polina angrily. "But where on earth did you pick up this Englishman?" She said this after a pause.

"I *knew* you would ask about him!" Whereupon I told her of my previous encounters with Astley while travelling.

"He is very shy," I said, "and susceptible. Also, he is in love with you."

"Yes, he *is* in love with me," she replied.

"And he is ten times richer than the Frenchman. In fact, what does the Frenchman possess? To me it seems at least doubtful that he possesses anything at all."

"Oh, no, there is no doubt about it. He does possess some château or other. Last night the General told me that for certain. *Now* are you satisfied?"

"Nevertheless, in your place I should marry the Englishman."

"And why?" asked Polina.

"Because, though the Frenchman is the handsomer of the two, he is also the baser; whereas the Englishman is not only a man of honour, but ten times the wealthier of the pair."

"Yes? But then the Frenchman is a marquis, and the cleverer of the two," remarked Polina imperturbably.

"Is that so?" I repeated.

"Yes; absolutely."

Polina was not at all pleased at my questions; I could see that she was doing her best to irritate me with the brusquerie of her answers. But I took no notice of this.

"It amuses me to see you grow angry," she continued. "However, inasmuch as I allow you to indulge in these questions and conjectures, you ought to pay me something for the privilege."

"I consider that I have a perfect right to put these questions to you," was my calm retort; "for the reason that I am ready to pay for them, and also care little what becomes of me."

Polina giggled.

"Last time you told me – when on the Shlangenberg – that at a word from me you would be ready to jump down a thousand feet into the abyss. Some day I may remind you of that saying, in order to see if you will be as good as your word. Yes, you may depend upon it that I shall do so. I hate you because I have allowed you to go to such lengths, and I also hate you and still more – because you are so necessary to me. For the time being I want you, so I must keep you."

Then she made a movement to rise. Her tone had sounded very angry. Indeed, of late her talks with me had invariably ended on a note of temper and irritation – yes, of real temper.

"May I ask you who is this Mlle. Blanche?" I inquired (since I did not wish Polina to depart without an explanation).

"You *know* who she is – just Mlle. Blanche. Nothing further has transpired. Probably she will soon be Madame General – that is to say, if the rumours that Grandmamma is nearing her end should prove true. Mlle. Blanche, with her mother and her cousin, the Marquis, know very well that, as things now stand, we are ruined."

"And is the General at last in love?"

"That has nothing to do with it. Listen to me. Take these 700 florins, and go and play roulette with them. Win as much for me as you can, for I am badly in need of money."

So saying, she called Nadia back to her side, and entered the Casino, where she joined the rest of our party. For myself, I took, in musing astonishment, the first path to the left. Something had seemed to strike my brain when she told me to go and play roulette. Strangely enough, that something had also seemed to make me hesitate, and to set me analysing my feelings with regard to her. In fact, during the two weeks of my absence I had felt far more at my ease than I did now, on the day of my return; although, while travelling, I had moped like an imbecile, rushed about like a man in a fever, and actually beheld her in my dreams. Indeed, on one occasion (this happened in Switzerland, when I was asleep in the train) I had spoken aloud to her, and set all my fellow-travellers laughing. Again, therefore, I put to myself the question: "Do I, or do I not love her?" and again I could return myself no answer or, rather, for the hundredth time I told myself that I detested her. Yes, I detested her; there were moments (more especially at the close of our talks together) when I would gladly have given half my life to have strangled her! I swear that, had there, at such moments, been a sharp knife ready to my hand, I would have seized that knife with pleasure, and plunged it into her breast. Yet I also swear that if, on the Shlangenberg, she had *really* said to me, "Leap into that abyss," I should have leapt into it, and with equal pleasure. Yes, this I knew well. One way or the other, the thing must soon be ended. She, too, knew it in some curious way; the thought that I was fully conscious of her inaccessibility, and of the impossibility of my ever realising my dreams, afforded her, I am certain, the keenest possible pleasure. Otherwise, is it likely that she, the cautious and clever woman that she was, would have indulged in this familiarity and openness with me? Hitherto (I concluded) she had looked upon me in the same light that the old Empress did upon her servant – the Empress who hesitated not to unrobe herself before her slave, since she did not account a slave a man. Yes, often Polina must have taken me for something less than a man!"

Still, she had charged me with a commission – to win what I could at roulette. Yet all the time I could not help wondering *why* it was so necessary for her to win something, and what new schemes could have sprung to birth in her ever-fertile brain. A host of new and unknown factors seemed to have arisen during the last two weeks. Well, it behoved me to divine them, and to probe them, and that as soon as possible. Yet not now: at the present moment I must repair to the roulette-table.

CHAPTER TWO

I CONFESS I DID not like it. Although I had made up my mind to play, I felt averse to doing so on behalf of some one else. In fact, it almost upset my balance, and I entered the gaming rooms with an angry feeling at my heart. At first glance the scene irritated me. Never at any time have I been able to bear the flunkeyishness which one meets in the Press of the world at large, but more especially in that of Russia, where, almost every evening, journalists write on two subjects in particular – namely, on the splendour and luxury of the casinos to be found in the Rhenish towns, and on the heaps of gold which are daily to be seen lying on their tables. Those journalists are not paid for doing so: they write thus merely out of a spirit of disinterested complaisance. For there is nothing splendid about the establishments in question; and, not only are there no heaps of gold to be seen lying on their tables, but also there is very little money to be seen at all. Of course, during the season, *some* madman or another may make his appearance – generally an Englishman, or an Asiatic, or a Turk – and (as had happened during the summer of which I write) win or lose a great deal; but, as regards the rest of the crowd, it plays only for petty gülden, and seldom does much wealth figure on the board.

When, on the present occasion, I entered the gaming-rooms (for the first time in my life), it was several moments before I could even make up my mind to play. For one thing, the crowd oppressed me. Had I been playing for myself, I think I should have left at once, and never have embarked upon gambling at all, for I could feel my heart beginning to beat, and my heart was anything but cold-blooded. Also, I knew, I had long ago made up my mind, that never should I depart from Roulettenberg until some radical, some final, change had taken place in my fortunes. Thus, it must and would be. However ridiculous it may seem to you that I was expecting to win at roulette, I look upon the generally accepted opinion concerning the folly and the grossness of hoping to win at gambling as a thing even more absurd. For why is gambling a whit worse than any other method of acquiring money? How, for instance, is it worse than trade? True, out of a hundred persons, only one can win; yet what business is that of yours or of mine?

At all events, I confined myself at first simply to looking on, and decided to attempt nothing serious. Indeed, I felt that, if I began to do anything at all, I should do it in an absent-minded, haphazard sort of way – of that I felt certain. Also, it behoved me to learn the game itself; since, despite a thousand descriptions of roulette which I had read with ceaseless avidity, I knew nothing of its rules, and had never even seen it played.

In the first place, everything about it seemed to me so foul – so morally mean and foul. Yet I am not speaking of the hungry, restless folk who, by scores nay, even by hundreds – could be seen crowded around the gaming-tables. For in a desire to win quickly and to win much I can see nothing sordid; I have always applauded the opinion of a certain dead and gone, but cocksure, moralist who replied to the excuse that "one may always gamble moderately", by saying that to do so makes things worse, since, in that case, the profits too will always be moderate.

Insignificant profits and sumptuous profits do not stand on the same footing. No, it is all a matter of proportion. What may seem a small sum to a Rothschild may seem a large sum to me, and it is not the fault of stakes or of winnings that everywhere men can be found winning, can be found depriving their fellows of something, just as they do at roulette. As to the question whether stakes and winnings are, in themselves, immoral is another question altogether, and I wish to express no opinion upon it. Yet the very fact that I was full of a strong desire to win caused this gambling for gain, in spite of its attendant squalor, to contain, if you will, something intimate, something sympathetic, to my eyes: for it is always pleasant to see men dispensing with ceremony, and acting naturally, and in an unbuttoned mood....

Yet why should I so deceive myself? I could see that the whole thing was a vain and unreasoning pursuit; and what, at the first glance, seemed to me the ugliest feature in this mob of roulette players was their respect for their occupation – the seriousness, and even the humility, with which they stood around the gaming tables. Moreover, I had always drawn sharp distinctions between a game which is *de mauvais genre* and a game which is permissible to a decent man. In fact, there are two sorts of gaming – namely, the game of the gentleman and the game of the plebs – the game for gain, and the game of the herd. Herein, as said, I draw sharp distinctions. Yet how essentially base are the distinctions! For instance, a gentleman may stake, say, five or ten louis d'or – seldom more, unless he is a very rich man, when he may stake, say, a thousand francs; but, he must do this simply for the love of the game itself – simply for sport, simply in order to observe the process of winning or of losing, and, above all things, as a man who remains quite uninterested in the possibility of his issuing a winner. If he wins, he will be at liberty, perhaps, to give vent to a laugh, or to pass a remark on the circumstance to a bystander, or to stake again, or to double his stake; but, even this he must do solely out of curiosity, and for the pleasure of watching the play of chances and of calculations, and not because of any vulgar desire to win. In a word, he must look upon the gaming-table, upon roulette, and upon trente et quarante, as mere relaxations which have been arranged solely for his amusement. Of the existence of the lures and gains upon which the bank is founded and maintained he must profess to have not an inkling. Best of all, he ought to imagine his fellow-gamblers and the rest of the mob which stands trembling over a coin to be equally rich and gentlemanly with himself, and playing solely for recreation and pleasure. This complete ignorance of the realities, this innocent view of mankind, is what, in my opinion, constitutes the truly aristocratic. For instance, I have seen even fond mothers so far indulge their guileless, elegant daughters – misses of fifteen or sixteen – as to give them a few gold coins and teach them how to play; and though the young ladies may have won or have lost, they have invariably laughed, and departed as though they were well pleased. In the same way, I saw our General once approach the table in a stolid, important manner. A lacquey darted to offer him a chair, but the General did not even notice him. Slowly he took out his money bags, and slowly extracted 300 francs in gold, which he staked on the black, and won. Yet he did not take up his winnings – he left them there on the table. Again the black turned up, and again he did not gather in what he had won; and when, in the third round, the *red* turned up he lost, at a stroke, 1200 francs. Yet even then he rose with a smile, and thus preserved his reputation; yet I knew that his money bags must be chafing his heart, as well as that, had the stake been twice or thrice as much again, he would still have restrained himself from venting his disappointment.

On the other hand, I saw a Frenchman first win, and then lose, 30,000 francs cheerfully, and without a murmur. Yes; even if a gentleman should lose his whole substance, he must never give way to annoyance. Money must be so subservient to gentility as never to be worth a thought. Of course, the *supremely* aristocratic thing is to be entirely oblivious of the mire of rabble, with its setting; but sometimes a reverse course may be aristocratic to remark, to scan, and even to gape at, the mob (for preference, through a lorgnette), even as though one were taking the crowd and its squalor for a sort of raree show which had been organised specially for a gentleman's diversion. Though one may be squeezed by the crowd, one must look as though one were fully assured of being the observer – of having neither part nor lot with the observed. At the same time, to stare fixedly about one is unbecoming; for that, again, is ungentlemanly, seeing that no spectacle is worth an open stare – are no spectacles in the world which merit from a gentleman too pronounced an inspection.

However, to me personally the scene *did* seem to be worth undisguised contemplation – more especially in view of the fact that I had come there not only to look at, but also to number myself sincerely and wholeheartedly with, the mob. As for my secret moral views, I had no room for them amongst my actual, practical opinions. Let that stand as written: I am writing only to relieve my conscience. Yet let me say also this: that from the first I have been consistent in having an intense aversion to any trial of my acts and thoughts by a moral standard. Another standard altogether has directed my life....

As a matter of fact, the mob was playing in exceedingly foul fashion. Indeed, I have an idea that sheer robbery was going on around that gaming-table. The croupiers who sat at the two ends of it had not only to watch the stakes, but also to calculate the game – an immense amount of work for two men! As for the crowd itself – well, it consisted mostly of Frenchmen. Yet I was not then taking notes merely in order to be able to give you a description of roulette, but in order to get my bearings as to my behaviour when I myself should begin to play. For example, I noticed that nothing was more common than for another's hand to stretch out and grab one's winnings whenever one had won. Then there would arise a dispute, and frequently an uproar; and it would be a case of "I beg of you to prove, and to produce witnesses to the fact, that the stake is yours."

At first the proceedings were pure Greek to me. I could only divine and distinguish that stakes were hazarded on numbers, on "odd" or "even," and on colours. Polina's money I decided to risk, that evening, only to the amount of 100 gülden. The thought that I was not going to play for myself quite unnerved me. It was an unpleasant sensation, and I tried hard to banish it. I had a feeling that, once I had begun to play for Polina, I should wreck my own fortunes. Also, I wonder if any one has *ever* approached a gaming-table without falling an immediate prey to superstition? I began by pulling out fifty gülden, and staking them on "even." The wheel spun and stopped at 13. I had lost! With a feeling like a sick qualm, as though I would like to make my way out of the crowd and go home, I staked another fifty gülden – this time on the red. The red turned up. Next time I staked the 100 gülden just where they lay – and again the red turned up. Again I staked the whole sum, and again the red turned up. Clutching my 400 gülden, I placed 200 of them on twelve figures, to see what would come of it. The result was that the croupier paid me out three times my total stake! Thus from 100 gülden my store had grown to 800! Upon that such a curious, such an inexplicable, unwonted feeling overcame me that I decided to depart. Always the thought kept recurring to me that if I had been playing for myself alone I should never have had such luck. Once more I staked the whole 800 gülden on the "even." The wheel stopped at 4. I was paid out another 800 gülden, and, snatching up my pile of 1600, departed in search of Polina Alexandrovna.

I found the whole party walking in the park, and was able to get an interview with her only after supper. This time the Frenchman was absent from the meal, and the General seemed to be in a more expansive vein. Among other things, he thought it necessary to remind me that he would be sorry to see me playing at the gaming-tables. In his opinion, such conduct would greatly compromise him – especially if I were to lose much. "And even if you were to *win* much I should be compromised," he added in a meaning sort of way. "Of course I have no *right* to order your actions, but you yourself will agree that..." As usual, he did not finish his sentence. I answered drily that I had very little money in my possession, and that, consequently, I was hardly in a position to indulge in any conspicuous play, even if I did gamble. At last, when ascending to my own room, I succeeded in handing Polina her winnings, and told her that, next time, I should not play for her.

"Why not?" she asked excitedly.

"Because I wish to play *for myself*," I replied with a feigned glance of astonishment. "That is my sole reason."

"Then are you so certain that your roulette-playing will get us out of our difficulties?" she inquired with a quizzical smile.

I said very seriously, "Yes," and then added: "Possibly my certainty about winning may seem to you ridiculous; yet, pray leave me in peace."

Nonetheless she insisted that I ought to go halves with her in the day's winnings, and offered me 800 gülden on condition that henceforth, I gambled only on those terms; but I refused to do so, once and for all – stating, as my reason, that I found myself unable to play on behalf of any one else, "I am not unwilling so to do," I added, "but in all probability I should lose."

"Well, absurd though it be, I place great hopes on your playing of roulette," she remarked musingly; "wherefore, you ought to play as my partner and on equal shares; wherefore, of course, you will do as I wish."

Then she left me without listening to any further protests on my part.

CHAPTER THREE

On the morrow she said not a word to me about gambling. In fact, she purposely avoided me, although her old manner to me had not changed: the same serene coolness was hers on meeting me – a coolness that was mingled even with a spice of contempt and dislike. In short, she was at no pains to conceal her aversion to me. That I could see plainly. Also, she did not trouble to conceal from me the fact that I was necessary to her, and that she was keeping me for some end which she had in view. Consequently there became established between us relations which, to a large extent, were incomprehensible to me, considering her general pride and aloofness. For example, although she knew that I was madly in love with her, she allowed me to speak to her of my passion (though she could not well have showed her contempt for me more than by permitting me, unhindered and unrebuked, to mention to her my love).

"You see," her attitude expressed, "how little I regard your feelings, as well as how little I care for what you say to me, or for what you feel for me." Likewise, though she spoke as before concerning her affairs, it was never with complete frankness. In her contempt for me there were refinements. Although she knew well that I was aware of a certain circumstance in her life of something which might one day cause her trouble, she would speak to me about her affairs (whenever she had need of me for a given end) as though I were a slave or a passing acquaintance – yet tell them me only in so far as one would need to know them if one were going to be made temporary use of. Had I not known the whole chain of events, or had she not seen how much I was pained and disturbed by her teasing insistency, she would never have thought it worthwhile to soothe me with this frankness – even though, since she not infrequently used me to execute commissions that were not only troublesome, but risky, she ought, in my opinion, to have been frank in *any* case. But, forsooth, it was not worth her while to trouble about *my* feelings – about the fact that *I* was uneasy, and, perhaps, thrice as put about by her cares and misfortunes as she was herself!

For three weeks I had known of her intention to take to roulette. She had even warned me that she would like me to play on her behalf, since it was unbecoming for her to play in person; and, from the tone of her words I had gathered that there was something on her mind besides a mere desire to win money. As if money could matter to *her!* No, she had some end in view, and there were circumstances at which I could guess, but which I did not know for certain. True, the slavery and abasement in which she held me might have given me (such things often do so) the power to question her with abrupt directness (seeing that, inasmuch as I figured in her eyes as a mere slave and nonentity, she could not very well have taken offence at any rude curiosity); but the fact was that, though she let me question her, she never returned me a single answer, and at times did not so much as notice me. That is how matters stood.

Next day there was a good deal of talk about a telegram which, four days ago, had been sent to St. Petersburg, but to which there had come no answer. The General was visibly disturbed and moody, for the matter concerned his mother. The Frenchman, too, was excited, and after dinner the whole party talked long and seriously together – the Frenchman's tone being extraordinarily presumptuous and offhand to everybody. It almost reminded one of the proverb, "Invite a man to your table, and soon he will place his feet upon it." Even to Polina he was brusque almost to the point of rudeness. Yet still he seemed glad to join us in our walks in the Casino, or in our rides and drives about the town. I had long been aware of certain circumstances which bound the General to him; I had long been aware that in Russia they had hatched some scheme together although I did not know whether the plot had come to anything, or whether it was still only in the stage of being talked of. Likewise I was aware, in part, of a family secret – namely, that, last year, the Frenchman had bailed the General out of debt, and given him 30,000 roubles wherewith to pay his Treasury dues on retiring from the service. And now, of course, the General was in a vice – although the chief part in the affair was being played by Mlle. Blanche. Yes, of this last I had no doubt.

But *who* was this Mlle. Blanche? It was said of her that she was a Frenchwoman of good birth who, living with her mother, possessed a colossal fortune. It was also said that she was some relation to the Marquis, but only a distant one a cousin, or cousin-german, or something of the sort. Likewise I knew that, up to the time of my journey to Paris, she and the Frenchman had been more ceremonious towards our party – they had stood on a much more precise and delicate footing with them; but that now their acquaintanceship – their friendship, their intimacy – had taken on a much more off-hand and rough-and-ready air. Perhaps they thought that our means were too modest for them, and, therefore, unworthy of politeness or reticence. Also, for the last three days I had noticed certain looks which Astley had kept throwing at Mlle. Blanche and her mother; and it had occurred to me that he must have had some previous acquaintance with the pair. I had even surmised that the Frenchman too must have met Mr. Astley before. Astley was a man so shy, reserved, and taciturn in his manner that one might have looked for anything from him. At all events the Frenchman accorded him only the slightest of greetings, and scarcely even looked at him. Certainly he did not seem to be afraid of him; which was intelligible enough. But why did Mlle. Blanche also never look at the Englishman? – particularly since, *à propos* of something or another, the Marquis had declared the Englishman to be immensely and indubitably rich? Was not that a sufficient reason to make Mlle. Blanche look at the Englishman? Anyway the General seemed extremely uneasy; and, one could well understand what a telegram to announce the death of his mother would mean for him!

Although I thought it probable that Polina was avoiding me for a definite reason, I adopted a cold and indifferent air; for I felt pretty certain that it would not be long before she herself approached me. For two days, therefore, I devoted my attention to Mlle. Blanche. The poor General was in despair! To fall in love at fifty-five, and with such vehemence, is indeed a misfortune! And add to that his widowerhood, his children, his ruined property, his debts, and the woman with whom he had fallen in love! Though Mlle. Blanche was extremely good-looking, I may or may not be understood when I say that she had one of those faces which one is afraid of. At all events, I myself have always feared such women. Apparently about twenty-five years of age, she was tall and broad-shouldered, with shoulders that sloped; yet though her neck and bosom were ample in their proportions, her skin was dull yellow in colour, while her hair (which was extremely abundant – sufficient to make two coiffures) was as black as Indian ink. Add to that a pair of black eyes with yellowish whites, a proud glance, gleaming teeth, and lips which were perennially pomaded and redolent of musk. As for her dress, it was invariably rich, effective, and chic, yet in good taste. Lastly, her feet and hands were astonishing, and her voice a deep contralto. Sometimes, when she laughed, she displayed her teeth, but at ordinary times her air was taciturn and haughty – especially in the presence of Polina and Maria Philipovna. Yet she seemed to me almost destitute of education, and even of wits, though cunning and suspicious. This, apparently, was not because her life had been lacking in incident. Perhaps, if all were known, the Marquis was not her kinsman at all, nor her mother, her mother; but there was evidence that, in Berlin, where we had first come across the pair, they had possessed acquaintances of good standing. As for the Marquis himself, I doubt to this day if he was a Marquis – although about the fact that he had formerly belonged to high society (for instance, in Moscow and Germany) there could be no doubt whatever. What he had formerly been in France I had not a notion. All I knew was that he was said to possess a château. During the last two weeks I had looked for much to transpire, but am still ignorant whether at that time anything decisive ever passed between Mademoiselle and the General. Everything seemed to depend upon our means – upon whether the General would be able to flourish sufficient money in her face. If ever the news should arrive that the grandmother was not dead, Mlle. Blanche, I felt sure, would disappear in a twinkling. Indeed, it surprised and amused me to observe what a passion for intrigue I was developing. But how I loathed it all! With what pleasure would I have given everybody and everything the go-by! Only – I could not leave Polina. How, then, could I show contempt for those who surrounded her? Espionage is a base thing, but – what have I to do with that?

Mr. Astley, too, I found a curious person. I was only sure that he had fallen in love with Polina. A remarkable and diverting circumstance is the amount which may lie in the mien of a shy and painfully modest man who has been touched with the divine passion – especially when he would rather sink into the earth than betray himself by a single word or look. Though Mr. Astley frequently met us when we were out walking, he would merely take off his hat and pass us by, though I knew he was dying to join us. Even when invited to do so, he would refuse. Again, in places of amusement – in the Casino, at concerts, or near the fountain – he was never far from the spot where we were sitting. In fact, *wherever* we were in the Park, in the forest, or on the Shlangenberg – one needed but to raise one's eyes and glance around to catch sight of at least a *portion* of Mr. Astley's frame sticking out – whether on an adjacent path or behind a bush. Yet never did he lose any chance of speaking to myself; and, one morning when we had met, and exchanged a couple of words, he burst out in his usual abrupt way, without saying "Good-morning."

"That Mlle. Blanche," he said. "Well, I have seen a good many women like her."

After that he was silent as he looked me meaningly in the face. What he meant I did not know, but to my glance of inquiry he returned only a dry nod, and a reiterated "It is so." Presently, however, he resumed:

"Does Mlle. Polina like flowers?"

"I really cannot say," was my reply.

"What? You cannot say?" he cried in great astonishment.

"No; I have never noticed whether she does so or not," I repeated with a smile.

"Hm! Then I have an idea in my mind," he concluded. Lastly, with a nod, he walked away with a pleased expression on his face. The conversation had been carried on in execrable French.

CHAPTER FOUR

Today has been a day of folly, stupidity, and ineptness. The time is now eleven o'clock in the evening, and I am sitting in my room and thinking. It all began, this morning, with my being forced to go and play roulette for Polina Alexandrovna. When she handed me over her store of six hundred gülden I exacted two conditions – namely, that I should not go halves with her in her winnings, if any (that is to say, I should not take anything for myself), and that she should explain to me, that same evening, why it was so necessary for her to win, and how much was the sum which she needed. For, I could not suppose that she was doing all this merely for the sake of money. Yet clearly she *did* need some money, and that as soon as possible, and for a special purpose. Well, she promised to explain matters, and I departed. There was a tremendous crowd in the gaming-rooms. What an arrogant, greedy crowd it was! I pressed forward towards the middle of the room until I had secured a seat at a croupier's elbow. Then I began to play in timid fashion, venturing only twenty or thirty gülden at a time. Meanwhile, I observed and took notes. It seemed to me that calculation was superfluous, and by no means possessed of the importance which certain other players attached to it, even though they sat with ruled papers in their hands, whereon they set down the coups, calculated the chances, reckoned, staked, and – lost exactly as we more simple mortals did who played without any reckoning at all.

However, I deduced from the scene one conclusion which seemed to me reliable – namely, that in the flow of fortuitous chances there is, if not a system, at all events a sort of order. This, of course, is a very strange thing. For instance, after a dozen middle figures there would always occur a dozen or so outer ones. Suppose the ball stopped twice at a dozen outer figures; it would then pass to a dozen of the first ones, and then, again, to a dozen of the middle ciphers, and fall upon them three or four times, and then revert to a dozen outers; whence, after another couple of rounds, the ball would again pass to the first figures, strike upon them once, and then return thrice to the middle series – continuing thus for an hour and a half, or two hours. One, three, two: one, three, two. It was all very curious. Again, for the whole of a day or a morning the red would alternate with the black, but almost without any order, and from moment to moment, so that scarcely two consecutive rounds would end upon either the one or the other. Yet, next day, or, perhaps, the next evening, the red alone would turn up, and attain a run of over two score, and continue so for quite a length of time – say, for a whole day. Of these circumstances the majority were pointed out to me by Mr. Astley, who stood by the gaming-table the whole morning, yet never once staked in person.

For myself, I lost all that I had on me, and with great speed. To begin with, I staked two hundred gülden on "even," and won. Then I staked the same amount again, and won: and so on some two or three times. At one moment I must have had in my hands – gathered there within a space of five minutes – about 4000 gülden. That, of course, was the proper moment for me to have departed, but there arose in me a strange sensation as of a challenge to Fate – as of a wish to deal her a blow on the cheek, and to put out my tongue at her. Accordingly I set down the largest stake allowed by the rules – namely, 4000 gülden – and lost. Fired by this mishap, I pulled out all the money left to me, staked it all on the same venture, and – again lost! Then I rose from the table, feeling as though I were stupefied. What had happened to me I did not know; but, before luncheon I told Polina of my losses – until which time I walked about the Park.

At luncheon I was as excited as I had been at the meal three days ago. Mlle. Blanche and the Frenchman were lunching with us, and it appeared that the former had been to the Casino that morning, and had seen my exploits there. So now she showed me more attention when talking to me; while, for his part, the Frenchman approached me, and asked outright if it had been my own money that I had lost. He appeared to be suspicious as to something being on foot between Polina and myself, but I merely fired up, and replied that the money had been all my own.

At this the General seemed extremely surprised, and asked me whence I had procured it; whereupon I replied that, though I had begun only with 100 gülden, six or seven rounds had increased my capital to 5000 or 6000 gülden, and that subsequently I had lost the whole in two rounds.

All this, of course, was plausible enough. During my recital I glanced at Polina, but nothing was to be discerned on her face. However, she had allowed me to fire up without correcting me, and from that I concluded that it was my *cue* to fire up, and to conceal the fact that I had been playing on her behalf. "At all events," I thought to myself, "she, in her turn, has promised to give me an explanation to-night, and to reveal to me something or another."

Although the General appeared to be taking stock of me, he said nothing. Yet I could see uneasiness and annoyance in his face. Perhaps his straitened circumstances made it hard for him to have to hear of piles of gold passing through the hands of an irresponsible fool like myself within the space of a quarter of an hour. Now, I have an idea that, last night, he and the Frenchman had a sharp encounter with one another. At all events they closeted themselves together, and then had a long and vehement discussion; after which the Frenchman departed in what appeared to be a passion, but returned, early this morning, to renew the combat. On hearing of my losses, however, he only remarked with a sharp, and even a malicious, air that "a man ought to go more carefully." Next, for some reason or another, he added that, "though a great many Russians go in for gambling, they are no good at the game."

"*I* think that roulette was devised specially for Russians," I retorted; and when the Frenchman smiled contemptuously at my reply I further remarked that I was sure I was right; also that, speaking of Russians in the capacity of gamblers, I had far more blame for them than praise – of that he could be quite sure.

"Upon what do you base your opinion?" he inquired.

"Upon the fact that to the virtues and merits of the civilised Westerner there has become historically added – though this is not his chief point – a capacity for acquiring capital; whereas, not only is the Russian incapable of acquiring capital, but also he exhausts it wantonly and of sheer folly. None the less we Russians often need money; wherefore, we are glad of, and greatly devoted to, a method of acquisition like roulette – whereby, in a couple of hours, one may grow rich without doing any work. This method, I repeat, has a great attraction for us, but since we play in wanton fashion, and without taking any trouble, we almost invariably lose."

"To a certain extent that is true," assented the Frenchman with a self-satisfied air.

"Oh no, it is not true," put in the General sternly. "And you," he added to me, "you ought to be ashamed of yourself for traducing your own country!"

"I beg pardon," I said. "Yet it would be difficult to say which is the worst of the two – Russian ineptitude or the German method of growing rich through honest toil."

"What an extraordinary idea," cried the General.

"And what a *Russian* idea!" added the Frenchman.

I smiled, for I was rather glad to have a quarrel with them.

"I would rather live a wandering life in tents," I cried, "than bow the knee to a German idol!"

"To *what* idol?" exclaimed the General, now seriously angry.

"To the German method of heaping up riches. I have not been here very long, but I can tell you that what I have seen and verified makes my Tartar blood boil. Good Lord! I wish for no virtues of that kind. Yesterday I went for a walk of about ten versts; and, everywhere I found that things were even as we read of them in good German picture-books – that every house has its 'Vater,' who is horribly beneficent and extraordinarily honourable. So honourable is he that it is dreadful to have anything to do with him; and I cannot bear people of that sort. Each such 'Vater' has his family, and in the evenings they read improving books aloud. Over their roof-trees there murmur elms and chestnuts; the sun has sunk to his rest; a stork is roosting on the gable; and all is beautifully poetic and touching. Do not be angry, General. Let me tell you something that is even more touching than that. I can remember how, of an evening, my own father, now dead, used to sit under the lime trees in his little garden, and to read books aloud to myself and my mother. Yes, I know how things ought to be done. Yet every German family is bound to slavery and to submission to its 'Vater.' They work like oxen, and amass wealth like Jews. Suppose the 'Vater' has put by a certain number of gülden which he hands over to his eldest son, in order that the said son may acquire a trade or a small plot of land. Well, one result is to deprive the daughter of a dowry, and so leave her among the unwedded. For the same reason, the parents will have to sell the younger son into bondage or the ranks of the army, in order that he may earn more towards the family capital. Yes, such things ARE done, for I have been making inquiries on the subject. It is all done out of sheer rectitude – out of a rectitude which is magnified to the point of the younger son believing that he has been *rightly* sold, and that it is simply idyllic for the victim to rejoice when he is made over into pledge. What more have I to tell? Well, this – that matters bear just as hardly upon the eldest son. Perhaps he has his Gretchen to whom his heart is bound; but he cannot marry her, for the reason that he has not yet amassed sufficient gülden. So, the pair wait on in a mood of sincere and virtuous expectation, and smilingly deposit themselves in pawn the while. Gretchen's cheeks grow sunken, and she begins to wither; until at last, after some twenty years, their substance has multiplied, and sufficient gülden have been honourably and virtuously accumulated. Then the 'Vater' blesses his forty-year-old heir and the thirty-five-year-old Gretchen with the sunken bosom and the scarlet nose; after which he bursts, into tears, reads the pair a lesson on morality, and dies. In turn the eldest son becomes a virtuous 'Vater,' and the old story begins again. In fifty or sixty years' time the grandson of the original 'Vater' will have amassed a considerable sum; and that sum he will hand over to, his son, and the latter to *his* son, and so on for several generations; until at length there will issue a Baron Rothschild, or a 'Hoppe and Company,' or the devil knows what! Is it not a beautiful spectacle – the spectacle of a century or two of inherited labour, patience, intellect, rectitude, character, perseverance, and calculation, with a stork sitting on the roof above it all? What is more; they think there can never be anything better than this; wherefore, from *their* point of view they begin to judge the rest of the world, and to censure all who are at fault – that is to say, who are not exactly like themselves. Yes, there you have it in a nutshell. For my own part, I would rather grow fat after the Russian manner, or squander my whole substance at roulette. I have no wish to be 'Hoppe and Company' at the end of five generations. I want the money for *myself*, for in no way do I look upon my personality as necessary to, or meet to be given over to, capital. I may be wrong, but there you have it. Those are *my* views."

"How far you may be right in what you have said I do not know," remarked the General moodily; "but I *do* know that you are becoming an insufferable *farçeur* whenever you are given the least chance."

As usual, he left his sentence unfinished. Indeed, whenever he embarked upon anything that in the least exceeded the limits of daily small-talk, he left unfinished what he was saying. The Frenchman had listened to me contemptuously, with a slight protruding of his eyes; but, he could not have understood very much of my harangue. As for Polina, she had looked on with serene indifference. She seemed to have heard neither my voice nor any other during the progress of the meal.

CHAPTER FIVE

YES, SHE HAD BEEN extraordinarily meditative. Yet, on leaving the table, she immediately ordered me to accompany her for a walk. We took the children with us, and set out for the fountain in the Park.

I was in such an irritated frame of mind that in rude and abrupt fashion I blurted out a question as to "why our Marquis de Griers had ceased to accompany her for strolls, or to speak to her for days together."

"Because he is a brute," she replied in rather a curious way. It was the first time that I had heard her speak so of De Griers: consequently, I was momentarily awed into silence by this expression of resentment.

"Have you noticed, too, that today he is by no means on good terms with the General?" I went on.

"Yes – and I suppose you want to know why," she replied with dry captiousness. "You are aware, are you not, that the General is mortgaged to the Marquis, with all his property? Consequently, if the General's mother does not die, the Frenchman will become the absolute possessor of everything which he now holds only in pledge."

"Then it is really the case that everything is mortgaged? I have heard rumours to that effect, but was unaware how far they might be true."

"Yes, they *are* true. What then?"

"Why, it will be a case of 'Farewell, Mlle. Blanche,'" I remarked; "for in such an event she would never become Madame General. Do you know, I believe the old man is so much in love with her that he will shoot himself if she should throw him over. At his age it is a dangerous thing to fall in love."

"Yes, something, I believe, *will* happen to him," assented Polina thoughtfully.

"And what a fine thing it all is!" I continued. "Could anything be more abominable than the way in which she has agreed to marry for money alone? Not one of the decencies has been observed; the whole affair has taken place without the least ceremony. And as for the grandmother, what could be more comical, yet more dastardly, than the sending of telegram after telegram to know if she is dead? What do you think of it, Polina Alexandrovna?"

"Yes, it is very horrible," she interrupted with a shudder. "Consequently, I am the more surprised that *you* should be so cheerful. What are *you* so pleased about? About the fact that you have gone and lost my money?"

"What? The money that you gave me to lose? I told you I should never win for other people – least of all for you. I obeyed you simply because you ordered me to; but you must not blame me for the result. I warned you that no good would ever come of it. You seem much depressed at having lost your money. Why do you need it so greatly?"

"Why do *you* ask me these questions?"

"Because you promised to explain matters to me. Listen. I am certain that, as soon as ever I 'begin to play for myself' (and I still have 120 gülden left), I shall win. You can then take of me what you require."

She made a contemptuous grimace.

"You must not be angry with me," I continued, "for making such a proposal. I am so conscious of being only a nonentity in your eyes that you need not mind accepting money from me. A gift from me could not possibly offend you. Moreover, it was I who lost your gülden."

She glanced at me, but, seeing that I was in an irritable, sarcastic mood, changed the subject.

"My affairs cannot possibly interest you," she said. "Still, if you *do* wish to know, I am in debt. I borrowed some money, and must pay it back again. I have a curious, senseless idea that I am bound to win at the gaming-tables. Why I think so I cannot tell, but I do think so, and with some assurance. Perhaps it is because of that assurance that I now find myself without any other resource."

"Or perhaps it is because it is so *necessary* for you to win. It is like a drowning man catching at a straw. You yourself will agree that, unless he were drowning he would not mistake a straw for the trunk of a tree."

Polina looked surprised.

"What?" she said. "Do not you also hope something from it? Did you not tell me again and again, two weeks ago, that you were certain of winning at roulette if you played here? And did you not ask me not to consider you a fool for doing so? Were you joking? You cannot have been, for I remember that you spoke with a gravity which forbade the idea of your jesting."

"True," I replied gloomily. "I always felt certain that I should win. Indeed, what you say makes me ask myself – Why have my absurd, senseless losses of today raised a doubt in my mind? Yet I am *still* positive that, so soon as ever I begin to play for myself, I shall infallibly win."

"And why are you so certain?"

"To tell the truth, I do not know. I only know that I *must* win – that it is the one resource I have left. Yes, why do I feel so assured on the point?"

"Perhaps because one cannot help winning if one is fanatically certain of doing so."

"Yet I dare wager that you do not think me capable of serious feeling in the matter?"

"I do not care whether you are so or not," answered Polina with calm indifference. "Well, since you ask me, I *do* doubt your ability to take anything seriously. You are capable of worrying, but not deeply. You are too ill-regulated and unsettled a person for that. But why do you want money? Not a single one of the reasons which you have given can be looked upon as serious."

"By the way," I interrupted, "you say you want to pay off a debt. It must be a large one. Is it to the Frenchman?"

"What do you mean by asking all these questions? You are very clever today. Surely you are not drunk?"

"You know that you and I stand on no ceremony, and that sometimes I put to you very plain questions. I repeat that I am your slave – and slaves cannot be shamed or offended."

"You talk like a child. It is always possible to comport oneself with dignity. If one has a quarrel it ought to elevate rather than to degrade one."

"A maxim straight from the copybook! Suppose I *cannot* comport myself with dignity. By that I mean that, though I am a man of self-respect, I am unable to carry off a situation properly. Do you know the reason? It is because we Russians are too richly and multifariously gifted to be able at once to find the proper mode of expression. It is all a question of mode. Most of us are so bounteously endowed with intellect as to require also a spice of genius to choose the right form of behaviour. And genius is lacking in us for the reason that so little genius at all exists. It belongs only to the French – though a few other Europeans have elaborated their forms so well as to be able to figure with extreme dignity, and yet be wholly undignified persons. That is why, with us, the mode is so all-important. The Frenchman may receive an insult – a real, a venomous insult: yet, he will not so much as frown. But a tweaking of the nose he cannot bear, for the reason that such an act is an infringement of the accepted, of the time-hallowed order of decorum. That is why our good ladies are so fond of Frenchmen – the Frenchman's manners, they say, are perfect! But in my opinion there is no such thing as a Frenchman's manners. The Frenchman is only a bird – the *coq gaulois*. At the same time, as I am not a woman, I do not properly understand the question. Cocks may be excellent birds. If I am wrong you must stop me. You ought to stop and correct me more often when I am speaking to you, for I am too apt to say everything that is in my head.

"You see, I have lost my manners. I agree that I have none, nor yet any dignity. I will tell you why. I set no store upon such things. Everything in me has undergone a cheek. You know the reason. I have not a single human thought in my head. For a long while I have been ignorant of what is going on in the world – here or in Russia. I have been to Dresden, yet am completely in the dark as to what Dresden is like. You know the cause of my obsession. I have no hope now, and am a mere cipher in your eyes; wherefore, I tell you outright that wherever I go I see only you – all the rest is a matter of indifference.

"Why or how I have come to love you I do not know. It may be that you are not altogether fair to look upon. Do you know, I am ignorant even as to what your face is like. In all probability, too, your heart is not comely, and it is possible that your mind is wholly ignoble."

"And because you do not believe in my nobility of soul you think to purchase me with money?" she said.

"*When* have I thought to do so?" was my reply.

"You are losing the thread of the argument. If you do not wish to purchase me, at all events you wish to purchase my respect."

"Not at all. I have told you that I find it difficult to explain myself. You are hard upon me. Do not be angry at my chattering. You know why you ought not to be angry with me – that I am simply an imbecile. However, I do not mind if you *are* angry. Sitting in my room, I need but to think of you, to imagine to myself the rustle of your dress, and at once I fall almost to biting my hands. Why should you be angry with me? Because I call myself your slave? Revel, I pray you, in my slavery – revel in it. Do you know that sometimes I could kill you? – not because I do not love you, or am jealous of you, but, because I feel as though I could simply devour you... You are laughing!"

"No, I am not," she retorted. "But I order you, nevertheless, to be silent."

She stopped, well nigh breathless with anger. God knows, she may not have been a beautiful woman, yet I loved to see her come to a halt like this, and was therefore, the more fond of arousing her temper. Perhaps she divined this, and for that very reason gave way to rage. I said as much to her.

"What rubbish!" she cried with a shudder.

"I do not care," I continued. "Also, do you know that it is not safe for us to take walks together? Often I have a feeling that I should like to strike you, to disfigure you, to strangle you. Are you certain that it will never come to that? You are driving me to frenzy. Am I afraid of a scandal, or of your anger? Why should I fear your anger? I love without hope, and know that hereafter I shall love you a thousand times more. If ever I should kill you I should have to kill myself too. But I shall put off doing so as long as possible, for I wish to continue enjoying the unbearable pain which your coldness gives me. Do you know a very strange thing? It is that, with every day, my love for you increases – though that would seem to be almost an impossibility. Why should I not become a fatalist? Remember how, on the third day that we ascended the Shlangenberg, I was moved to whisper in your ear: 'Say but the word, and I will leap into the abyss.' Had you said it, I should have leapt. Do you not believe me?"

"What stupid rubbish!" she cried.

"I care not whether it be wise or stupid," I cried in return. "I only know that in your presence I must speak, speak, speak. Therefore, I am speaking. I lose all conceit when I am with you, and everything ceases to matter."

"Why should I have wanted you to leap from the Shlangenberg?" she said drily, and (I think) with wilful offensiveness. "*That* would have been of no use to me."

"Splendid!" I shouted. "I know well that you must have used the words 'of no use' in order to crush me. *I* can see through you. 'Of no use,' did you say? Why, to give pleasure is *always* of use; and, as for barbarous, unlimited power – even if it be only over a fly – why, it is a kind of luxury. Man is a despot by nature, and loves to torture. You, in particular, love to do so."

I remember that at this moment she looked at me in a peculiar way. The fact is that my face must have been expressing all the maze of senseless, gross sensations which were seething within me. To this day I can remember, word for word, the conversation as I have written it down. My eyes were suffused with blood, and the foam had caked itself on my lips. Also, on my honour I swear that, had she bidden me cast myself from the summit of the Shlangenberg, I should have done it. Yes, had she bidden me in jest, or only in contempt and with a spit in my face, I should have cast myself down.

"Oh no! Why so? I believe you," she said, but in such a manner – in the manner of which, at times, she was a mistress – and with such a note of disdain and viperish arrogance in her tone, that God knows I could have killed her.

Yes, at that moment she stood in peril. I had not lied to her about that.

"Surely you are not a coward?" suddenly she asked me.

"I do not know," I replied. "Perhaps I am, but I do not know. I have long given up thinking about such things."

"If I said to you, 'Kill that man,' would you kill him?"

"Whom?"

"Whomsoever I wish?"

"The Frenchman?"

"Do not ask me questions; return me answers. I repeat, whomsoever I wish? I desire to see if you were speaking seriously just now."

She awaited my reply with such gravity and impatience that I found the situation unpleasant.

"Do *you*, rather, tell me," I said, "what is going on here? Why do you seem half-afraid of me? I can see for myself what is wrong. You are the step-daughter of a ruined and insensate man who is smitten with love for this devil of a Blanche. And there is this Frenchman, too, with his mysterious influence over you. Yet, you actually ask me such a question! If you do not tell me how things stand, I shall have to put in my oar and do something. Are you ashamed to be frank with me? Are you shy of me?"

"I am not going to talk to you on that subject. I have asked you a question, and am waiting for an answer."

"Well, then – I will kill whomsoever you wish," I said. "But are you *really* going to bid me do such deeds?"

"Why should you think that I am going to let you off? I shall bid you do it, or else renounce me. Could you ever do the latter? No, you know that you couldn't. You would first kill whom I had bidden you, and then kill *me* for having dared to send you away!"

Something seemed to strike upon my brain as I heard these words. Of course, at the time I took them half in jest and half as a challenge; yet, she had spoken them with great seriousness. I felt thunderstruck that she should so express herself, that she should assert such a right over me, that she should assume such authority and say outright: "Either you kill whom I bid you, or I will have nothing more to do with you." Indeed, in what she had said there was something so cynical and unveiled as to pass all bounds. For how could she ever regard me as the same after the killing was done? This was more than slavery and abasement; it was sufficient to bring a man back to his right senses. Yet, despite the outrageous improbability of our conversation, my heart shook within me.

Suddenly, she burst out laughing. We were seated on a bench near the spot where the children were playing – just opposite the point in the alley-way before the Casino where the carriages drew up in order to set down their occupants.

"Do you see that fat Baroness?" she cried. "It is the Baroness Burmergelm. She arrived three days ago. Just look at her husband – that tall, wizened Prussian there, with the stick in his hand. Do you remember how he stared at us the other day? Well, go to the Baroness, take off your hat to her, and say something in French."

"Why?"

"Because you have sworn that you would leap from the Shlangenberg for my sake, and that you would kill any one whom I might bid you kill. Well, instead of such murders and tragedies, I wish only for a good laugh. Go without answering me, and let me see the Baron give you a sound thrashing with his stick."

"Then you throw me out a challenge? – you think that I will not do it?"

"Yes, I do challenge you. Go, for such is my will."

"Then I *will* go, however mad be your fancy. Only, look here: shall you not be doing the General a great disservice, as well as, through him, a great disservice to yourself? It is not about myself I am worrying – it is about you and the General. Why, for a mere fancy, should I go and insult a woman?"

"Ah! Then I can see that you are only a trifler," she said contemptuously. "Your eyes are swimming with blood – but only because you have drunk a little too much at luncheon. Do I not know that what I have asked you to do is foolish and wrong, and that the General will be angry about it? But I want to have a good laugh, all the same. I want that, and nothing else. Why should you insult a woman, indeed? Well, you will be given a sound thrashing for so doing."

I turned away, and went silently to do her bidding. Of course the thing was folly, but I could not get out of it. I remember that, as I approached the Baroness, I felt as excited as a schoolboy. I was in a frenzy, as though I were drunk.

CHAPTER SIX

Two days have passed since that day of lunacy. What a noise and a fuss and a chattering and an uproar there was! And what a welter of unseemliness and disorder and stupidity and bad manners! And *I* the cause of it all! Yet part of the scene was also ridiculous – at all events to myself it was so. I am not quite sure what was the matter with me – whether I was merely stupefied or whether I purposely broke loose and ran amok. At times my mind seems all confused; while at other times I seem almost to be back in my childhood, at the school desk, and to have done the deed simply out of mischief.

It all came of Polina – yes, of Polina. But for her, there might never have been a fracas. Or perhaps I did the deed in a fit of despair (though it may be foolish of me to think so)? What there is so attractive about her I cannot think. Yet there *is* something attractive about her – something passing fair, it would seem. Others besides myself she has driven to distraction. She is tall and straight, and very slim. Her body looks as though it could be tied into a knot, or bent double, like a cord. The imprint of her foot is long and narrow. It is, a maddening imprint – yes, simply a maddening one! And her hair has a reddish tint about it, and her eyes are like cat's eyes – though able also to glance with proud, disdainful mien. On the evening of my first arrival, four months ago, I remember that she was sitting and holding an animated conversation with De Griers in the salon. And the way in which she looked at him was such that later, when I retired to my own room upstairs, I kept fancying that she had smitten him in the face – that she had smitten him right on the cheek, so peculiar had been her look as she stood confronting him. Ever since that evening I have loved her.

But to my tale.

I stepped from the path into the carriage-way, and took my stand in the middle of it. There I awaited the Baron and the Baroness.

When they were but a few paces distant from me I took off my hat, and bowed.

I remember that the Baroness was clad in a voluminous silk dress, pale grey in colour, and adorned with flounces and a crinoline and train. Also, she was short and inordinately stout, while her gross, flabby chin completely concealed her neck. Her face was purple, and the little eyes in it had an impudent, malicious expression. Yet she walked as though she were conferring a favour upon everybody by so doing. As for the Baron, he was tall, wizened, bony-faced after the German fashion, spectacled, and, apparently, about forty-five years of age. Also, he had legs which seemed to begin almost at his chest – or, rather, at his chin! Yet, for all his air of peacock-like conceit, his clothes sagged a little, and his face wore a sheepish air which might have passed for profundity.

These details I noted within a space of a few seconds.

At first my bow and the fact that I had my hat in my hand barely caught their attention. The Baron only scowled a little, and the Baroness swept straight on.

"Madame la Baronne," said I, loudly and distinctly – embroidering each word, as it were – "j'ai l'honneur d'être votre esclave."

Then I bowed again, put on my hat, and walked past the Baron with a rude smile on my face.

Polina had ordered me merely to take off my hat: the bow and the general effrontery were of my own invention. God knows what instigated me to perpetrate the outrage! In my frenzy I felt as though I were walking on air.

"Hein!" ejaculated – or, rather, growled – the Baron as he turned towards me in angry surprise.

I too turned round, and stood waiting in pseudo-courteous expectation. Yet still I wore on my face an impudent smile as I gazed at him. He seemed to hesitate, and his brows contracted to their utmost limits. Every moment his visage was growing darker. The Baroness also turned in my direction, and gazed at me in wrathful perplexity, while some of the passers-by also began to stare at us, and others of them halted outright.

"Hein!" the Baron vociferated again, with a redoubled growl and a note of growing wrath in his voice.

"Ja wohl!" I replied, still looking him in the eyes.

"Sind Sie rasend?" he exclaimed, brandishing his stick, and, apparently, beginning to feel nervous. Perhaps it was my costume which intimidated him, for I was well and fashionably dressed, after the manner of a man who belongs to indisputably good society.

"Ja wo-o-ohl!" cried I again with all my might with a longdrawn rolling of the "ohl" sound after the fashion of the Berliners (who constantly use the phrase "Ja wohl!" in conversation, and more or less prolong the syllable "ohl" according as they desire to express different shades of meaning or of mood).

At this the Baron and the Baroness faced sharply about, and almost fled in their alarm. Some of the bystanders gave vent to excited exclamations, and others remained staring at me in astonishment. But I do not remember the details very well.

Wheeling quietly about, I returned in the direction of Polina Alexandrovna. But, when I had got within a hundred paces of her seat, I saw her rise and set out with the children towards the hotel.

At the portico I caught up to her.

"I have perpetrated the – the piece of idiocy," I said as I came level with her.

"Have you? Then you can take the consequences," she replied without so much as looking at me. Then she moved towards the staircase.

I spent the rest of the evening walking in the park. Thence I passed into the forest, and walked on until I found myself in a neighbouring principality. At a wayside restaurant I partook of an omelette and some wine, and was charged for the idyllic repast a thaler and a half.

Not until eleven o'clock did I return home – to find a summons awaiting me from the General.

Our party occupied two suites in the hotel; each of which contained two rooms. The first (the larger suite) comprised a salon and a smoking-room, with, adjoining the latter, the General's study. It was here that he was awaiting me as he stood posed in a majestic attitude beside his writing-table. Lolling on a divan close by was De Griers.

"My good sir," the General began, "may I ask you what this is that you have gone and done?"

"I should be glad," I replied, "if we could come straight to the point. Probably you are referring to my encounter of today with a German?"

"With a German? Why, the German was the Baron Burmergelm – a most important personage! I hear that you have been rude both to him and to the Baroness?"

"No, I have not."

"But I understand that you simply terrified them, my good sir?" shouted the General.

"Not in the least," I replied. "You must know that when I was in Berlin I frequently used to hear the Berliners repeat, and repellently prolong, a certain phrase – namely, 'Ja wohl!'; and, happening to meet this couple in the carriage-drive, I found, for some reason or another, that this phrase suddenly recurred to my memory, and exercised a rousing effect upon my spirits. Moreover, on the three previous occasions that I have met the Baroness she has walked towards me as though I were a worm which could easily be crushed with the foot. Not unnaturally, I too possess a measure of self-respect; wherefore, on *this* occasion I took off my hat, and said politely (yes, I assure you it was said politely): 'Madame, j'ai l'honneur d'être votre esclave.' Then the Baron turned round, and said 'Hein!'; whereupon I felt moved to ejaculate in answer 'Ja wohl!' Twice I shouted it at him – the first time in an ordinary tone, and the second time with the greatest prolonging of the words of which I was capable. That is all."

I must confess that this puerile explanation gave me great pleasure. I felt a strong desire to overlay the incident with an even added measure of grossness; so, the further I proceeded, the more did the gusto of my proceeding increase.

"You are only making fun of me!" vociferated the General as, turning to the Frenchman, he declared that my bringing about of the incident had been gratuitous. De Griers smiled contemptuously, and shrugged his shoulders.

"Do not think *that*," I put in. "It was not so at all. I grant you that my behaviour was bad – I fully confess that it was so, and make no secret of the fact. I would even go so far as to grant you that my behaviour might well be called stupid and indecent tomfoolery; but, *more* than that it was not. Also, let me tell you that I am very sorry for my conduct. Yet there is one circumstance which, in my eyes, almost absolves me from regret in the matter. Of late – that is to say, for the last two or three weeks – I have been feeling not at all well. That is to say, I have been in a sick, nervous, irritable, fanciful condition, so that I have periodically lost control over myself. For instance, on more than one occasion I have tried to pick a quarrel even with Monsieur le Marquise here; and, under the circumstances, he had no choice but to answer me. In short, I have recently been showing signs of ill-health. Whether the Baroness Burmergelm will take this circumstance into consideration when I come to beg her pardon (for I *do* intend to make her amends) I do not know; but I doubt if she will, and the less so since, so far as I know, the circumstance is one which, of late, has begun to be abused in the legal world, in that advocates in criminal cases have taken to justifying their clients on the ground that, at the moment of the crime, they (the clients) were unconscious of what they were doing – that, in short, they were out of health. 'My client committed the murder – that is true; but he has no recollection of having committed it.' And doctors actually support these advocates by affirming that there really is such a malady – that there really *can* arise temporary delusions which make a man remember nothing of a given deed, or only a half or a quarter of it! But the Baron and Baroness are members of an older generation, as well as Prussian Junkers and landowners. To them such a process in the medico-judicial world will be unknown, and therefore, they are the more unlikely to accept any such explanation. What is *your* opinion about it, General?"

"Enough, sir!" he thundered with barely restrained fury. "Enough, I say! Once and for all I must endeavour to rid myself of you and your impertinence. To justify yourself in the eyes of the Baron and Baroness will be impossible. Any intercourse with you, even though it be confined to a begging of their pardons, they would look upon as a degradation. I may tell you that, on learning that you formed part of my household, the Baron approached me in the Casino, and demanded of me additional satisfaction. Do you understand, then, what it is that you have entailed upon me – upon *me*, my good sir? You have entailed upon me the fact of my being forced to sue humbly to the Baron, and to give him my word of honour that this very day you shall cease to belong to my establishment!"

"Excuse me, General," I interrupted, "but did he make an express point of it that I should 'cease to belong to your establishment,' as you call it?"

"No; I, of my own initiative, thought that I ought to afford him that satisfaction; and, with it he was satisfied. So we must part, good sir. It is my duty to hand over to you forty gülden, three florins, as per the accompanying statement. Here is the money, and here the account, which you are at liberty to verify. Farewell. From henceforth we are strangers. From you I have never had anything but trouble and unpleasantness. I am about to call the landlord, and explain to him that from tomorrow onwards I shall no longer be responsible for your hotel expenses. Also I have the honour to remain your obedient servant."

I took the money and the account (which was indicted in pencil), and, bowing low to the General, said to him very gravely:

"The matter cannot end here. I regret very much that you should have been put to unpleasantness at the Baron's hands; but, the fault (pardon me) is your own. How came you to answer for me to the Baron? And what did you mean by saying that I formed part of your household? I am merely your family tutor – not a son of yours, nor yet your ward, nor a person of any kind for whose acts you need be responsible. I am a judicially competent person, a man of twenty-five years of age, a university graduate, a gentleman, and, until I met yourself, a complete stranger to you. Only my boundless respect for your merits restrains me from demanding satisfaction at your hands, as well as a further explanation as to the reasons which have led you to take it upon yourself to answer for my conduct."

So struck was he with my words that, spreading out his hands, he turned to the Frenchman, and interpreted to him that I had challenged himself (the General) to a duel. The Frenchman laughed aloud.

"Nor do I intend to let the Baron off," I continued calmly, but with not a little discomfiture at De Griers' merriment. "And since you, General, have today been so good as to listen to the Baron's complaints, and to enter into his concerns – since you have made yourself a participator in the affair – I have the honour to inform you that, tomorrow morning at the latest, I shall, in my own name, demand of the said Baron a formal explanation as to the reasons which have led him to disregard the fact that the matter lies between him and myself alone, and to put a slight upon me by referring it to another person, as though I were unworthy to answer for my own conduct."

Then there happened what I had foreseen. The General on hearing of this further intended outrage, showed the white feather.

"What?" he cried. "Do you intend to go on with this damned nonsense? Do you not realise the harm that it is doing me? I beg of you not to laugh at me, sir – not to laugh at me, for we have police authorities here who, out of respect for my rank, and for that of the Baron... In short, sir, I swear to you that I will have you arrested, and marched out of the place, to prevent any further brawling on your part. Do you understand what I say?" He was almost breathless with anger, as well as in a terrible fright.

"General," I replied with that calmness which he never could abide, "one cannot arrest a man for brawling until he has brawled. I have not so much as begun my explanations to the Baron, and you are altogether ignorant as to the form and time which my intended procedure is likely to assume. I wish but to disabuse the Baron of what is, to me, a shameful supposition – namely, that I am under the guardianship of a person who is qualified to exercise control over my free will. It is vain for you to disturb and alarm yourself."

"For God's sake, Alexis Ivanovitch, do put an end to this senseless scheme of yours!" he muttered, but with a sudden change from a truculent tone to one of entreaty as he caught me by the hand. "Do you know what is likely to come of it? Merely further unpleasantness. You will agree with me, I am sure, that at present I ought to move with especial care – yes, with very especial care. You cannot be fully aware of how I am situated. When we leave this place I shall be ready to receive you back into my household; but, for the time being I – Well, I cannot tell you all my reasons." With that he wound up in a despairing voice: "O Alexis Ivanovitch, Alexis Ivanovitch!"

I moved towards the door – begging him to be calm, and promising that everything should be done decently and in order; whereafter I departed.

Russians, when abroad, are over-apt to play the poltroon, to watch all their words, and to wonder what people are thinking of their conduct, or whether such and such a thing is *comme il faut*. In short, they are over-apt to cosset themselves, and to lay claim to great importance. Always they prefer the form of behaviour which has once and for all become accepted and established. This they will follow slavishly whether in hotels, on promenades, at meetings, or when on a journey. But the General had avowed to me that, over and above such considerations as these, there were circumstances which compelled him to "move with especial care at present", and that the fact had actually made him poor-spirited and a coward – it had made him altogether change his tone towards me. This fact I took into my calculations, and duly noted it, for, of course, he *might* apply to the authorities tomorrow, and it behoved me to go carefully.

Yet it was not the General but Polina that I wanted to anger. She had treated me with such cruelty, and had got me into such a hole, that I felt a longing to force her to beseech me to stop. Of course, my tomfoolery might compromise her; yet certain other feelings and desires had begun to form themselves in my brain. If I was never to rank in her eyes as anything but a nonentity, it would not greatly matter if I figured as a draggle-tailed cockerel, and the Baron were to give me a good thrashing; but, the fact was that I desired to have the laugh of them all, and to come out myself unscathed. Let people see what they *would* see. Let Polina, for once, have a good fright, and be forced to whistle me to heel again. But, however much she might whistle, she should see that I was at least no draggle-tailed cockerel!

I have just received a surprising piece of news. I have just met our chambermaid on the stairs, and been informed by her that Maria Philipovna departed today, by the night train, to stay with a cousin at Carlsbad. What can that mean? The maid declares that Madame packed her trunks early in the day. Yet how is it that no one else seems to have been aware of the circumstance? Or is it that *I* have been the only person to be unaware of it? Also, the maid has just told me that, three days ago, Maria Philipovna had some high words with the General. I understand, then! Probably the words were concerning Mlle. Blanche. Certainly something decisive is approaching.

CHAPTER SEVEN

In the morning I sent for the maître d'hôtel, and explained to him that, in future, my bill was to be rendered to me personally. As a matter of fact, my expenses had never been so large as to alarm me, nor to lead me to quit the hotel; while, moreover, I still had 160 gülden left to me, and – in them – yes, in them, perhaps, riches awaited me. It was a curious fact, that, though I had not yet won anything at play, I nevertheless acted, thought, and felt as though I were sure, before long, to become wealthy – since I could not imagine myself otherwise.

Next, I bethought me, despite the earliness of the hour, of going to see Mr. Astley, who was staying at the Hôtel de l'Angleterre (a hostelry at no great distance from our own). But suddenly De Griers entered my room. This had never before happened, for of late that gentleman and I had stood on the most strained and distant of terms – he attempting no concealment of his contempt for me (he even made an express point of showing it), and I having no reason to desire his company. In short, I detested him. Consequently, his entry at the present moment the more astounded me. At once I divined that something out of the way was on the carpet.

He entered with marked affability, and began by complimenting me on my room. Then, perceiving that I had my hat in my hands, he inquired whither I was going so early; and, no sooner did he hear that I was bound for Mr. Astley's than he stopped, looked grave, and seemed plunged in thought.

He was a true Frenchman insofar as that, though he could be lively and engaging when it suited him, he became insufferably dull and wearisome as soon as ever the need for being lively and engaging had passed. Seldom is a Frenchman *naturally* civil: he is civil only as though to order and of set purpose. Also, if he thinks it incumbent upon him to be fanciful, original, and out of the way, his fancy always assumes a foolish, unnatural vein, for the reason that it is compounded of trite, hackneyed forms. In short, the natural Frenchman is a conglomeration of commonplace, petty, everyday positiveness, so that he is the most tedious person in the world. Indeed, I believe that none but greenhorns and excessively Russian people feel an attraction towards the French; for, to any man of sensibility, such a compendium of outworn forms – a compendium which is built up of drawing-room manners, expansiveness, and gaiety – becomes at once over-noticeable and unbearable.

"I have come to see you on business," De Griers began in a very offhand, yet polite, tone; "nor will I seek to conceal from you the fact that I have come in the capacity of an emissary, of an intermediary, from the General. Having small knowledge of the Russian tongue, I lost most of what was said last night; but, the General has now explained matters, and I must confess that – "

"See here, Monsieur de Griers," I interrupted. "I understand that you have undertaken to act in this affair as an intermediary. Of course I am only 'un utchitel,' a tutor, and have never claimed to be an intimate of this household, nor to stand on at all familiar terms with it. Consequently, I do not know the whole of its circumstances. Yet pray explain to me this: have you yourself become one of its members, seeing that you are beginning to take such a part in everything, and are now present as an intermediary?"

The Frenchman seemed not over-pleased at my question. It was one which was too outspoken for his taste – and he had no mind to be frank with me.

"I am connected with the General," he said drily, "partly through business affairs, and partly through special circumstances. My principal has sent me merely to ask you to forego your intentions of last evening. What you contemplate is, I have no doubt, very clever; yet he has charged me to represent to you that you have not the slightest chance of succeeding in your end, since not only will the Baron refuse to receive you, but also he (the Baron) has at his disposal every possible means for obviating further unpleasantness from you. Surely you can see that yourself? What, then, would be the good of going on with it all? On the other hand, the General promises that at the first favourable opportunity he will receive you back into his household, and, in the meantime, will credit you with your salary – with 'vos appointements.' Surely that will suit you, will it not?"

Very quietly I replied that he (the Frenchman) was labouring under a delusion; that perhaps, after all, I should not be expelled from the Baron's presence, but, on the contrary, be listened to; finally, that I should be glad if Monsieur de Griers would confess that he was now visiting me merely in order to see how far I intended to go in the affair.

"Good heavens!" cried de Griers. "Seeing that the General takes such an interest in the matter, is there anything very unnatural in his desiring also to know your plans?"

Again I began my explanations, but the Frenchman only fidgeted and rolled his head about as he listened with an expression of manifest and unconcealed irony on his face. In short, he adopted a supercilious attitude. For my own part, I endeavoured to pretend that I took the affair very seriously. I declared that, since the Baron had gone and complained of me to the General, as though I were a mere servant of the General's, he had, in the first place, lost me my post, and, in the second place, treated me like a person to whom, as to one not qualified to answer for himself, it was not even worth while to speak. Naturally, I said, I felt insulted at this. Yet, comprehending as I did, differences of years, of social status, and so forth (here I could scarcely help smiling), I was not anxious to bring about further scenes by going personally to demand or to request satisfaction of the Baron. All that I felt was that I had a right to go in person and beg the Baron's and the Baroness's pardon – the more so since, of late, I had been feeling unwell and unstrung, and had been in a fanciful condition. And so forth, and so forth. Yet (I continued) the Baron's offensive behaviour to me of yesterday (that is to say, the fact of his referring the matter to the General) as well as his insistence that the General should deprive me of my post, had placed me in such a position that I could not well express my regret to him (the Baron) and to his good lady, for the reason that in all probability both he and the Baroness, with the world at large, would imagine that I was doing so merely because I hoped, by my action, to recover my post. Hence, I found myself forced to request the Baron to express to me *his own* regrets, as well as to express them in the most unqualified manner – to say, in fact, that he had never had any wish to insult me. After the Baron had done *that*, I should, for my part, at once feel free to express to him, whole-heartedly and without reserve, my own regrets. "In short," I declared in conclusion, "my one desire is that the Baron may make it possible for me to adopt the latter course."

"Oh fie! What refinements and subtleties!" exclaimed De Griers. "Besides, what have you to express regret for? Confess, Monsieur, Monsieur – pardon me, but I have forgotten your name – confess, I say, that all this is merely a plan to annoy the General? Or perhaps, you have some other and special end in view? Eh?"

"In return you must pardon *me*, mon cher Marquis, and tell me what *you* have to do with it."

"The General – "

"But what of the General? Last night he said that, for some reason or another, it behoved him to 'move with especial care at present;' wherefore, he was feeling nervous. But I did not understand the reference."

"Yes, there *do* exist special reasons for his doing so," assented De Griers in a conciliatory tone, yet with rising anger. "You are acquainted with Mlle. de Cominges, are you not?"

"Mlle. Blanche, you mean?"

"Yes, Mlle. Blanche de Cominges. Doubtless you know also that the General is in love with this young lady, and may even be about to marry her before he leaves here? Imagine, therefore, what any scene or scandal would entail upon him!"

"I cannot see that the marriage scheme need, be affected by scenes or scandals."

"Mais le Baron est si irascible – un caractère prussien, vous savez! Enfin il fera une querelle d'Allemand."

"I do not care," I replied, "seeing that I no longer belong to his household" (of set purpose I was trying to talk as senselessly as possible). "But is it quite settled that Mlle. is to marry the General? What are they waiting for? Why should they conceal such a matter – at all events from ourselves, the General's own party?"

"I cannot tell you. The marriage is not yet a settled affair, for they are awaiting news from Russia. The General has business transactions to arrange."

"Ah! Connected, doubtless, with madame his mother?"

De Griers shot at me a glance of hatred.

"To cut things short," he interrupted, "I have complete confidence in your native politeness, as well as in your tact and good sense. I feel sure that you will do what I suggest, even if it is only for the sake of this family which has received you as a kinsman into its bosom and has always loved and respected you."

"Be so good as to observe," I remarked, "that the same family has just *expelled* me from its bosom. All that you are saying you are saying but for show; but, when people have just said to you, 'Of course we do not wish to turn you out, yet, for the sake of appearance's, you must *permit* yourself to be turned out,' nothing can matter very much."

"Very well, then," he said, in a sterner and more arrogant tone. "Seeing that my solicitations have had no effect upon you, it is my duty to mention that other measures will be taken. There exist here police, you must remember, and this very day they shall send you packing. Que diable! To think of a blanc bec like yourself challenging a person like the Baron to a duel! Do you suppose that you will be *allowed* to do such things? Just try doing them, and see if any one will be afraid of you! The reason why I have asked you to desist is that I can see that your conduct is causing the General annoyance. Do you believe that the Baron could not tell his lacquey simply to put you out of doors?"

"Nevertheless I should not GO out of doors," I retorted with absolute calm. "You are labouring under a delusion, Monsieur de Griers. The thing will be done in far better trim than you imagine. I was just about to start for Mr. Astley's, to ask him to be my intermediary – in other words, my second. He has a strong liking for me, and I do not think that he will refuse. He will go and see the Baron on MY behalf, and the Baron will certainly not decline to receive him. Although I am only a tutor – a kind of subaltern, Mr. Astley is known to all men as the nephew of a real English lord, the Lord Piebroch, as well as a lord in his own right. Yes, you may be pretty sure that the Baron will be civil to Mr. Astley, and listen to him. Or, should he decline to do so, Mr. Astley will take the refusal as a personal affront to himself (for you know how persistent the English are?) and thereupon introduce to the Baron a friend of his own (and he has many friends in a good position). That being so, picture to yourself the issue of the affair – an affair which will not quite end as you think it will."

This caused the Frenchman to bethink him of playing the coward. "Really things may be as this fellow says," he evidently thought. "Really he *might* be able to engineer another scene."

"Once more I beg of you to let the matter drop," he continued in a tone that was now entirely conciliatory. "One would think that it actually *pleased* you to have scenes! Indeed, it is a brawl rather than genuine satisfaction that you are seeking. I have said that the affair may prove to be diverting, and even clever, and that possibly you may attain something by it; yet none the less I tell you" (he said this only because he saw me rise and reach for my hat) "that I have come hither also to hand you these few words from a certain person. Read them, please, for I must take her back an answer."

So saying, he took from his pocket a small, compact, wafer-sealed note, and handed it to me. In Polina's handwriting I read:

"I hear that you are thinking of going on with this affair. You have lost your temper now, and are beginning to play the fool! Certain circumstances, however, I may explain to you later. Pray cease from your folly, and put a check upon yourself. For folly it all is. I have need of you, and, moreover, you have promised to obey me. Remember the Shlangenberg. I ask you to be obedient. If necessary, I shall even *bid* you be obedient. – Your own

POLINA.

"*P.S.* – If so be that you still bear a grudge against me for what happened last night, pray forgive me."

Everything, to my eyes, seemed to change as I read these words. My lips grew pale, and I began to tremble. Meanwhile, the cursed Frenchman was eyeing me discreetly and askance, as though he wished to avoid witnessing my confusion. It would have been better if he had laughed outright.

"Very well," I said, "you can tell Mlle. not to disturb herself. But," I added sharply, "I would also ask you why you have been so long in handing me this note? Instead of chattering about trifles, you ought to have delivered me the missive at once – if you have really come commissioned as you say."

"Well, pardon some natural haste on my part, for the situation is so strange. I wished first to gain some personal knowledge of your intentions; and, moreover, I did not know the contents of the note, and thought that it could be given you at any time."

"I understand," I replied. "So you were ordered to hand me the note only in the last resort, and if you could not otherwise appease me? Is it not so? Speak out, Monsieur de Griers."

"Perhaps," said he, assuming a look of great forbearance, but gazing at me in a meaning way.

I reached for my hat; whereupon he nodded, and went out. Yet on his lips I fancied that I could see a mocking smile. How could it have been otherwise?

"You and I are to have a reckoning later, Master Frenchman," I muttered as I descended the stairs. "Yes, we will measure our strength together." Yet my thoughts were all in confusion, for again something seemed to have struck me dizzy. Presently the air revived me a little, and, a couple of minutes later, my brain had sufficiently cleared to enable two ideas in particular to stand out in it. Firstly, I asked myself, which of the absurd, boyish, and extravagant threats which I had uttered at random last night had made everybody so alarmed? Secondly, what was the influence which this Frenchman appeared to exercise over Polina? He had but to give the word, and at once she did as he desired – at once she wrote me a note to beg of me to forbear! Of course, the relations between the pair had, from the first, been a riddle to me – they had been so ever since I had first made their acquaintance. But of late I had remarked in her a strong aversion for, even a contempt for – him, while, for his part, he had scarcely even looked at her, but had behaved towards her always in the most churlish fashion. Yes, I had noted that. Also, Polina herself had mentioned to me her dislike for him, and delivered herself of some remarkable confessions on the subject. Hence, he must have got her into his power somehow – somehow he must be holding her as in a vice.

CHAPTER EIGHT

All at once, on the Promenade, as it was called – that is to say, in the Chestnut Avenue – I came face to face with my Englishman.

"I was just coming to see you," he said; "and you appear to be out on a similar errand. So you have parted with your employers?"

"How do you know that?" I asked in astonishment. "Is *every one* aware of the fact?"

"By no means. Not every one would consider such a fact to be of moment. Indeed, I have never heard any one speak of it."

"Then how come you to know it?"

"Because I have had occasion to do so. Whither are you bound? I like you, and was therefore coming to pay you a visit."

"What a splendid fellow you are, Mr. Astley!" I cried, though still wondering how he had come by his knowledge. "And since I have not yet had my coffee, and you have, in all probability, scarcely tasted yours, let us adjourn to the Casino Café, where we can sit and smoke and have a talk."

The café in question was only a hundred paces away; so, when coffee had been brought, we seated ourselves, and I lit a cigarette. Astley was no smoker, but, taking a seat by my side, he prepared himself to listen.

"I do not intend to go away," was my first remark. "I intend, on the contrary, to remain here."

"That I never doubted," he answered good-humouredly.

It is a curious fact that, on my way to see him, I had never even thought of telling him of my love for Polina. In fact, I had purposely meant to avoid any mention of the subject. Nor, during our stay in the place, had I ever made aught but the scantiest reference to it. You see, not only was Astley a man of great reserve, but also from the first I had perceived that Polina had made a great impression upon him, although he never spoke of her. But now, strangely enough, he had no sooner seated himself and bent his steely gaze upon me, than, for some reason or another, I felt moved to tell him everything – to speak to him of my love in all its phases. For an hour and a half did I discourse on the subject, and found it a pleasure to do so, even though this was the first occasion on which I had referred to the matter. Indeed, when, at certain moments, I perceived that my more ardent passages confused him, I purposely increased my ardour of narration. Yet one thing I regret: and that is that I made references to the Frenchman which were a little over-personal.

Mr. Astley sat without moving as he listened to me. Not a word nor a sound of any kind did he utter as he stared into my eyes. Suddenly, however, on my mentioning the Frenchman, he interrupted me, and inquired sternly whether I did right to speak of an extraneous matter (he had always been a strange man in his mode of propounding questions).

"No, I fear not," I replied.

"And concerning this Marquis and Mlle. Polina you know nothing beyond surmise?"

Again I was surprised that such a categorical question should come from such a reserved individual.

"No, I know nothing *for certain* about them" was my reply. "No – nothing."

"Then you have done very wrong to speak of them to me, or even to imagine things about them."

"Quite so, quite so," I interrupted in some astonishment. "I admit that. Yet that is not the question." Whereupon I related to him in detail the incident of two days ago. I spoke of Polina's outburst, of my encounter with the Baron, of my dismissal, of the General's extraordinary pusillanimity, and of the call which De Griers had that morning paid me. In conclusion, I showed Astley the note which I had lately received.

"What do you make of it?" I asked. "When I met you I was just coming to ask you your opinion. For myself, I could have killed this Frenchman, and am not sure that I shall not do so even yet."

"I feel the same about it," said Mr. Astley. "As for Mlle. Polina – well, you yourself know that, if necessity drives, one enters into relation with people whom one simply detests. Even between this couple there may be something which, though unknown to you, depends upon extraneous circumstances. For, my own part, I think that you may reassure yourself – or at all events partially. And as for Mlle. Polina's proceedings of two days ago, they were, of course, strange; not because she can have meant to get rid of you, or to earn for you a thrashing from the Baron's cudgel (which for some curious reason, he did not use, although he had it ready in his hands), but because such proceedings on the part of such – well, of such a refined lady as Mlle. Polina are, to say the least of it, unbecoming. But she cannot have guessed that you would carry out her absurd wish to the letter?"

"Do you know what?" suddenly I cried as I fixed Mr. Astley with my gaze. "I believe that you have already heard the story from some one – very possibly from Mlle. Polina herself?"

In return he gave me an astonished stare.

"Your eyes look very fiery," he said with a return of his former calm, "and in them I can read suspicion. Now, you have no right whatever to be suspicious. It is not a right which I can for a moment recognise, and I absolutely refuse to answer your questions."

"Enough! You need say no more," I cried with a strange emotion at my heart, yet not altogether understanding what had aroused that emotion in my breast. Indeed, when, where, and how could Polina have chosen Astley to be one of her confidants? Of late I had come rather to overlook him in this connection, even though Polina had always been a riddle to me – so much so that now, when I had just permitted myself to tell my friend of my infatuation in all its aspects, I had found myself struck, during the very telling, with the fact that in my relations with her I could specify nothing that was explicit, nothing that was positive. On the contrary, my relations had been purely fantastic, strange, and unreal; they had been unlike anything else that I could think of.

"Very well, very well," I replied with a warmth equal to Astley's own. "Then I stand confounded, and have no further opinions to offer. But you are a good fellow, and I am glad to know what you think about it all, even though I do not need your advice."

Then, after a pause, I resumed:

"For instance, what reason should you assign for the General taking fright in this way? Why should my stupid clowning have led the world to elevate it into a serious incident? Even De Griers has found it necessary to put in his oar (and he only interferes on the most important occasions), and to visit me, and to address to me the most earnest supplications. Yes, *he*, De Griers, has actually been playing the suppliant to *me!* And, mark you, although he came to me as early as nine o'clock, he had ready-prepared in his hand Mlle. Polina's note. When, I would ask, was that note written? Mlle. Polina must have been aroused from sleep for the express purpose of writing it. At all events the circumstance shows that she is an absolute slave to the Frenchman, since she actually begs my pardon in the note – actually begs my pardon! Yet what is her personal concern in the matter? Why is she interested in it at all? Why, too, is the whole party so afraid of this precious Baron? And what sort of a business do you call it for the General to be going to marry Mlle. Blanche de Cominges? He told me last night that, because of the circumstance, he must 'move with especial care at present.' What is your opinion of it all? Your look convinces me that you know more about it than I do."

Mr. Astley smiled and nodded.

"Yes, I think I *do* know more about it than you do," he assented. "The affair centres around this Mlle. Blanche. Of that I feel certain."

"And what of Mlle. Blanche?" I cried impatiently (for in me there had dawned a sudden hope that this would enable me to discover something about Polina).

"Well, my belief is that at the present moment Mlle. Blanche has, in very truth, a special reason for wishing to avoid any trouble with the Baron and the Baroness. It might lead not only to some unpleasantness, but even to a scandal."

"Oh, oh!"

"Also I may tell you that Mlle. Blanche has been in Roulettenberg before, for she was staying here three seasons ago. I myself was in the place at the time, and in those days Mlle. Blanche was not known as Mlle. de Cominges, nor was her mother, the Widow de Cominges, even in existence. In any case no one ever mentioned the latter. De Griers, too, had not materialised, and I am convinced that not only do the parties stand in no relation to one another, but also they have not long enjoyed one another's acquaintance. Likewise, the *Marquisate* de Griers is of recent creation. Of that I have reason to be sure, owing to a certain circumstance. Even the name De Griers itself may be taken to be a new invention, seeing that I have a friend who once met the said 'Marquis' under a different name altogether."

"Yet he possesses a good circle of friends?"

"Possibly. Mlle. Blanche also may possess that. Yet it is not three years since she received from the local police, at the instance of the Baroness, an invitation to leave the town. And she left it."

"But why?"

"Well, I must tell you that she first appeared here in company with an Italian – a prince of some sort, a man who bore an historic name (Barberini or something of the kind). The fellow was simply a mass of rings and diamonds – real diamonds, too – and the couple used to drive out in a marvellous carriage. At first Mlle. Blanche played 'trente et quarante' with fair success, but, later, her luck took a marked change for the worse. I distinctly remember that in a single evening she lost an enormous sum. But worse was to ensue, for one fine morning her prince disappeared – horses, carriage, and all. Also, the hotel bill which he left unpaid was enormous. Upon this Mlle. Zelma (the name which she assumed after figuring as Madame Barberini) was in despair. She shrieked and howled all over the hotel, and even tore her clothes in her frenzy. In the hotel there was staying also a Polish count (you must know that ALL travelling Poles are counts!), and the spectacle of Mlle. Zelma tearing her clothes and, catlike, scratching her face with her beautiful, scented nails produced upon him a strong impression. So the pair had a talk together, and, by luncheon time, she was consoled. Indeed, that evening the couple entered the Casino arm-in-arm – Mlle. Zelma laughing loudly, according to her custom, and showing even more expansiveness in her manners than she had before shown. For instance, she thrust her way into the file of women roulette-players in the exact fashion of those ladies who, to clear a space for themselves at the tables, push their fellow-players roughly aside. Doubtless you have noticed them?"

"Yes, certainly."

"Well, they are not worth noticing. To the annoyance of the decent public they are allowed to remain here – at all events such of them as daily change 4000 franc notes at the tables (though, as soon as ever these women cease to do so, they receive an invitation to depart). However, Mlle. Zelma continued to change notes of this kind, but her play grew more and more unsuccessful, despite the fact that such ladies' luck is frequently good, for they have a surprising amount of cash at their disposal. Suddenly, the Count too disappeared, even as the Prince had done, and that same evening Mlle. Zelma was forced to appear in the Casino alone. On this occasion no one offered her a greeting. Two days later she had come to the end of her resources; whereupon, after staking and losing her last louis d'or she chanced to look around her, and saw standing by her side the Baron Burmergelm, who had been eyeing her with fixed disapproval. To his distaste, however, Mlle. paid no attention, but, turning to him with her well-known smile, requested him to stake, on her behalf, ten louis on the red. Later that evening a complaint from the Baroness led the authorities to request Mlle. not to re-enter the Casino. If you feel in any way surprised that I should know these petty and unedifying details, the reason is that I had them from a relative of mine who, later that evening, drove Mlle. Zelma in his carriage from Roulettenberg to Spa. Now, mark you, Mlle. wants to become Madame General, in order that, in future, she may be spared the receipt of such invitations from Casino authorities as she received three years ago. At present she is not playing; but that is only because, according to the signs, she is lending money to other players. Yes, that is a much more paying game. I even suspect that the unfortunate General is himself in her debt, as well as, perhaps, also De Griers. Or, it may be that the latter has entered into a partnership with her. Consequently you yourself will see that, until the marriage shall have been consummated, Mlle. would scarcely like to have the attention of the Baron and the Baroness drawn to herself. In short, to any one in her position, a scandal would be most detrimental. You form a member of the ménage of these people; wherefore, any act of yours might cause such a scandal – and the more so since daily she appears in public arm in arm with the General or with Mlle. Polina. *Now* do you understand?"

"No, I do not!" I shouted as I banged my fist down upon the table – banged it with such violence that a frightened waiter came running towards us. "Tell me, Mr. Astley, why, if you knew this history all along, and, consequently, always knew who this Mlle. Blanche is, you never warned either myself or the General, nor, most of all, Mlle. Polina" (who is accustomed to appear in the Casino – in public everywhere with Mlle. Blanche). "How could you do it?"

"It would have done no good to warn you," he replied quietly, "for the reason that you could have effected nothing. Against what was I to warn you? As likely as not, the General knows more about Mlle. Blanche even than I do; yet the unhappy man still walks about with her and Mlle. Polina. Only yesterday I saw this Frenchwoman riding, splendidly mounted, with De Griers, while the General was careering in their wake on a roan horse. He had said, that morning, that his legs were hurting him, yet his riding-seat was easy enough. As he passed I looked at him, and the thought occurred to me that he was a man lost for ever. However, it is no affair of mine, for I have only recently had the happiness to make Mlle. Polina's acquaintance. Also" – he added this as an afterthought – "I have already told you that I do not recognise your right to ask me certain questions, however sincere be my liking for you."

"Enough," I said, rising. "To me it is as clear as day that Mlle. Polina knows all about this Mlle. Blanche, but cannot bring herself to part with her Frenchman; wherefore, she consents also to be seen in public with Mlle. Blanche. You may be sure that nothing else would ever have induced her either to walk about with this Frenchwoman or to send me a note not to touch the Baron. Yes, it is *there* that the influence lies before which everything in the world must bow! Yet she herself it was who launched me at the Baron! The devil take it, but I was left no choice in the matter."

"You forget, in the first place, that this Mlle. de Cominges is the General's inamorata, and, in the second place, that Mlle. Polina, the General's step-daughter, has a younger brother and sister who, though they are the General's own children, are completely neglected by this madman, and robbed as well."

"Yes, yes; that is so. For me to go and desert the children now would mean their total abandonment; whereas, if I remain, I should be able to defend their interests, and, perhaps, to save a moiety of their property. Yes, yes; that is quite true. And yet, and yet – Oh, I can well understand why they are all so interested in the General's mother!"

"In whom?" asked Mr. Astley.

"In the old woman of Moscow who declines to die, yet concerning whom they are for ever expecting telegrams to notify the fact of her death."

"Ah, then of course their interests centre around her. It is a question of succession. Let that but be settled, and the General will marry, Mlle. Polina will be set free, and De Griers – "

"Yes, and De Griers?"

"Will be repaid his money, which is what he is now waiting for."

"What? You think that he is waiting for *that?*"

"I know of nothing else," asserted Mr. Astley doggedly.

"But, I do, I do!" I shouted in my fury. "He is waiting also for the old woman's will, for the reason that it awards Mlle. Polina a dowry. As soon as ever the money is received, she will throw herself upon the Frenchman's neck. All women are like that. Even the proudest of them become abject slaves where marriage is concerned. What Polina is good for is to fall head over ears in love. That is *my* opinion. Look at her – especially when she is sitting alone, and plunged in thought. All this was pre-ordained and foretold, and is accursed. Polina could perpetrate any mad act. She – she – But who called me by name?" I broke off. "Who is shouting for me? I heard some one calling in Russian, 'Alexis Ivanovitch!' It was a woman's voice. Listen!"

At the moment, we were approaching my hotel. We had left the café long ago, without even noticing that we had done so.

"Yes, I *did* hear a woman's voice calling, but whose I do not know. The someone was calling you in Russian. Ah! NOW I can see whence the cries come. They come from that lady there – the one who is sitting on the settee, the one who has just been escorted to the verandah by a crowd of lacqueys. Behind her see that pile of luggage! She must have arrived by train."

"But why should she be calling *me?* Hear her calling again! See! She is beckoning to us!"

"Yes, so she is," assented Mr. Astley.

"Alexis Ivanovitch, Alexis Ivanovitch! Good heavens, what a stupid fellow!" came in a despairing wail from the verandah.

We had almost reached the portico, and I was just setting foot upon the space before it, when my hands fell to my sides in limp astonishment, and my feet glued themselves to the pavement!

CHAPTER NINE

For on the topmost tier of the hotel verandah, after being carried up the steps in an armchair amid a bevy of footmen, maid-servants, and other menials of the hotel, headed by the landlord (that functionary had actually run out to meet a visitor who arrived with so much stir and din, attended by her own retinue, and accompanied by so great a pile of trunks and portmanteaux) – on the topmost tier of the verandah, I say, there was sitting – *the grandmother!* Yes, it was *she* – rich, and imposing, and seventy-five years of age – Antonida Vassilievna Tarassevitcha, landowner and *grande dame* of Moscow – the "La Baboulenka" who had caused so many telegrams to be sent off and received – who had been dying, yet not dying – who had, in her own person, descended upon us even as snow might fall from the clouds! Though unable to walk, she had arrived borne aloft in an armchair (her mode of conveyance for the last five years), as brisk, aggressive, self-satisfied, bolt-upright, loudly imperious, and generally abusive as ever. In fact, she looked exactly as she had on the only two occasions when I had seen her since my appointment to the General's household. Naturally enough, I stood petrified with astonishment. She had sighted me a hundred paces off! Even while she was being carried along in her chair she had recognised me, and called me by name and surname (which, as usual, after hearing once, she had remembered ever afterwards).

"And this is the woman whom they had thought to see in her grave after making her will!" I thought to myself. "Yet she will outlive us, and every one else in the hotel. Good Lord! what is going to become of us now? What on earth is to happen to the General? She will turn the place upside down!"

"My good sir," the old woman continued in a stentorian voice, "what are you standing *there* for, with your eyes almost falling out of your head? Cannot you come and say how-do-you-do? Are you too proud to shake hands? Or do you not recognise me? Here, Potapitch!" she cried to an old servant who, dressed in a frock coat and white waistcoat, had a bald, red head (he was the chamberlain who always accompanied her on her journeys). "Just think! Alexis Ivanovitch does not recognise me! They have buried me for good and all! Yes, and after sending hosts of telegrams to know if I were dead or not! Yes, yes, I have heard the whole story. I am very much alive, though, as you may see."

"Pardon me, Antonida Vassilievna," I replied good humouredly as I recovered my presence of mind. "*I* have no reason to wish you ill. I am merely rather astonished to see you. Why should I not be so, seeing how unexpected – "

"*Why* should you be astonished? I just got into my chair, and came. Things are quiet enough in the train, for there is no one there to chatter. Have you been out for a walk?"

"Yes. I have just been to the Casino."

"Oh? Well, it is quite nice here," she went on as she looked about her. "The place seems comfortable, and all the trees are out. I like it very well. Are your people at home? Is the General, for instance, indoors?"

"Yes; and probably all of them."

"Do they observe the convenances, and keep up appearances? Such things always give one tone. I have heard that they are keeping a carriage, even as Russian gentlefolks ought to do. When abroad, our Russian people always cut a dash. Is Prascovia here too?"

"Yes. Polina Alexandrovna is here."

"And the Frenchwoman? However, I will go and look for them myself. Tell me the nearest way to their rooms. Do *you* like being here?"

"Yes, I thank you, Antonida Vassilievna."

"And you, Potapitch, you go and tell that fool of a landlord to reserve me a suitable suite of rooms. They must be handsomely decorated, and not too high up. Have my luggage taken up to them. But what are you tumbling over yourselves for? Why are you all tearing about? What scullions these fellows are! – Who is that with you?" she added to myself.

"A Mr. Astley," I replied.

"And who is Mr. Astley?"

"A fellow-traveller, and my very good friend, as well as an acquaintance of the General's."

"Oh, an Englishman? Then that is why he stared at me without even opening his lips. However, I like Englishmen. Now, take me upstairs, direct to their rooms. Where are they lodging?"

Madame was lifted up in her chair by the lacqueys, and I preceded her up the grand staircase. Our progress was exceedingly effective, for everyone whom we met stopped to stare at the cortège. It happened that the hotel had the reputation of being the best, the most expensive, and the most aristocratic in all the spa, and at every turn on the staircase or in the corridors we encountered fine ladies and important-looking Englishmen – more than one of whom hastened downstairs to inquire of the awestruck landlord who the newcomer was. To all such questions he returned the same answer – namely, that the old lady was an influential foreigner, a Russian, a Countess, and a *grande dame*, and that she had taken the suite which, during the previous week, had been tenanted by the Grande Duchesse de N.

Meanwhile the cause of the sensation – the Grandmother – was being borne aloft in her armchair. Every person whom she met she scanned with an inquisitive eye, after first of all interrogating me about him or her at the top of her voice. She was stout of figure, and, though she could not leave her chair, one felt, the moment that one first looked at her, that she was also tall of stature. Her back was as straight as a board, and never did she lean back in her seat. Also, her large grey head, with its keen, rugged features, remained always erect as she glanced about her in an imperious, challenging sort of way, with looks and gestures that clearly were unstudied. Though she had reached her seventy-sixth year, her face was still fresh, and her teeth had not decayed. Lastly, she was dressed in a black silk gown and white mobcap.

"She interests me tremendously," whispered Mr. Astley as, still smoking, he walked by my side. Meanwhile I was reflecting that probably the old lady knew all about the telegrams, and even about De Griers, though little or nothing about Mlle. Blanche. I said as much to Mr. Astley.

But what a frail creature is man! No sooner was my first surprise abated than I found myself rejoicing in the shock which we were about to administer to the General. So much did the thought inspire me that I marched ahead in the gayest of fashions.

Our party was lodging on the third floor. Without knocking at the door, or in any way announcing our presence, I threw open the portals, and the Grandmother was borne through them in triumph. As though of set purpose, the whole party chanced at that moment to be assembled in the General's study. The time was eleven o'clock, and it seemed that an outing of some sort (at which a portion of the party were to drive in carriages, and others to ride on horseback, accompanied by one or two extraneous acquaintances) was being planned. The General was present, and also Polina, the children, the latter's nurses, De Griers, Mlle. Blanche (attired in a riding-habit), her mother, the young Prince, and a learned German whom I beheld for the first time. Into the midst of this assembly the lacqueys conveyed Madame in her chair, and set her down within three paces of the General!

Good heavens! Never shall I forget the spectacle which ensued! Just before our entry, the General had been holding forth to the company, with De Griers in support of him. I may also mention that, for the last two or three days, Mlle. Blanche and De Griers had been making a great deal of the young Prince, under the very nose of the poor General. In short, the company, though decorous and conventional, was in a gay, familiar mood. But no sooner did the Grandmother appear than the General stopped dead in the middle of a word, and, with jaw dropping, stared hard at the old lady – his eyes almost starting out of his head, and his expression as spellbound as though he had just seen a basilisk. In return, the Grandmother stared at him silently and without moving – though with a look of mingled challenge, triumph, and ridicule in her eyes. For ten seconds did the pair remain thus eyeing one another, amid the profound silence of the company; and even De Griers sat petrified – an extraordinary look of uneasiness dawning on his face. As for Mlle. Blanche, she too stared wildly at the Grandmother, with eyebrows raised and her lips parted – while the Prince and the German savant contemplated the tableau in profound amazement. Only Polina looked anything but perplexed or surprised. Presently, however, she too turned as white as a sheet, and then reddened to her temples. Truly the Grandmother's arrival seemed to be a catastrophe for everybody! For my own part, I stood looking from the Grandmother to the company, and back again, while Mr. Astley, as usual, remained in the background, and gazed calmly and decorously at the scene.

"Well, here I am – and instead of a telegram, too!" the Grandmother at last ejaculated, to dissipate the silence. "What? You were not expecting me?"

"Antonida Vassilievna! O my dearest mother! But how on earth did you, did you – ?" The mutterings of the unhappy General died away.

I verily believe that if the Grandmother had held her tongue a few seconds longer she would have had a stroke.

"How on earth did I *what?*" she exclaimed. "Why, I just got into the train and came here. What else is the railway meant for? But you thought that I had turned up my toes and left my property to the lot of you. Oh, I know *all* about the telegrams which you have been dispatching. They must have cost you a pretty sum, I should think, for telegrams are not sent from abroad for nothing. Well, I picked up my heels, and came here. Who is this Frenchman? Monsieur de Griers, I suppose?"

"Oui, madame," assented De Griers. "Et, croyez, je suis si enchanté! Votre santé – c'est un miracle vous voir ici. Une surprise charmante!"

"Just so. 'Charmante!' I happen to know you as a mountebank, and therefore trust you no more than *this*." She indicated her little finger. "And who is *that?*" she went on, turning towards Mlle. Blanche. Evidently the Frenchwoman looked so becoming in her riding-habit, with her whip in her hand, that she had made an impression upon the old lady. "Who is that woman there?"

"Mlle. de Cominges," I said. "And this is her mother, Madame de Cominges. They also are staying in the hotel."

"Is the daughter married?" asked the old lady, without the least semblance of ceremony.

"No," I replied as respectfully as possible, but under my breath.

"Is she good company?"

I failed to understand the question.

"I mean, is she or is she not a bore? Can she speak Russian? When this De Griers was in Moscow he soon learnt to make himself understood."

I explained to the old lady that Mlle. Blanche had never visited Russia.

"Bonjour, then," said Madame, with sudden brusquerie.

"Bonjour, madame," replied Mlle. Blanche with an elegant, ceremonious bow as, under cover of an unwonted modesty, she endeavoured to express, both in face and figure, her extreme surprise at such strange behaviour on the part of the Grandmother.

"How the woman sticks out her eyes at me! How she mows and minces!" was the Grandmother's comment. Then she turned suddenly to the General, and continued: "I have taken up my abode here, so am going to be your next-door neighbour. Are you glad to hear that, or are you not?"

"My dear mother, believe me when I say that I am sincerely delighted," returned the General, who had now, to a certain extent, recovered his senses; and inasmuch as, when occasion arose, he could speak with fluency, gravity, and a certain effect, he set himself to be expansive in his remarks, and went on: "We have been so dismayed and upset by the news of your indisposition! We had received such hopeless telegrams about you! Then suddenly – "

"Fibs, fibs!" interrupted the Grandmother.

"How on earth, too, did you come to decide upon the journey?" continued the General, with raised voice as he hurried to overlook the old lady's last remark. "Surely, at your age, and in your present state of health, the thing is so unexpected that our surprise is at least intelligible. However, I am glad to see you (as indeed, are we all" – he said this with a dignified, yet conciliatory, smile), "and will use my best endeavours to render your stay here as pleasant as possible."

"Enough! All this is empty chatter. You are talking the usual nonsense. I shall know quite well how to spend my time. How did I come to undertake the journey, you ask? Well, is there anything so very surprising about it? It was done quite simply. What is every one going into ecstasies about? – How do you do, Prascovia? What are *you* doing here?"

"And how are *you*, Grandmother?" replied Polina, as she approached the old lady. "Were you long on the journey?"

"The most sensible question that I have yet been asked! Well, you shall hear for yourself how it all happened. I lay and lay, and was doctored and doctored, until at last I drove the physicians from me, and called in an apothecary from Nicolai who had cured an old woman of a malady similar to my own – cured her merely with a little hayseed. Well, he did me a great deal of good, for on the third day I broke into a sweat, and was able to leave my bed. Then my German doctors held another consultation, put on their spectacles, and told me that if I would go abroad, and take a course of the waters, the indisposition would finally pass away. 'Why should it not?' I thought to myself. So I had got things ready, and on the following day, a Friday, set out for here. I occupied a special compartment in the train, and where ever I had to change I found at the station bearers who were ready to carry me for a few coppers. You have nice quarters here," she went on as she glanced around the room. "But where on earth did you get the money for them, my good sir? I thought that everything of yours had been mortgaged? This Frenchman alone must be your creditor for a good deal. Oh, I know all about it, all about it."

"I-I am surprised at you, my dearest mother," said the General in some confusion. "I-I am greatly surprised. But I do not need any extraneous control of my finances. Moreover, my expenses do not exceed my income, and we – "

"They do not exceed it? Fie! Why, you are robbing your children of their last kopeck – you, their guardian!"

"After this," said the General, completely taken aback, " – after what you have just said, I do not know whether – "

"You do not know *what?* By heavens, are you *never* going to drop that roulette of yours? Are you going to whistle all your property away?"

This made such an impression upon the General that he almost choked with fury.

"Roulette, indeed? *I* play roulette? Really, in view of my position – Recollect what you are saying, my dearest mother. You must still be unwell."

"Rubbish, rubbish!" she retorted. "The truth is that you *cannot* be got away from that roulette. You are simply telling lies. This very day I mean to go and see for myself what roulette is like. Prascovia, tell me what there is to be seen here; and do you, Alexis Ivanovitch, show me everything; and do you, Potapitch, make me a list of excursions. What *is* there to be seen?" again she inquired of Polina.

"There is a ruined castle, and the Shlangenberg."

"The Shlangenberg? What is it? A forest?"

"No, a mountain on the summit of which there is a place fenced off. From it you can get a most beautiful view."

"Could a chair be carried up that mountain of yours?"

"Doubtless we could find bearers for the purpose," I interposed.

At this moment Theodosia, the nursemaid, approached the old lady with the General's children.

"No, I *don't* want to see them," said the Grandmother. "I hate kissing children, for their noses are always wet. How are you getting on, Theodosia?"

"I am very well, thank you, Madame," replied the nursemaid. "And how is your ladyship? We have been feeling so anxious about you!"

"Yes, I know, you simple soul – But who are those other guests?" the old lady continued, turning again to Polina. "For instance, who is that old rascal in the spectacles?"

"Prince Nilski, Grandmamma," whispered Polina.

"Oh, a Russian? Why, I had no idea that he could understand me! Surely he did not hear what I said? As for Mr. Astley, I have seen him already, and I see that he is here again. How do you do?" she added to the gentleman in question.

Mr. Astley bowed in silence.

"Have you *nothing* to say to me?" the old lady went on. "Say something, for goodness' sake! Translate to him, Polina."

Polina did so.

"I have only to say," replied Mr. Astley gravely, but also with alacrity, "that I am indeed glad to see you in such good health." This was interpreted to the Grandmother, and she seemed much gratified.

"How well English people know how to answer one!" she remarked. "That is why I like them so much better than French. Come here," she added to Mr. Astley. "I will try not to bore you too much. Polina, translate to him that I am staying in rooms on a lower floor.

Yes, on a lower floor," she repeated to Astley, pointing downwards with her finger.

Astley looked pleased at receiving the invitation.

Next, the old lady scanned Polina, from head to foot with minute attention.

"I could almost have liked you, Prascovia," suddenly she remarked, "for you are a nice girl – the best of the lot. You have some character about you. I too have character. Turn round. Surely that is not false hair that you are wearing?"

"No, Grandmamma. It is my own."

"Well, well. I do not like the stupid fashions of today. You are very good looking. I should have fallen in love with you if I had been a man. Why do you not get married? It is time now that I was going. I want to walk, yet I always have to ride. Are you still in a bad temper?" she added to the General.

"No, indeed," rejoined the now mollified General.

"I quite understand that at your time of life – "

"Cette vieille est tombée en enfance," De Griers whispered to me.

"But I want to look round a little," the old lady added to the General. Will you lend me Alexis Ivanovitch for the purpose?

"As much as you like. But I myself – yes, and Polina and Monsieur de Griers too – we all of us hope to have the pleasure of escorting you."

"Mais, madame, cela sera un plaisir," De Griers commented with a bewitching smile.

"'Plaisir' indeed! Why, I look upon you as a perfect fool, monsieur." Then she remarked to the General: "I am not going to let you have any of my money. I must be off to my rooms now, to see what they are like. Afterwards we will look round a little. Lift me up."

Again the Grandmother was borne aloft and carried down the staircase amid a perfect bevy of followers – the General walking as though he had been hit over the head with a cudgel, and De Griers seeming to be plunged in thought. Endeavouring to be left behind, Mlle. Blanche next thought better of it, and followed the rest, with the Prince in her wake. Only the German savant and Madame de Cominges did not leave the General's apartments.

CHAPTER TEN

AT SPAS – AND, PROBABLY, all over Europe – hotel landlords and managers are guided in their allotment of rooms to visitors, not so much by the wishes and requirements of those visitors, as by their personal estimate of the same. It may also be said that these landlords and managers seldom make a mistake. To the Grandmother, however, our landlord, for some reason or another, allotted such a sumptuous suite that he fairly overreached himself; for he assigned her a suite consisting of four magnificently appointed rooms, with bathroom, servants' quarters, a separate room for her maid, and so on. In fact, during the previous week the suite had been occupied by no less a personage than a Grand Duchess: which circumstance was duly explained to the new occupant, as an excuse for raising the price of these apartments. The Grandmother had herself carried – or, rather, wheeled – through each room in turn, in order that she might subject the whole to a close and attentive scrutiny; while the landlord – an elderly, bald-headed man – walked respectfully by her side.

What every one took the Grandmother to be I do not know, but it appeared, at least, that she was accounted a person not only of great importance, but also, and still more, of great wealth; and without delay they entered her in the hotel register as "Madame la générale, Princesse de Tarassevitcheva," although she had never been a princess in her life. Her retinue, her reserved compartment in the train, her pile of unnecessary trunks, portmanteaux, and strong-boxes, all helped to increase her prestige; while her wheeled chair, her sharp tone and voice, her eccentric questions (put with an air of the most overbearing and unbridled imperiousness), her whole figure – upright, rugged, and commanding as it was – completed the general awe in which she was held. As she inspected her new abode she ordered her chair to be stopped at intervals in order that, with finger extended towards some article of furniture, she might ply the respectfully smiling, yet secretly apprehensive, landlord with unexpected questions. She addressed them to him in French, although her pronunciation of the language was so bad that sometimes I had to translate them. For the most part, the landlord's answers were unsatisfactory, and failed to please her; nor were the questions themselves of a practical nature, but related, generally, to God knows what.

For instance, on one occasion she halted before a picture which, a poor copy of a well-known original, had a mythological subject.

"Of whom is this a portrait?" she inquired.

The landlord explained that it was probably that of a countess.

"But how know you that?" the old lady retorted.

"You live here, yet you cannot say for certain! And why is the picture there at all? And why do its eyes look so crooked?"

To all these questions the landlord could return no satisfactory reply, despite his floundering endeavours.

"The blockhead!" exclaimed the Grandmother in Russian.

Then she proceeded on her way – only to repeat the same story in front of a Saxon statuette which she had sighted from afar, and had commanded, for some reason or another, to be brought to her. Finally, she inquired of the landlord what was the value of the carpet in her bedroom, as well as where the said carpet had been manufactured; but, the landlord could do no more than promise to make inquiries.

"What donkeys these people are!" she commented. Next, she turned her attention to the bed.

"What a huge counterpane!" she exclaimed. "Turn it back, please." The lacqueys did so.

"Further yet, further yet," the old lady cried. "Turn it *right* back. Also, take off those pillows and bolsters, and lift up the feather bed."

The bed was opened for her inspection.

"Mercifully it contains no bugs," she remarked.

"Pull off the whole thing, and then put on my own pillows and sheets. The place is too luxurious for an old woman like myself. It is too large for any one person. Alexis Ivanovitch, come and see me whenever you are not teaching your pupils."

"After tomorrow I shall no longer be in the General's service," I replied, "but merely living in the hotel on my own account."

"Why so?"

"Because, the other day, there arrived from Berlin a German and his wife – persons of some importance; and, it chanced that, when taking a walk, I spoke to them in German without having properly compassed the Berlin accent."

"Indeed?"

"Yes: and this action on my part the Baron held to be an insult, and complained about it to the General, who yesterday dismissed me from his employ."

"But I suppose you must have threatened that precious Baron, or something of the kind? However, even if you did so, it was a matter of no moment."

"No, I did not. The Baron was the aggressor by raising his stick at me."

Upon that the Grandmother turned sharply to the General.

"What? You permitted yourself to treat your tutor thus, you nincompoop, and to dismiss him from his post? You are a blockhead – an utter blockhead! I can see that clearly."

"Do not alarm yourself, my dear mother," the General replied with a lofty air – an air in which there was also a tinge of familiarity. "I am quite capable of managing my own affairs. Moreover, Alexis Ivanovitch has not given you a true account of the matter."

"What did you do next?" The old lady inquired of me.

"I wanted to challenge the Baron to a duel," I replied as modestly as possible; "but the General protested against my doing so."

"And *why* did you so protest?" she inquired of the General. Then she turned to the landlord, and questioned him as to whether *he* would not have fought a duel, if challenged. "For," she added, "I can see no difference between you and the Baron; nor can I bear that German visage of yours." Upon this the landlord bowed and departed, though he could not have understood the Grandmother's compliment.

"Pardon me, Madame," the General continued with a sneer, "but are duels really feasible?"

"Why not? All men are crowing cocks, and that is why they quarrel. *You*, though, I perceive, are a blockhead – a man who does not even know how to carry his breeding. Lift me up. Potapitch, see to it that you always have *two* bearers ready. Go and arrange for their hire. But we shall not require more than two, for I shall need only to be carried upstairs. On the level or in the street I can be *wheeled* along. Go and tell them that, and pay them in advance, so that they may show me some respect. You too, Potapitch, are always to come with me, and *you*, Alexis Ivanovitch, are to point out to me this Baron as we go along, in order that I may get a squint at the precious 'Von.' And where is that roulette played?"

I explained to her that the game was carried on in the salons of the Casino; whereupon there ensued a string of questions as to whether there were many such salons, whether many people played in them, whether those people played a whole day at a time, and whether the game was managed according to fixed rules. At length, I thought it best to say that the most advisable course would be for her to go and see it for herself, since a mere description of it would be a difficult matter.

"Then take me straight there," she said, "and do you walk on in front of me, Alexis Ivanovitch."

"What, mother? Before you have so much as rested from your journey?" the General inquired with some solicitude. Also, for some reason which I could not divine, he seemed to be growing nervous; and, indeed, the whole party was evincing signs of confusion, and exchanging glances with one another. Probably they were thinking that it would be a ticklish – even an embarrassing – business to accompany the Grandmother to the Casino, where, very likely, she would perpetrate further eccentricities, and in public too! Yet on their own initiative they had offered to escort her!

"Why should I rest?" she retorted. "I am not tired, for I have been sitting still these past five days. Let us see what your medicinal springs and waters are like, and where they are situated. What, too, about that, that – what did you call it, Prascovia? – oh, about that mountain top?"

"Yes, we are going to see it, Grandmamma."

"Very well. Is there anything else for me to see here?"

"Yes! Quite a number of things," Polina forced herself to say.

"Martha, *you* must come with me as well," went on the old lady to her maid.

"No, no, mother!" ejaculated the General. "Really she cannot come. They would not admit even Potapitch to the Casino."

"Rubbish! Because she is my servant, is that a reason for turning her out? Why, she is only a human being like the rest of us; and as she has been travelling for a week she might like to look about her. With whom else could she go out but myself? She would never dare to show her nose in the street alone."

"But, mother – "

"Are you ashamed to be seen with me? Stop at home, then, and you will be asked no questions. A pretty General *you* are, to be sure! I am a general's widow myself. But, after all, why should I drag the whole party with me? I will go and see the sights with only Alexis Ivanovitch as my escort."

De Griers strongly insisted that *every one* ought to accompany her. Indeed, he launched out into a perfect shower of charming phrases concerning the pleasure of acting as her cicerone, and so forth. Every one was touched with his words.

"Mais elle est tombée en enfance," he added aside to the General. "Seule, elle fera des bêtises." More than this I could not overhear, but he seemed to have got some plan in his mind, or even to be feeling a slight return of his hopes.

The distance to the Casino was about half a verst, and our route led us through the Chestnut Avenue until we reached the square directly fronting the building. The General, I could see, was a trifle reassured by the fact that, though our progress was distinctly eccentric in its nature, it was, at least, correct and orderly. As a matter of fact, the spectacle of a person who is unable to walk is not anything to excite surprise at a spa. Yet it was clear that the General had a great fear of the Casino itself: for why should a person who had lost the use of her limbs – more especially an old woman – be going to rooms which were set apart only for roulette? On either side of the wheeled chair walked Polina and Mlle. Blanche – the latter smiling, modestly jesting, and, in short, making herself so agreeable to the Grandmother that in the end the old lady relented towards her. On the other side of the chair Polina had to answer an endless flow of petty questions – such as "Who was it passed just now?" "Who is that coming along?" "Is the town a large one?" "Are the public gardens extensive?" "What sort of trees are those?" "What is the name of those hills?" "Do I see eagles flying yonder?" "What is that absurd-looking building?" and so forth. Meanwhile Astley whispered to me, as he walked by my side, that he looked for much to happen that morning. Behind the old lady's chair marched Potapitch and Martha – Potapitch in his frockcoat and white waistcoat, with a cloak over all, and the forty-year-old and rosy, but slightly grey-headed, Martha in a mob-cap, cotton dress, and squeaking shoes. Frequently the old lady would twist herself round to converse with these servants. As for De Griers, he spoke as though he had made up his mind to do something (though it is also possible that he spoke in this manner merely in order to hearten the General, with whom he appeared to have held a conference). But, alas, the Grandmother had uttered the fatal words, "I am not going to give you any of my money;" and though De Griers might regard these words lightly, the General knew his mother better. Also, I noticed that De Griers and Mlle. Blanche were still exchanging looks; while of the Prince and the German savant I lost sight at the end of the Avenue, where they had turned back and left us.

Into the Casino we marched in triumph. At once, both in the person of the commissionaire and in the persons of the footmen, there sprang to life the same reverence as had arisen in the lacqueys of the hotel. Yet it was not without some curiosity that they eyed us.

Without loss of time, the Grandmother gave orders that she should be wheeled through every room in the establishment; of which apartments she praised a few, while to others she remained indifferent. Concerning everything, however, she asked questions. Finally we reached the gaming-salons, where a lacquey who was, acting as guard over the doors, flung them open as though he were a man possessed.

The Grandmother's entry into the roulette-salon produced a profound impression upon the public. Around the tables, and at the further end of the room where the trente-et-quarante table was set out, there may have been gathered from 150 to 200 gamblers, ranged in several rows. Those who had succeeded in pushing their way to the tables were standing with their feet firmly planted, in order to avoid having to give up their places until they should have finished their game (since merely to stand looking on – thus occupying a gambler's place for nothing – was not permitted). True, chairs were provided around the tables, but few players made use of them – more especially if there was a large attendance of the general public; since to stand allowed of a closer approach; and, therefore, of greater facilities for calculation and staking. Behind the foremost row were herded a second and a third row of people awaiting their turn; but sometimes their impatience led these people to stretch a hand through the first row, in order to deposit their stakes. Even third-row individuals would dart forward to stake; whence seldom did more than five or ten minutes pass without a scene over disputed money arising at one or another end of the table. On the other hand, the police of the Casino were an able body of men; and though to escape the crush was an impossibility, however much one might wish it, the eight croupiers apportioned to each table kept an eye upon the stakes, performed the necessary reckoning, and decided disputes as they arose.

In the last resort they always called in the Casino police, and the disputes would immediately come to an end. Policemen were stationed about the Casino in ordinary costume, and mingled with the spectators so as to make it impossible to recognise them. In particular they kept a lookout for pickpockets and swindlers, who simply swanned in the roulette salons, and reaped a rich harvest. Indeed, in every direction money was being filched from pockets or purses – though, of course, if the attempt miscarried, a great uproar ensued. One had only to approach a roulette table, begin to play, and then openly grab some one else's winnings, for a din to be raised, and the thief to start vociferating that the stake was *his;* and, if the coup had been carried out with sufficient skill, and the witnesses wavered at all in their testimony, the thief would as likely as not succeed in getting away with the money, provided that the sum was not a large one – not large enough to have attracted the attention of the croupiers or some fellow-player. Moreover, if it were a stake of insignificant size, its true owner would sometimes decline to continue the dispute, rather than become involved in a scandal. Conversely, if the thief was detected, he was ignominiously expelled the building.

Upon all this the Grandmother gazed with open-eyed curiosity; and, on some thieves happening to be turned out of the place, she was delighted. Trente-et-quarante interested her but little; she preferred roulette, with its ever-revolving wheel. At length she expressed a wish to view the game closer; whereupon in some mysterious manner, the lacqueys and other officious agents (especially one or two ruined Poles of the kind who keep offering their services to successful gamblers and foreigners in general) at once found and cleared a space for the old lady among the crush, at the very centre of one of the tables, and next to the chief croupier; after which they wheeled her chair thither. Upon this a number of visitors who were not playing, but only looking on (particularly some Englishmen with their families), pressed closer forward towards the table, in order to watch the old lady from among the ranks of the gamblers. Many a lorgnette I saw turned in her direction, and the croupiers' hopes rose high that such an eccentric player was about to provide them with something out of the common. An old lady of seventy-five years who, though unable to walk, desired to play was not an everyday phenomenon. I too pressed forward towards the table, and ranged myself by the Grandmother's side; while Martha and Potapitch remained somewhere in the background among the crowd, and the General, Polina, and De Griers, with Mlle. Blanche, also remained hidden among the spectators.

At first the old lady did no more than watch the gamblers, and ply me, in a half-whisper, with sharp-broken questions as to who was so-and-so. Especially did her favour light upon a very young man who was plunging heavily, and had won (so it was whispered) as much as 40,000 francs, which were lying before him on the table in a heap of gold and bank-notes. His eyes kept flashing, and his hands shaking; yet all the while he staked without any sort of calculation – just what came to his hand, as he kept winning and winning, and raking and raking in his gains. Around him lacqueys fussed – placing chairs just behind where he was standing – and clearing the spectators from his vicinity, so that he should have more room, and not be crowded – the whole done, of course, in expectation of a generous largesse. From time to time other gamblers would hand him part of their winnings – being glad to let him stake for them as much as his hand could grasp; while beside him stood a Pole in a state of violent, but respectful, agitation, who, also in expectation of a generous largesse, kept whispering to him at intervals (probably telling him what to stake, and advising and directing his play). Yet never once did the player throw him a glance as he staked and staked, and raked in his winnings. Evidently, the player in question was dead to all besides.

For a few minutes the Grandmother watched him.

"Go and tell him," suddenly she exclaimed with a nudge at my elbow, " – go and tell him to stop, and to take his money with him, and go home. Presently he will be losing – yes, losing everything that he has now won." She seemed almost breathless with excitement.

"Where is Potapitch?" she continued. "Send Potapitch to speak to him. No, *you* must tell him, *you* must tell him," – here she nudged me again – "for I have not the least notion where Potapitch is. Sortez, sortez," she shouted to the young man, until I leant over in her direction and whispered in her ear that no shouting was allowed, nor even loud speaking, since to do so disturbed the calculations of the players, and might lead to our being ejected.

"How provoking!" she retorted. "Then the young man is done for! I suppose he *wishes* to be ruined. Yet I could not bear to see him have to return it all. What a fool the fellow is!" and the old lady turned sharply away.

On the left, among the players at the other half of the table, a young lady was playing, with, beside her, a dwarf. Who the dwarf may have been – whether a relative or a person whom she took with her to act as a foil – I do not know; but I had noticed her there on previous occasions, since, everyday, she entered the Casino at one o'clock precisely, and departed at two – thus playing for exactly one hour. Being well-known to the attendants, she always had a seat provided for her; and, taking some gold and a few thousand-franc notes out of her pocket – would begin quietly, coldly, and after much calculation, to stake, and mark down the figures in pencil on a paper, as though striving to work out a system according to which, at given moments, the odds might group themselves. Always she staked large coins, and either lost or won one, two, or three thousand francs a day, but not more; after which she would depart. The Grandmother took a long look at her.

"*That* woman is not losing," she said. "To whom does she belong? Do you know her? Who is she?"

"She is, I believe, a Frenchwoman," I replied.

"Ah! A bird of passage, evidently. Besides, I can see that she has her shoes polished. Now, explain to me the meaning of each round in the game, and the way in which one ought to stake."

Upon this I set myself to explain the meaning of all the combinations – of "rouge et noir," of "pair et impair," of "manque et passe," with, lastly, the different values in the system of numbers. The Grandmother listened attentively, took notes, put questions in various forms, and laid the whole thing to heart. Indeed, since an example of each system of stakes kept constantly occurring, a great deal of information could be assimilated with ease and celerity. The Grandmother was vastly pleased.

"But what is zero?" she inquired. "Just now I heard the flaxen-haired croupier call out 'zero!' And why does he keep raking in all the money that is on the table? To think that he should grab the whole pile for himself! What does zero mean?"

"Zero is what the bank takes for itself. If the wheel stops at that figure, everything lying on the table becomes the absolute property of the bank. Also, whenever the wheel has begun to turn, the bank ceases to pay out anything."

"Then I should receive nothing if I were staking?"

"No; unless by any chance you had *purposely* staked on zero; in which case you would receive thirty-five times the value of your stake."

"Why thirty-five times, when zero so often turns up? And if so, why do not more of these fools stake upon it?"

"Because the number of chances against its occurrence is thirty-six."

"Rubbish! Potapitch, Potapitch! Come here, and I will give you some money." The old lady took out of her pocket a tightly-clasped purse, and extracted from its depths a ten-gülden piece. "Go at once, and stake that upon zero."

"But, Madame, zero has only this moment turned up," I remonstrated; "wherefore, it may not do so again for ever so long. Wait a little, and you may then have a better chance."

"Rubbish! Stake, please."

"Pardon me, but zero might not turn up again until, say, tonight, even though you had staked thousands upon it. It often happens so."

"Rubbish, rubbish! Who fears the wolf should never enter the forest. What? We have lost? Then stake again."

A second ten-gülden piece did we lose, and then I put down a third. The Grandmother could scarcely remain seated in her chair, so intent was she upon the little ball as it leapt through the notches of the ever-revolving wheel. However, the third ten-gülden piece followed the first two. Upon this the Grandmother went perfectly crazy. She could no longer sit still, and actually struck the table with her fist when the croupier cried out, "Trente-six," instead of the desiderated zero.

"To listen to him!" fumed the old lady. "When will that accursed zero ever turn up? I cannot breathe until I see it. I believe that that infernal croupier is *purposely* keeping it from turning up. Alexis Ivanovitch, stake TWO golden pieces this time. The moment we cease to stake, that cursed zero will come turning up, and we shall get nothing."

"My good Madame – "

"Stake, stake! It is not *your* money."

Accordingly I staked two ten-gülden pieces. The ball went hopping round the wheel until it began to settle through the notches. Meanwhile the Grandmother sat as though petrified, with my hand convulsively clutched in hers.

"Zero!" called the croupier.

"There! You see, you see!" cried the old lady, as she turned and faced me, wreathed in smiles. "I told you so! It was the Lord God himself who suggested to me to stake those two coins. Now, how much ought I to receive? Why do they not pay it out to me? Potapitch! Martha! Where are they? What has become of our party? Potapitch, Potapitch!"

"Presently, Madame," I whispered. "Potapitch is outside, and they would decline to admit him to these rooms. See! You are being paid out your money. Pray take it." The croupiers were making up a heavy packet of coins, sealed in blue paper, and containing fifty ten gülden pieces, together with an unsealed packet containing another twenty. I handed the whole to the old lady in a money-shovel.

"Faites le jeu, messieurs! Faites le jeu, messieurs! Rien ne va plus," proclaimed the croupier as once more he invited the company to stake, and prepared to turn the wheel.

"We shall be too late! He is going to spin again! Stake, stake!" The Grandmother was in a perfect fever. "Do not hang back! Be quick!" She seemed almost beside herself, and nudged me as hard as she could.

"Upon what shall I stake, Madame?"

"Upon zero, upon zero! Again upon zero! Stake as much as ever you can. How much have we got? Seventy ten-gülden pieces? We shall not miss them, so stake twenty pieces at a time."

"Think a moment, Madame. Sometimes zero does not turn up for two hundred rounds in succession. I assure you that you may lose all your capital."

"You are wrong – utterly wrong. Stake, I tell you! What a chattering tongue you have! I know perfectly well what I am doing." The old lady was shaking with excitement.

"But the rules do not allow of more than 120 gülden being staked upon zero at a time."

"How 'do not allow'? Surely you are wrong? Monsieur, monsieur – " here she nudged the croupier who was sitting on her left, and preparing to spin – "combien zero? Douze? Douze?"

I hastened to translate.

"Oui, Madame," was the croupier's polite reply. "No single stake must exceed four thousand florins. That is the regulation."

"Then there is nothing else for it. We must risk in gülden."

"Le jeu est fait!" the croupier called. The wheel revolved, and stopped at thirty. We had lost!

"Again, again, again! Stake again!" shouted the old lady. Without attempting to oppose her further, but merely shrugging my shoulders, I placed twelve more ten-gülden pieces upon the table. The wheel whirled around and around, with the Grandmother simply quaking as she watched its revolutions.

"Does she again think that zero is going to be the winning coup?" thought I, as I stared at her in astonishment. Yet an absolute assurance of winning was shining on her face; she looked perfectly convinced that zero was about to be called again. At length the ball dropped off into one of the notches.

"Zero!" cried the croupier.

"Ah!!!" screamed the old lady as she turned to me in a whirl of triumph.

I myself was at heart a gambler. At that moment I became acutely conscious both of that fact and of the fact that my hands and knees were shaking, and that the blood was beating in my brain. Of course this was a rare occasion – an occasion on which zero had turned up no less than three times within a dozen rounds; yet in such an event there was nothing so very surprising, seeing that, only three days ago, I myself had been a witness to zero turning up *three times in succession*, so that one of the players who was recording the coups on paper was moved to remark that for several days past zero had never turned up at all!

With the Grandmother, as with any one who has won a very large sum, the management settled up with great attention and respect, since she was fortunate to have to receive no less than 4200 gülden. Of these gülden the odd 200 were paid her in gold, and the remainder in bank notes.

This time the old lady did not call for Potapitch; for that she was too preoccupied. Though not outwardly shaken by the event (indeed, she seemed perfectly calm), she was trembling inwardly from head to foot. At length, completely absorbed in the game, she burst out:

"Alexis Ivanovitch, did not the croupier just say that 4000 florins were the most that could be staked at any one time? Well, take these 4000, and stake them upon the red."

To oppose her was useless. Once more the wheel revolved.

"Rouge!" proclaimed the croupier.

Again 4000 florins – in all 8000!

"Give me them," commanded the Grandmother, "and stake the other 4000 upon the red again."

I did so.

"Rouge!" proclaimed the croupier.

"Twelve thousand!" cried the old lady. "Hand me the whole lot. Put the gold into this purse here, and count the bank notes. Enough! Let us go home. Wheel my chair away."

CHAPTER ELEVEN

The chair, with the old lady beaming in it, was wheeled away towards the doors at the further end of the salon, while our party hastened to crowd around her, and to offer her their congratulations. In fact, eccentric as was her conduct, it was also overshadowed by her triumph; with the result that the General no longer feared to be publicly compromised by being seen with such a strange woman, but, smiling in a condescending, cheerfully familiar way, as though he were soothing a child, he offered his greetings to the old lady. At the same time, both he and the rest of the spectators were visibly impressed. Everywhere people kept pointing to the Grandmother, and talking about her. Many people even walked beside her chair, in order to view her the better while, at a little distance, Astley was carrying on a conversation on the subject with two English acquaintances of his. De Griers was simply overflowing with smiles and compliments, and a number of fine ladies were staring at the Grandmother as though she had been something curious.

"Quelle victoire!" exclaimed De Griers.

"Mais, Madame, c'était du feu!" added Mlle. Blanche with an elusive smile.

"Yes, I have won twelve thousand florins," replied the old lady. "And then there is all this gold. With it the total ought to come to nearly thirteen thousand. How much is that in Russian money? Six thousand roubles, I think?"

However, I calculated that the sum would exceed seven thousand roubles – or, at the present rate of exchange, even eight thousand.

"Eight thousand roubles! What a splendid thing! And to think of you simpletons sitting there and doing nothing! Potapitch! Martha! See what I have won!"

"How *did* you do it, Madame?" Martha exclaimed ecstatically. "Eight thousand roubles!"

"And I am going to give you fifty gülden apiece. There they are."

Potapitch and Martha rushed towards her to kiss her hand.

"And to each bearer also I will give a ten-gülden piece. Let them have it out of the gold, Alexis Ivanovitch. But why is this footman bowing to me, and that other man as well? Are they congratulating me? Well, let them have ten gülden apiece."

"Madame la princesse – Un pauvre expatrié – Malheur continuel – Les princes russes sont si généreux!" said a man who for some time past had been hanging around the old lady's chair – a personage who, dressed in a shabby frockcoat and coloured waistcoat, kept taking off his cap, and smiling pathetically.

"Give him ten gülden," said the Grandmother. "No, give him twenty. Now, enough of that, or I shall never get done with you all. Take a moment's rest, and then carry me away. Prascovia, I mean to buy a new dress for you tomorrow. Yes, and for you too, Mlle. Blanche. Please translate, Prascovia."

"Merci, Madame," replied Mlle. Blanche gratefully as she twisted her face into the mocking smile which usually she kept only for the benefit of De Griers and the General. The latter looked confused, and seemed greatly relieved when we reached the Avenue.

"How surprised Theodosia too will be!" went on the Grandmother (thinking of the General's nursemaid). "She, like yourselves, shall have the price of a new gown. Here, Alexis Ivanovitch! Give that beggar something" (a crooked-backed ragamuffin had approached to stare at us).

"But perhaps he is *not* a beggar – only a rascal," I replied.

"Never mind, never mind. Give him a gülden."

I approached the beggar in question, and handed him the coin. Looking at me in great astonishment, he silently accepted the gülden, while from his person there proceeded a strong smell of liquor.

"Have you never tried your luck, Alexis Ivanovitch?"

"No, Madame."

"Yet just now I could see that you were burning to do so?"

"I *do* mean to try my luck presently."

"Then stake everything upon zero. You have seen how it ought to be done? How much capital do you possess?"

"Two hundred gülden, Madame."

"Not very much. See here; I will lend you five hundred if you wish. Take this purse of mine." With that she added sharply to the General: "But *you* need not expect to receive any."

This seemed to upset him, but he said nothing, and De Griers contented himself by scowling.

"Que diable!" he whispered to the General. "C'est une terrible vieille."

"Look! Another beggar, another beggar!" exclaimed the grandmother. "Alexis Ivanovitch, go and give him a gülden."

As she spoke I saw approaching us a grey-headed old man with a wooden leg – a man who was dressed in a blue frockcoat and carrying a staff. He looked like an old soldier. As soon as I tendered him the coin he fell back a step or two, and eyed me threateningly.

"Was ist der Teufel!" he cried, and appended thereto a round dozen of oaths.

"The man is a perfect fool!" exclaimed the Grandmother, waving her hand. "Move on now, for I am simply famished. When we have lunched we will return to that place."

"What?" cried I. "You are going to play *again?*"

"What else do you suppose?" she retorted. "Are you going only to sit here, and grow sour, and let me look at you?"

"Madame," said De Griers confidentially, "les chances peuvent tourner. Une seule mauvaise chance, et vous perdrez tout – surtout avec votre jeu. C'était terrible!"

"Oui; vous perdrez absolument," put in Mlle. Blanche.

"What has that got to do with *you?*" retorted the old lady. "It is not *your* money that I am going to lose; it is my own. And where is that Mr. Astley of yours?" she added to myself.

"He stayed behind in the Casino."

"What a pity! He is such a nice sort of man!"

Arriving home, and meeting the landlord on the staircase, the Grandmother called him to her side, and boasted to him of her winnings – thereafter doing the same to Theodosia, and conferring upon her thirty gülden; after which she bid her serve luncheon. The meal over, Theodosia and Martha broke into a joint flood of ecstasy.

"I was watching you all the time, Madame," quavered Martha, "and I asked Potapitch what mistress was trying to do. And, my word! the heaps and *heaps* of money that were lying upon the table! Never in my life have I seen so much money. And there were gentlefolk around it, and other gentlefolk sitting down. So, I asked Potapitch where all these gentry had come from; for, thought I, maybe the Holy Mother of God will help our mistress among them. Yes, I prayed for you, Madame, and my heart died within me, so that I kept trembling and trembling. The Lord be with her, I thought to myself; and in answer to my prayer He has now sent you what He has done! Even yet I tremble – I tremble to think of it all."

"Alexis Ivanovitch," said the old lady, "after luncheon, – that is to say, about four o'clock – get ready to go out with me again. But in the meanwhile, good-bye. Do not forget to call a doctor, for I must take the waters. Now go and get rested a little."

I left the Grandmother's presence in a state of bewilderment.

Vainly I endeavoured to imagine what would become of our party, or what turn the affair would next take. I could perceive that none of the party had yet recovered their presence of mind – least of all the General. The factor of the Grandmother's appearance in place of the hourly expected telegram to announce her death (with, of course, resultant legacies) had so upset the whole scheme of intentions and projects that it was with a decided feeling of apprehension and growing paralysis that the conspirators viewed any future performances of the old lady at roulette. Yet this second factor was not quite so important as the first, since, though the Grandmother had twice declared that she did not intend to give the General any money, that declaration was not a complete ground for the abandonment of hope. Certainly De Griers, who, with the General, was up to the neck in the affair, had not wholly lost courage; and I felt sure that Mlle. Blanche also – Mlle. Blanche who was not only as deeply involved as the other two, but also expectant of becoming Madame General and an important legatee – would not lightly surrender the position, but would use her every resource of coquetry upon the old lady, in order to afford a contrast to the impetuous Polina, who was difficult to understand, and lacked the art of pleasing.

Yet now, when the Grandmother had just performed an astonishing feat at roulette; now, when the old lady's personality had been so clearly and typically revealed as that of a rugged, arrogant woman who was "tombée en enfance"; now, when everything appeared to be lost, – why, now the Grandmother was as merry as a child which plays with thistle-down. "Good Lord!" I thought with, may God forgive me, a most malicious smile, "every ten-gülden piece which the Grandmother staked must have raised a blister on the General's heart, and maddened De Griers, and driven Mlle. de Cominges almost to frenzy with the sight of this spoon dangling before her lips." Another factor is the circumstance that even when, overjoyed at winning, the Grandmother was distributing alms right and left, and taking every one to be a beggar, she again snapped out to the General that he was not going to be allowed any of her money – which meant that the old lady had quite made up her mind on the point, and was sure of it. Yes, danger loomed ahead.

All these thoughts passed through my mind during the few moments that, having left the old lady's rooms, I was ascending to my own room on the top storey. What most struck me was the fact that, though I had divined the chief, the stoutest, threads which united the various actors in the drama, I had, until now, been ignorant of the methods and secrets of the game. For Polina had never been completely open with me. Although, on occasions, it had happened that involuntarily, as it were, she had revealed to me something of her heart, I had noticed that in most cases – in fact, nearly always – she had either laughed away these revelations, or grown confused, or purposely imparted to them a false guise. Yes, she must have concealed a great deal from me. But, I had a presentiment that now the end of this strained and mysterious situation was approaching. Another stroke, and all would be finished and exposed. Of my own fortunes, interested though I was in the affair, I took no account. I was in the strange position of possessing but two hundred gülden, of being at a loose end, of lacking both a post, the means of subsistence, a shred of hope, and any plans for the future, yet of caring nothing for these things. Had not my mind been so full of Polina, I should have given myself up to the comical piquancy of the impending denouement, and laughed my fill at it. But the thought of Polina was torture to me. That her fate was settled I already had an inkling; yet *that* was not the thought which was giving me so much uneasiness. What I really wished for was to penetrate her secrets. I wanted her to come to me and say, "I love you," and, if she would not so come, or if to hope that she would ever do so was an unthinkable absurdity – why, then there was nothing else for me to want. Even now I do not know what I am wanting. I feel like a man who has lost his way. I yearn but to be in her presence, and within the circle of her light and splendour – to be there now, and forever, and for the whole of my life. More I do not know. How can I ever bring myself to leave her?

On reaching the third storey of the hotel I experienced a shock. I was just passing the General's suite when something caused me to look round. Out of a door about twenty paces away there was coming Polina! She hesitated for a moment on seeing me, and then beckoned me to her.

"Polina Alexandrovna!"

"Hush! Not so loud."

"Something startled me just now," I whispered, "and I looked round, and saw you. Some electrical influence seems to emanate from your form."

"Take this letter," she went on with a frown (probably she had not even heard my words, she was so preoccupied), "and hand it personally to Mr. Astley. Go as quickly as ever you can, please. No answer will be required. He himself – " She did not finish her sentence.

"To Mr. Astley?" I asked, in some astonishment.

But she had vanished again.

Aha! So the two were carrying on a correspondence! However, I set off to search for Astley – first at his hotel, and then at the Casino, where I went the round of the salons in vain. At length, vexed, and almost in despair, I was on my way home when I ran across him among a troop of English ladies and gentlemen who had been out for a ride. Beckoning to him to stop, I handed him the letter. We had barely time even to look at one another, but I suspected that it was of set purpose that he restarted his horse so quickly.

Was jealousy, then, gnawing at me? At all events, I felt exceedingly depressed, despite the fact that I had no desire to ascertain what the correspondence was about. To think that *he* should be her confidant! "My friend, mine own familiar friend!" passed through my mind. Yet *was* there any love in the matter? "Of course not," reason whispered to me. But reason goes for little on such occasions. I felt that the matter must be cleared up, for it was becoming unpleasantly complex.

I had scarcely set foot in the hotel when the commissionaire and the landlord (the latter issuing from his room for the purpose) alike informed me that I was being searched for high and low – that three separate messages to ascertain my whereabouts had come down from the General. When I entered his study I was feeling anything but kindly disposed. I found there the General himself, De Griers, and Mlle. Blanche, but not Mlle.'s mother, who was a person whom her reputed daughter used only for show purposes, since in all matters of business the daughter fended for herself, and it is unlikely that the mother knew anything about them.

Some very heated discussion was in progress, and meanwhile the door of the study was open – an unprecedented circumstance. As I approached the portals I could hear loud voices raised, for mingled with the pert, venomous accents of De Griers were Mlle. Blanche's excited, impudently abusive tongue and the General's plaintive wail as, apparently, he sought to justify himself in something. But on my appearance every one stopped speaking, and tried to put a better face upon matters. De Griers smoothed his hair, and twisted his angry face into a smile – into the mean, studiedly polite French smile which I so detested; while the downcast, perplexed General assumed an air of dignity – though only in a mechanical way. On the other hand, Mlle. Blanche did not trouble to conceal the wrath that was sparkling in her countenance, but bent her gaze upon me with an air of impatient expectancy. I may remark that hitherto she had treated me with absolute superciliousness, and, so far from answering my salutations, had always ignored them.

"Alexis Ivanovitch," began the General in a tone of affectionate upbraiding, "may I say to you that I find it strange, exceedingly strange, that – In short, your conduct towards myself and my family – In a word, your – er – extremely – "

"Eh! Ce n'est pas ça," interrupted De Griers in a tone of impatience and contempt (evidently he was the ruling spirit of the conclave). "Mon cher monsieur, notre général se trompe. What he means to say is that he warns you – he begs of you most earnestly – not to ruin him. I use the expression because – "

"Why? Why?" I interjected.

"Because you have taken upon yourself to act as guide to this, to this – how shall I express it? – to this old lady, à cette pauvre terrible vieille. But she will only gamble away all that she has – gamble it away like thistledown. You yourself have seen her play. Once she has acquired the taste for gambling, she will never leave the roulette-table, but, of sheer perversity and temper, will stake her all, and lose it. In cases such as hers a gambler can never be torn away from the game; and then – and then – "

"And then," asseverated the General, "you will have ruined my whole family. I and my family are her heirs, for she has no nearer relatives than ourselves. I tell you frankly that my affairs are in great – very great disorder; how much they are so you yourself are partially aware. If she should lose a large sum, or, maybe, her whole fortune, what will become of us – of my children" (here the General exchanged a glance with De Griers) "or of me?" (here he looked at Mlle. Blanche, who turned her head contemptuously away). "Alexis Ivanovitch, I beg of you to save us."

"Tell me, General, how am I to do so? On what footing do I stand here?"

"Refuse to take her about. Simply leave her alone."

"But she would soon find some one else to take my place?"

"Ce n'est pas ça, ce n'est pas ça," again interrupted De Griers. "Que diable! Do not leave her alone so much as advise her, persuade her, draw her away. In any case do not let her gamble; find her some counter-attraction."

"And how am I to do that? If only you would undertake the task, Monsieur de Griers!" I said this last as innocently as possible, but at once saw a rapid glance of excited interrogation pass from Mlle. Blanche to De Griers, while in the face of the latter also there gleamed something which he could not repress.

"Well, at the present moment she would refuse to accept my services," said he with a gesture. "But if, later – "

Here he gave Mlle. Blanche another glance which was full of meaning; whereupon she advanced towards me with a bewitching smile, and seized and pressed my hands. Devil take it, but how that devilish visage of hers could change! At the present moment it was a visage full of supplication, and as gentle in its expression as that of a smiling, roguish infant. Stealthily, she drew me apart from the rest as though the more completely to separate me from them; and, though no harm came of her doing so – for it was merely a stupid manoeuvre, and no more – I found the situation very unpleasant.

The General hastened to lend her his support.

"Alexis Ivanovitch," he began, "pray pardon me for having said what I did just now – for having said more than I meant to do. I beg and beseech you, I kiss the hem of your garment, as our Russian saying has it, for you, and only you, can save us. I and Mlle. de Cominges, we all of us beg of you – But you understand, do you not? Surely you understand?" and with his eyes he indicated Mlle. Blanche. Truly he was cutting a pitiful figure!

At this moment three low, respectful knocks sounded at the door; which, on being opened, revealed a chambermaid, with Potapitch behind her – come from the Grandmother to request that I should attend her in her rooms. "She is in a bad humour," added Potapitch.

The time was half-past three.

"My mistress was unable to sleep," explained Potapitch; "so, after tossing about for a while, she suddenly rose, called for her chair, and sent me to look for you. She is now in the verandah."

"Quelle mégère!" exclaimed De Griers.

True enough, I found Madame in the hotel verandah – much put about at my delay, for she had been unable to contain herself until four o'clock.

"Lift me up," she cried to the bearers, and once more we set out for the roulette-salons.

CHAPTER TWELVE

The Grandmother was in an impatient, irritable frame of mind. Without doubt the roulette had turned her head, for she appeared to be indifferent to everything else, and, in general, seemed much distraught. For instance, she asked me no questions about objects *en route*, except that, when a sumptuous barouche passed us and raised a cloud of dust, she lifted her hand for a moment, and inquired, "What was that?" Yet even then she did not appear to hear my reply, although at times her abstraction was interrupted by sallies and fits of sharp, impatient fidgeting. Again, when I pointed out to her the Baron and Baroness Burmergelm walking to the Casino, she merely looked at them in an absent-minded sort of way, and said with complete indifference, "Ah!" Then, turning sharply to Potapitch and Martha, who were walking behind us, she rapped out:

"Why have *you* attached yourselves to the party? We are not going to take you with us every time. Go home at once." Then, when the servants had pulled hasty bows and departed, she added to me: "You are all the escort I need."

At the Casino the Grandmother seemed to be expected, for no time was lost in procuring her former place beside the croupier. It is my opinion that though croupiers seem such ordinary, humdrum officials – men who care nothing whether the bank wins or loses – they are, in reality, anything but indifferent to the bank's losing, and are given instructions to attract players, and to keep a watch over the bank's interests; as also, that for such services, these officials are awarded prizes and premiums. At all events, the croupiers of Roulettenberg seemed to look upon the Grandmother as their lawful prey – whereafter there befell what our party had foretold.

It happened thus:

As soon as ever we arrived the Grandmother ordered me to stake twelve ten-gülden pieces in succession upon zero. Once, twice, and thrice I did so, yet zero never turned up.

"Stake again," said the old lady with an impatient nudge of my elbow, and I obeyed.

"How many times have we lost?" she inquired – actually grinding her teeth in her excitement.

"We have lost 144 ten-gülden pieces," I replied. "I tell you, Madame, that zero may not turn up until nightfall."

"Never mind," she interrupted. "Keep on staking upon zero, and also stake a thousand gülden upon rouge. Here is a banknote with which to do so."

The red turned up, but zero missed again, and we only got our thousand gülden back.

"But you see, you see," whispered the old lady. "We have now recovered almost all that we staked. Try zero again. Let us do so another ten times, and then leave off."

By the fifth round, however, the Grandmother was weary of the scheme.

"To the devil with that zero!" she exclaimed. "Stake four thousand gülden upon the red."

"But, Madame, that will be so much to venture!" I remonstrated. "Suppose the red should not turn up?" The Grandmother almost struck me in her excitement. Her agitation was rapidly making her quarrelsome. Consequently, there was nothing for it but to stake the whole four thousand gülden as she had directed.

The wheel revolved while the Grandmother sat as bolt upright, and with as proud and quiet a mien, as though she had not the least doubt of winning.

"Zero!" cried the croupier.

At first the old lady failed to understand the situation; but, as soon as she saw the croupier raking in her four thousand gülden, together with everything else that happened to be lying on the table, and recognised that the zero which had been so long turning up, and on which we had lost nearly two hundred ten-gülden pieces, had at length, as though of set purpose, made a sudden reappearance – why, the poor old lady fell to cursing it, and to throwing herself about, and wailing and gesticulating at the company at large. Indeed, some people in our vicinity actually burst out laughing.

"To think that that accursed zero should have turned up *now!*" she sobbed. "The accursed, accursed thing! And, it is all *your* fault," she added, rounding upon me in a frenzy. "It was *you* who persuaded me to cease staking upon it."

"But, Madame, I only explained the game to you. How am *I* to answer for every mischance which may occur in it?"

"You and your mischances!" she whispered threateningly. "Go! Away at once!"

"Farewell, then, Madame." And I turned to depart.

"No – stay," she put in hastily. "Where are you going to? Why should you leave me? You fool! No, no... stay here. It is *I* who was the fool. Tell me what I ought to do."

"I cannot take it upon myself to advise you, for you will only blame me if I do so. Play at your own discretion. Say exactly what you wish staked, and I will stake it."

"Very well. Stake another four thousand gülden upon the red. Take this banknote to do it with. I have still got twenty thousand roubles in actual cash."

"But," I whispered, "such a quantity of money – "

"Never mind. I cannot rest until I have won back my losses. Stake!"

I staked, and we lost.

"Stake again, stake again – eight thousand at a stroke!"

"I cannot, Madame. The largest stake allowed is four thousand gülden."

"Well, then; stake four thousand."

This time we won, and the Grandmother recovered herself a little.

"You see, you see!" she exclaimed as she nudged me. "Stake another four thousand."

I did so, and lost. Again, and yet again, we lost. "Madame, your twelve thousand gülden are now gone," at length I reported.

"I see they are," she replied with, as it were, the calmness of despair. "I see they are," she muttered again as she gazed straight in front of her, like a person lost in thought. "Ah well, I do not mean to rest until I have staked another four thousand."

"But you have no money with which to do it, Madame. In this satchel I can see only a few five percent bonds and some transfers – no actual cash."

"And in the purse?"

"A mere trifle."

"But there is a money-changer's office here, is there not? They told me I should be able to get any sort of paper security changed!"

"Quite so; to any amount you please. But you will lose on the transaction what would frighten even a Jew."

"Rubbish! I am *determined* to retrieve my losses. Take me away, and call those fools of bearers."

I wheeled the chair out of the throng, and, the bearers making their appearance, we left the Casino.

"Hurry, hurry!" commanded the Grandmother. "Show me the nearest way to the money-changer's. Is it far?"

"A couple of steps, Madame."

At the turning from the square into the Avenue we came face to face with the whole of our party – the General, De Griers, Mlle. Blanche, and her mother. Only Polina and Mr. Astley were absent.

"Well, well, well!" exclaimed the Grandmother. "But we have no time to stop. What do you want? I can't talk to you here."

I dropped behind a little, and immediately was pounced upon by De Griers.

"She has lost this morning's winnings," I whispered, "and also twelve thousand gülden of her original money. At the present moment we are going to get some bonds changed."

De Griers stamped his foot with vexation, and hastened to communicate the tidings to the General. Meanwhile we continued to wheel the old lady along.

"Stop her, stop her," whispered the General in consternation.

"You had better try and stop her yourself," I returned – also in a whisper.

"My good mother," he said as he approached her, " – my good mother, pray let, let – " (his voice was beginning to tremble and sink) " – let us hire a carriage, and go for a drive. Near here there is an enchanting view to be obtained. We-we-we were just coming to invite you to go and see it."

"Begone with you and your views!" said the Grandmother angrily as she waved him away.

"And there are trees there, and we could have tea under them," continued the General – now in utter despair.

"Nous boirons du lait, sur l'herbe fraiche," added De Griers with the snarl almost of a wild beast.

"Du lait, de l'herbe fraiche" – the idyll, the ideal of the Parisian bourgeois – his whole outlook upon "la nature et la verité"!

"Have done with you and your milk!" cried the old lady. "Go and stuff *yourself* as much as you like, but my stomach simply recoils from the idea. What are you stopping for? I have nothing to say to you."

"Here we are, Madame," I announced. "Here is the moneychanger's office."

I entered to get the securities changed, while the Grandmother remained outside in the porch, and the rest waited at a little distance, in doubt as to their best course of action. At length the old lady turned such an angry stare upon them that they departed along the road towards the Casino.

The process of changing involved complicated calculations which soon necessitated my return to the Grandmother for instructions.

"The thieves!" she exclaimed as she clapped her hands together. "Never mind, though. Get the documents cashed – No; send the banker out to me," she added as an afterthought.

"Would one of the clerks do, Madame?"

"Yes, one of the clerks. The thieves!"

The clerk consented to come out when he perceived that he was being asked for by an old lady who was too infirm to walk; after which the Grandmother began to upbraid him at length, and with great vehemence, for his alleged usuriousness, and to bargain with him in a mixture of Russian, French, and German – I acting as interpreter. Meanwhile, the grave-faced official eyed us both, and silently nodded his head. At the Grandmother, in particular, he gazed with a curiosity which almost bordered upon rudeness. At length, too, he smiled.

"Pray recollect yourself!" cried the old lady. "And may my money choke you! Alexis Ivanovitch, tell him that we can easily repair to someone else."

"The clerk says that others will give you even less than he."

Of what the ultimate calculations consisted I do not exactly remember, but at all events they were alarming. Receiving twelve thousand florins in gold, I took also the statement of accounts, and carried it out to the Grandmother.

"Well, well," she said, "I am no accountant. Let us hurry away, hurry away." And she waved the paper aside.

"Neither upon that accursed zero, however, nor upon that equally accursed red do I mean to stake a cent," I muttered to myself as I entered the Casino.

This time I did all I could to persuade the old lady to stake as little as possible – saying that a turn would come in the chances when she would be at liberty to stake more. But she was so impatient that, though at first she agreed to do as I suggested, nothing could stop her when once she had begun. By way of prelude she won stakes of a hundred and two hundred gülden.

"There you are!" she said as she nudged me. "See what we have won! Surely it would be worth our while to stake four thousand instead of a hundred, for we might win another four thousand, and then – ! Oh, it was YOUR fault before – all your fault!"

I felt greatly put out as I watched her play, but I decided to hold my tongue, and to give her no more advice.

Suddenly De Griers appeared on the scene. It seemed that all this while he and his companions had been standing beside us – though I noticed that Mlle. Blanche had withdrawn a little from the rest, and was engaged in flirting with the Prince. Clearly the General was greatly put out at this. Indeed, he was in a perfect agony of vexation. But Mlle. was careful never to look his way, though he did his best to attract her notice. Poor General! By turns his face blanched and reddened, and he was trembling to such an extent that he could scarcely follow the old lady's play. At length Mlle. and the Prince took their departure, and the General followed them.

"Madame, Madame," sounded the honeyed accents of De Griers as he leant over to whisper in the Grandmother's ear. "That stake will never win. No, no, it is impossible," he added in Russian with a writhe. "No, no!"

"But why not?" asked the Grandmother, turning round. "Show me what I ought to do."

Instantly De Griers burst into a babble of French as he advised, jumped about, declared that such and such chances ought to be waited for, and started to make calculations of figures. All this he addressed to me in my capacity as translator – tapping the table the while with his finger, and pointing hither and thither. At length he seized a pencil, and began to reckon sums on paper until he had exhausted the Grandmother's patience.

"Away with you!" she interrupted. "You talk sheer nonsense, for, though you keep on saying 'Madame, Madame,' you haven't the least notion what ought to be done. Away with you, I say!"

"Mais, Madame," cooed De Griers – and straightway started afresh with his fussy instructions.

"Stake just *once*, as he advises," the Grandmother said to me, "and then we shall see what we *shall* see. Of course, his stake *might* win."

As a matter of fact, De Grier's one object was to distract the old lady from staking large sums; wherefore, he now suggested to her that she should stake upon certain numbers, singly and in groups. Consequently, in accordance with his instructions, I staked a ten-gülden piece upon several odd numbers in the first twenty, and five ten-gülden pieces upon certain groups of numbers-groups of from twelve to eighteen, and from eighteen to twenty-four. The total staked amounted to 160 gülden.

The wheel revolved. "Zero!" cried the croupier.

We had lost it all!

"The fool!" cried the old lady as she turned upon De Griers. "You infernal Frenchman, to think that *you* should advise! Away with you! Though you fuss and fuss, you don't even know what you're talking about."

Deeply offended, De Griers shrugged his shoulders, favoured the Grandmother with a look of contempt, and departed. For some time past he had been feeling ashamed of being seen in such company, and this had proved the last straw.

An hour later we had lost everything in hand.

"Home!" cried the Grandmother.

Not until we had turned into the Avenue did she utter a word; but from that point onwards, until we arrived at the hotel, she kept venting exclamations of "What a fool I am! What a silly old fool I am, to be sure!"

Arrived at the hotel, she called for tea, and then gave orders for her luggage to be packed.

"We are off again," she announced.

"But whither, Madame?" inquired Martha.

"What business is that of *yours?* Let the cricket stick to its hearth.[2] Potapitch, have everything packed, for we are returning to Moscow at once. I have fooled away fifteen thousand roubles."

"Fifteen thousand roubles, good mistress? My God!" And Potapitch spat upon his hands – probably to show that he was ready to serve her in any way he could.

"Now then, you fool! At once you begin with your weeping and wailing! Be quiet, and pack. Also, run downstairs, and get my hotel bill."

"The next train leaves at 9:30, Madame," I interposed, with a view to checking her agitation.

"And what is the time now?"

"Half-past eight."

"How vexing! But, never mind. Alexis Ivanovitch, I have not a kopeck left; I have but these two bank notes. Please run to the office and get them changed. Otherwise I shall have nothing to travel with."

Departing on her errand, I returned half an hour later to find the whole party gathered in her rooms. It appeared that the news of her impending departure for Moscow had thrown the conspirators into consternation even greater than her losses had done. For, said they, even if her departure should save her fortune, what will become of the General later? And who is to repay De Griers? Clearly Mlle. Blanche would never consent to wait until the Grandmother was dead, but would at once elope with the Prince or someone else. So they had all gathered

2 The Russian form of "Mind your own business."

together – endeavouring to calm and dissuade the Grandmother. Only Polina was absent. For her part the Grandmother had nothing for the party but abuse.

"Away with you, you rascals!" she was shouting. "What have my affairs to do with you? Why, in particular, do *you*" – here she indicated De Griers – "come sneaking here with your goat's beard? And what do *you*" – here she turned to Mlle. Blanche "want of me? What are *you* finicking for?"

"Diantre!" muttered Mlle. under her breath, but her eyes were flashing. Then all at once she burst into a laugh and left the room – crying to the General as she did so: "Elle vivra cent ans!"

"So you have been counting upon my death, have you?" fumed the old lady. "Away with you! Clear them out of the room, Alexis Ivanovitch. What business is it of *theirs?* It is not *their* money that I have been squandering, but my own."

The General shrugged his shoulders, bowed, and withdrew, with De Griers behind him.

"Call Prascovia," commanded the Grandmother, and in five minutes Martha reappeared with Polina, who had been sitting with the children in her own room (having purposely determined not to leave it that day). Her face looked grave and careworn.

"Prascovia," began the Grandmother, "is what I have just heard through a side wind true – namely, that this fool of a stepfather of yours is going to marry that silly whirligig of a Frenchwoman – that actress, or something worse? Tell me, is it true?"

"I do not know *for certain*, Grandmamma," replied Polina; "but from Mlle. Blanche's account (for she does not appear to think it necessary to conceal anything) I conclude that – "

"You need not say any more," interrupted the Grandmother energetically. "I understand the situation. I always thought we should get something like this from him, for I always looked upon him as a futile, frivolous fellow who gave himself unconscionable airs on the fact of his being a general (though he only became one because he retired as a colonel). Yes, I know *all* about the sending of the telegrams to inquire whether 'the old woman is likely to turn up her toes soon.' Ah, they were looking for the legacies! Without money that wretched woman (what is her name? – Oh, De Cominges) would never dream of accepting the General and his false teeth – no, not even for him to be her lacquey – since she herself, they say, possesses a pile of money, and lends it on interest, and makes a good thing out of it. However, it is not *you*, Prascovia, that I am blaming; it was not *you* who sent those telegrams. Nor, for that matter, do I wish to recall old scores. True, I know that you are a vixen by nature – that you are a wasp which will sting one if one touches it – yet, my heart is sore for you, for I loved your mother, Katerina. Now, will you leave everything here, and come away with me? Otherwise, I do not know what is to become of you, and it is not right that you should continue living with these people. Nay," she interposed, the moment that Polina attempted to speak, "I have not yet finished. I ask of you nothing in return. My house in Moscow is, as you know, large enough for a palace, and you could occupy a whole floor of it if you liked, and keep away from me for weeks together. Will you come with me or will you not?"

"First of all, let me ask of *you*," replied Polina, "whether you are intending to depart at once?"

"What? You suppose me to be jesting? I have said that I am going, and I *am* going. Today I have squandered fifteen thousand roubles at that accursed roulette of yours, and though, five years ago, I promised the people of a certain suburb of Moscow to build them a stone church in place of a wooden one, I have been fooling away my money here! However, I am going back now to build my church."

"But what about the waters, Grandmamma? Surely you came here to take the waters?"

"You and your waters! Do not anger me, Prascovia. Surely you are trying to? Say, then: will you, or will you not, come with me?"

"Grandmamma," Polina replied with deep feeling, "I am very, very grateful to you for the shelter which you have so kindly offered me. Also, to a certain extent you have guessed my position aright, and I am beholden to you to such an extent that it may be that I *will* come and live with you, and that very soon; yet there are important reasons why – why I cannot make up my mind just yet. If you would let me have, say, a couple of weeks to decide in – ?"

"You mean that you are *not* coming?"

"I mean only that I cannot come just yet. At all events, I could not well leave my little brother and sister here, since, since – if I were to leave them – they would be abandoned altogether. But if, Grandmamma, you would take the little ones *and* myself, then, of course, I could come with you, and would do all I could to serve you" (this she said with great earnestness). "Only, without the little ones I *cannot* come."

"Do not make a fuss" (as a matter of fact Polina never at any time either fussed or wept). "The Great Foster-Father[3] can find for all his chicks a place. You are not coming without the children? But see here,

3 Translated literally – The Great Poulterer.

Prascovia. I wish you well, and nothing but well: yet I have divined the reason why you will not come. Yes, I know all, Prascovia. That Frenchman will never bring you good of any sort."

Polina coloured hotly, and even I started. "For," thought I to myself, "every one seems to know about that affair. Or perhaps I am the only one who does not know about it?"

"Now, now! Do not frown," continued the Grandmother. "But I do not intend to slur things over. You will take care that no harm befalls you, will you not? For you are a girl of sense, and I am sorry for you – I regard you in a different light to the rest of them. And now, please, leave me. Good-bye."

"But let me stay with you a little longer," said Polina.

"No," replied the other; "you need not. Do not bother me, for you and all of them have tired me out."

Yet when Polina tried to kiss the Grandmother's hand, the old lady withdrew it, and herself kissed the girl on the cheek. As she passed me, Polina gave me a momentary glance, and then as swiftly averted her eyes.

"And good-bye to you, also, Alexis Ivanovitch. The train starts in an hour's time, and I think that you must be weary of me. Take these five hundred gülden for yourself."

"I thank you humbly, Madame, but I am ashamed to – "

"Come, come!" cried the Grandmother so energetically, and with such an air of menace, that I did not dare refuse the money further.

"If, when in Moscow, you have no place where you can lay your head," she added, "come and see me, and I will give you a recommendation. Now, Potapitch, get things ready."

I ascended to my room, and lay down upon the bed. A whole hour I must have lain thus, with my head resting upon my hand. So the crisis had come! I needed time for its consideration. To-morrow I would have a talk with Polina. Ah! The Frenchman! So, it was true? But how could it be so? Polina and De Griers! What a combination!

No, it was too improbable. Suddenly I leapt up with the idea of seeking Astley and forcing him to speak. There could be no doubt that he knew more than I did. Astley? Well, he was another problem for me to solve.

Suddenly there came a knock at the door, and I opened it to find Potapitch awaiting me.

"Sir," he said, "my mistress is asking for you."

"Indeed? But she is just departing, is she not? The train leaves in ten minutes' time."

"She is uneasy, sir; she cannot rest. Come quickly, sir; do not delay."

I ran downstairs at once. The Grandmother was just being carried out of her rooms into the corridor. In her hands she held a roll of bank-notes.

"Alexis Ivanovitch," she cried, "walk on ahead, and we will set out again."

"But whither, Madame?"

"I cannot rest until I have retrieved my losses. March on ahead, and ask me no questions. Play continues until midnight, does it not?"

For a moment I stood stupefied – stood deep in thought; but it was not long before I had made up my mind.

"With your leave, Madame," I said, "I will not go with you."

"And why not? What do you mean? Is every one here a stupid good-for-nothing?"

"Pardon me, but I have nothing to reproach myself with. I merely will not go. I merely intend neither to witness nor to join in your play. I also beg to return you your five hundred gülden. Farewell."

Laying the money upon a little table which the Grandmother's chair happened to be passing, I bowed and withdrew.

"What folly!" the Grandmother shouted after me. "Very well, then. Do not come, and I will find my way alone. Potapitch, you must come with me. Lift up the chair, and carry me along."

I failed to find Mr. Astley, and returned home. It was now growing late – it was past midnight, but I subsequently learnt from Potapitch how the Grandmother's day had ended. She had lost all the money which, earlier in the day, I had got for her paper securities – a sum amounting to about ten thousand roubles. This she did under the direction of the Pole whom, that afternoon, she had dowered with two ten-gülden pieces. But before his arrival on the scene, she had commanded Potapitch to stake for her; until at length she had told him also to go about his business. Upon that the Pole had leapt into the breach. Not only did it happen that he knew the Russian language, but also he could speak a mixture of three different dialects, so that the pair were able to understand one another. Yet the old lady never ceased to abuse him, despite his deferential manner, and to compare him unfavourably with myself (so, at all events, Potapitch declared). "*You*," the old chamberlain said to me, "treated her as a gentleman should, but he – he robbed her right and left, as I could see with my own eyes. Twice she caught him at it, and rated him soundly. On one occasion she even pulled his hair, so that the bystanders burst out laughing. Yet she lost everything, sir – that is to say, she lost all that you had changed for her. Then we brought her home, and, after asking for some water and saying her prayers, she went to bed. So worn out was she that she fell asleep at once. May God send her dreams of angels! And *this* is all that foreign travel has done for us! Oh, my own Moscow! For what have we not at home there, in Moscow? Such a garden and flowers as you could never see here, and fresh air and apple-trees coming into blossom, – and a beautiful view to look upon. Ah, but what must she do but go travelling abroad? Alack, alack!"

CHAPTER THIRTEEN

Almost a month has passed since I last touched these notes – notes which I began under the influence of impressions at once poignant and disordered. The crisis which I then felt to be approaching has now arrived, but in a form a hundred times more extensive and unexpected than I had looked for. To me it all seems strange, uncouth, and tragic. Certain occurrences have befallen me which border upon the marvellous. At all events, that is how I view them. I view them so in one regard at least. I refer to the whirlpool of events in which, at the time, I was revolving. But the most curious feature of all is my relation to those events, for hitherto I had never clearly understood myself. Yet now the actual crisis has passed away like a dream. Even my passion for Polina is dead. *Was* it ever so strong and genuine as I thought? If so, what has become of it now? At times I fancy that I must be mad; that somewhere I am sitting in a madhouse; that these events have merely *seemed* to happen; that still they merely *seem* to be happening.

I have been arranging and re-perusing my notes (perhaps for the purpose of convincing myself that I am not in a madhouse). At present I am lonely and alone. Autumn is coming – already it is mellowing the leaves; and, as I sit brooding in this melancholy little town (and how melancholy the little towns of Germany can be!), I find myself taking no thought for the future, but living under the influence of passing moods, and of my recollections of the tempest which recently drew me into its vortex, and then cast me out again. At times I seem still to be caught within that vortex. At times, the tempest seems once more to be gathering, and, as it passes overhead, to be wrapping me in its folds, until I have lost my sense of order and reality, and continue whirling and whirling and whirling around.

Yet, it may be that I shall be able to stop myself from revolving if once I can succeed in rendering myself an exact account of what has happened within the month just past. Somehow I feel drawn towards the pen; on many and many an evening I have had nothing else in the world to do. But, curiously enough, of late I have taken to amusing myself with the works of M. Paul de Kock, which I read in German translations obtained from a wretched local library. These works I cannot abide, yet I read them, and find myself marvelling that I should be doing so. Somehow I seem to be afraid of any *serious* book – afraid of permitting any *serious* preoccupation to break the spell of the passing moment. So dear to me is the formless dream of which I have spoken, so dear to me are the impressions which it has left behind it, that I fear to touch the vision with anything new, lest it should dissolve in smoke. But is it so dear to me? Yes, it *is* dear to me, and will ever be fresh in my recollections – even forty years hence....

So let me write of it, but only partially, and in a more abridged form than my full impressions might warrant.

First of all, let me conclude the history of the Grandmother. Next day she lost every gülden that she possessed. Things were bound to happen so, for persons of her type who have once entered upon that road descend it with ever-increasing rapidity, even as a sledge descends a toboggan-slide. All day until eight o'clock that evening did she play; and, though I personally did not witness her exploits, I learnt of them later through report.

All that day Potapitch remained in attendance upon her; but the Poles who directed her play she changed more than once. As a beginning she dismissed her Pole of the previous day – the Pole whose hair she had pulled – and took to herself another one; but the latter proved worse even than the former, and incurred dismissal in favour of the first Pole, who, during the time of his unemployment, had nevertheless hovered around the Grandmother's chair, and from time to time obtruded his head over her shoulder. At length the old lady became desperate, for the second Pole, when dismissed, imitated his predecessor by declining to go away; with the result that one Pole remained standing on the right of the victim, and the other on her left; from which vantage points the pair quarrelled, abused each other concerning the stakes and rounds, and exchanged the epithet "laidak"[4] and other Polish terms of endearment. Finally, they effected a mutual reconciliation, and, tossing the money about anyhow, played simply at random. Once more quarrelling, each of them staked money on his own side of the Grandmother's chair (for instance, the one Pole staked upon the red, and the other one upon the

4 Rascal

black), until they had so confused and browbeaten the old lady that, nearly weeping, she was forced to appeal to the head croupier for protection, and to have the two Poles expelled. No time was lost in this being done, despite the rascals' cries and protestations that the old lady was in their debt, that she had cheated them, and that her general behaviour had been mean and dishonourable. The same evening the unfortunate Potapitch related the story to me with tears complaining that the two men had filled their pockets with money (he himself had seen them do it) which had been shamelessly pilfered from his mistress. For instance, one Pole demanded of the Grandmother fifty gülden for his trouble, and then staked the money by the side of her stake. She happened to win; whereupon he cried out that the winning stake was his, and hers the loser. As soon as the two Poles had been expelled, Potapitch left the room, and reported to the authorities that the men's pockets were full of gold; and, on the Grandmother also requesting the head croupier to look into the affair, the police made their appearance, and, despite the protests of the Poles (who, indeed, had been caught redhanded), their pockets were turned inside out, and the contents handed over to the Grandmother. In fact, in, view of the circumstance that she lost all day, the croupiers and other authorities of the Casino showed her every attention; and on her fame spreading through the town, visitors of every nationality – even the most knowing of them, the most distinguished – crowded to get a glimpse of "la vieille comtesse russe, tombée en enfance," who had lost "so many millions."

Yet with the money which the authorities restored to her from the pockets of the Poles the Grandmother effected very, very little, for there soon arrived to take his countrymen's place, a third Pole – a man who could speak Russian fluently, was dressed like a gentleman (albeit in lacqueyish fashion), and sported a huge moustache. Though polite enough to the old lady, he took a high hand with the bystanders. In short, he offered himself less as a servant than as an *entertainer*. After each round he would turn to the old lady, and swear terrible oaths to the effect that he was a "Polish gentleman of honour" who would scorn to take a kopeck of her money; and, though he repeated these oaths so often that at length she grew alarmed, he had her play in hand, and began to win on her behalf; wherefore, she felt that she could not well get rid of him. An hour later the two Poles who, earlier in the day, had been expelled from the Casino, made a reappearance behind the old lady's chair, and renewed their offers of service – even if it were only to be sent on messages; but from Potapitch I subsequently had it that between these rascals and the said "gentleman of honour" there passed a wink, as well as that the latter put something into their hands. Next, since the Grandmother had not yet lunched – she had scarcely for a moment left her chair – one of the two Poles ran to the restaurant of the Casino, and brought her thence a cup of soup, and afterwards some tea. In fact, *both* the Poles hastened to perform this office. Finally, towards the close of the day, when it was clear that the Grandmother was about to play her last bank-note, there could be seen standing behind her chair no fewer than six natives of Poland – persons who, as yet, had been neither audible nor visible; and as soon as ever the old lady played the note in question, they took no further notice of her, but pushed their way past her chair to the table; seized the money, and staked it – shouting and disputing the while, and arguing with the "gentleman of honour" (who also had forgotten the Grandmother's existence), as though he were their equal. Even when the Grandmother had lost her all, and was returning (about eight o'clock) to the hotel, some three or four Poles could not bring themselves to leave her, but went on running beside her chair and volubly protesting that the Grandmother had cheated them, and that she ought to be made to surrender what was not her own. Thus the party arrived at the hotel; whence, presently, the gang of rascals was ejected neck and crop.

According to Potapitch's calculations, the Grandmother lost, that day, a total of ninety thousand roubles, in addition to the money which she had lost the day before. Every paper security which she had brought with her – five percent bonds, internal loan scrip, and what not – she had changed into cash. Also, I could not but marvel at the way in which, for seven or eight hours at a stretch, she sat in that chair of hers, almost never leaving the table. Again, Potapitch told me that there were three occasions on which she really began to win; but that, led on by false hopes, she was unable to tear herself away at the right moment. Every gambler knows how a person may sit a day and a night at cards without ever casting a glance to right or to left.

Meanwhile, that day some other very important events were passing in our hotel. As early as eleven o'clock – that is to say, before the Grandmother had quitted her rooms – the General and De Griers decided upon their last stroke. In other words, on learning that the old lady had changed her mind about departing, and was bent on setting out for the Casino again, the whole of our gang (Polina only excepted) proceeded en masse to her rooms, for the purpose of finally and frankly treating with her. But the General, quaking and greatly apprehensive as to his possible future, overdid things. After half an hour's prayers and entreaties, coupled with a full confession of his debts, and even of his passion for Mlle. Blanche (yes, he had quite lost his head), he suddenly adopted a tone of menace, and started to rage at the old lady – exclaiming that she was sullying the family honour, that she was making a public scandal of herself, and that she was smirching the fair name of Russia. The upshot was that the Grandmother turned him out of the room with her stick (it was a real stick, too!). Later in the morning he held several consultations with De Griers – the question which occupied him being: Is it in any way possible to make use of the police – to tell them that "this respected, but unfortunate, old lady has gone out of her mind, and is squandering her last kopeck," or something of the kind? In short, is it in any way possible to engineer a species of supervision over, or of restraint upon, the old lady? De Griers, however, shrugged his shoulders at this, and laughed in the General's face, while the old warrior went on chattering volubly, and running up and down his study. Finally De Griers waved his hand, and disappeared from view; and by evening it became known that he had left the hotel, after holding a very secret and important conference with Mlle. Blanche. As for the latter, from early morning she had taken decisive measures, by completely excluding the General from her presence, and bestowing upon him not a glance. Indeed, even when the General pursued her to the Casino, and met her walking arm in arm with the Prince, he (the General) received from her and her mother not the slightest recognition. Nor did the Prince himself bow. The rest of the day Mlle. spent in probing the Prince, and trying to make him declare himself; but in this she made a woeful mistake. The little incident occurred in the evening. Suddenly Mlle. Blanche realised that the Prince had not even a copper to his name, but, on the contrary, was minded to borrow of her money wherewith to play at roulette. In high displeasure she drove him from her presence, and shut herself up in her room.

The same morning I went to see – or, rather, to look for – Mr. Astley, but was unsuccessful in my quest. Neither in his rooms nor in the Casino nor in the Park was he to be found; nor did he, that day, lunch at his hotel as usual. However, at about five o'clock I caught sight of him walking from the railway station to the Hôtel d'Angleterre. He seemed to be in a great hurry and much preoccupied, though in his face I could discern no actual traces of worry or perturbation. He held out to me a friendly hand, with his usual ejaculation of "Ah!" but did not check his stride. I turned and walked beside him, but found, somehow, that his answers forbade any putting of definite questions. Moreover, I felt reluctant to speak to him of Polina; nor, for his part, did he ask me any questions concerning her, although, on my telling him of the

Grandmother's exploits, he listened attentively and gravely, and then shrugged his shoulders.

"She is gambling away everything that she has," I remarked.

"Indeed? She arrived at the Casino even before I had taken my departure by train, so I knew she had been playing. If I should have time I will go to the Casino to-night, and take a look at her. The thing interests me."

"Where have you been today?" I asked – surprised at myself for having, as yet, omitted to put to him that question.

"To Frankfort."

"On business?"

"On business."

What more was there to be asked after that? I accompanied him until, as we drew level with the Hotel des Quatre Saisons, he suddenly nodded to me and disappeared. For myself, I returned home, and came to the conclusion that, even had I met him at two o'clock in the afternoon, I should have learnt no more from him than I had done at five o'clock, for the reason that I had no definite question to ask. It was bound to have been so. For me to formulate the query which I really wished to put was a simple impossibility.

Polina spent the whole of that day either in walking about the park with the nurse and children or in sitting in her own room. For a long while past she had avoided the General and had scarcely had a word to say to him (scarcely a word, I mean, on any *serious* topic). Yes, that I had noticed. Still, even though I was aware of the position in which the General was placed, it had never occurred to me that he would have any reason to avoid *her*, or to trouble her with family explanations. Indeed, when I was returning to the hotel after my conversation with Astley, and chanced to meet Polina and the children, I could see that her face was as calm as though the family disturbances had never touched her. To my salute she responded with a slight bow, and I retired to my room in a very bad humour.

Of course, since the affair with the Burmergelms I had exchanged not a word with Polina, nor had with her any kind of intercourse. Yet I had been at my wits' end, for, as time went on, there was arising in me an ever-seething dissatisfaction. Even if she did not love me she ought not to have trampled upon my feelings, nor to have accepted my confessions with such contempt, seeing that she must have been aware that I loved her (of her own accord she had allowed me to tell her as much). Of course the situation between us had arisen in a curious manner. About two months ago, I had noticed that she had a desire to make me her friend, her confidant – that she was making trial of me for the purpose; but, for some reason or another, the desired result had never come about, and we had fallen into the present strange relations, which had led me to address her as I had done. At the same time, if my love was distasteful to her, why had she not *forbidden* me to speak of it to her?

But she had not so forbidden me. On the contrary, there had been occasions when she had even *invited* me to speak. Of course, this might have been done out of sheer wantonness, for I well knew – I had remarked it only too often – that, after listening to what I had to say, and angering me almost beyond endurance, she loved suddenly to torture me with some fresh outburst of contempt and aloofness! Yet she must have known that I could not live without her. Three days had elapsed since the affair with the Baron, and I could bear the severance no longer. When, that afternoon, I met her near the Casino, my heart almost made me faint, it beat so violently. She too could not live without me, for had she not said that she had *need* of me? Or had that too been spoken in jest?

That she had a secret of some kind there could be no doubt. What she had said to the Grandmother had stabbed me to the heart. On a thousand occasions I had challenged her to be open with me, nor could she have been ignorant that I was ready to give my very life for her. Yet always she had kept me at a distance with that contemptuous air of hers; or else she had demanded of me, in lieu of the life which I offered to lay at her feet, such escapades as I had perpetrated with the Baron. Ah, was it not torture to me, all this? For could it be that her whole world was bound up with the Frenchman? What, too, about Mr. Astley? The affair was inexplicable throughout. My God, what distress it caused me!

Arrived home, I, in a fit of frenzy, indited the following:

"Polina Alexandrovna, I can see that there is approaching us an exposure which will involve you too. For the last time I ask of you – have you, or have you not, any need of my life? If you have, then make such dispositions as you wish, and I shall always be discoverable in my room if required. If you have need of my life, write or send for me."

I sealed the letter, and dispatched it by the hand of a corridor lacquey, with orders to hand it to the addressee in person. Though I expected no answer, scarcely three minutes had elapsed before the lacquey returned with "the compliments of a certain person."

Next, about seven o'clock, I was sent for by the General. I found him in his study, apparently preparing to go out again, for his hat and stick were lying on the sofa. When I entered he was standing in the middle of the room – his feet wide apart, and his head bent down. Also, he appeared to be talking to himself. But as soon as ever he saw me at the door he came towards me in such a curious manner that involuntarily I retreated a step, and was for leaving the room; whereupon he seized me by both hands, and, drawing me towards the sofa, and seating himself thereon, he forced me to sit down on a chair opposite him. Then, without letting go of my hands, he exclaimed with quivering lips and a sparkle of tears on his eyelashes:

"Oh, Alexis Ivanovitch! Save me, save me! Have some mercy upon me!"

For a long time I could not make out what he meant, although he kept talking and talking, and constantly repeating to himself, "Have mercy, mercy!" At length, however, I divined that he was expecting me to give him something in the nature of advice – or, rather, that, deserted by every one, and overwhelmed with grief and apprehension, he had bethought himself of my existence, and sent for me to relieve his feelings by talking and talking and talking.

In fact, he was in such a confused and despondent state of mind that, clasping his hands together, he actually went down upon his knees and begged me to go to Mlle. Blanche, and beseech and advise her to return to him, and to accept him in marriage.

"But, General," I exclaimed, "possibly Mlle. Blanche has scarcely even remarked my existence? What could *I* do with her?"

It was in vain that I protested, for he could understand nothing that was said to him, Next he started talking about the Grandmother, but always in a disconnected sort of fashion – his one thought being to send for the police.

"In Russia," said he, suddenly boiling over with indignation, "or in any well-ordered State where there exists a government, old women like my mother are placed under proper guardianship. Yes, my good sir," he went on, relapsing into a scolding tone as he leapt to his feet and started to pace the room, "do you not know this" (he seemed to be addressing some imaginary auditor in the corner) " – do you not know this, that in Russia old women like her are subjected to restraint, the devil take them?" Again he threw himself down upon the sofa.

A minute later, though sobbing and almost breathless, he managed to gasp out that Mlle. Blanche had refused to marry him, for the reason that the Grandmother had turned up in place of a telegram, and it was therefore clear that he had no inheritance to look for. Evidently, he supposed that I had hitherto been in entire ignorance of all this. Again, when I referred to De Griers, the General made a gesture of despair.

"He has gone away," he said, "and everything which I possess is mortgaged to him. I stand stripped to my skin. Even of the money which you brought me from Paris, I know not if seven hundred francs be left. Of course that sum will do to go on with, but, as regards the future, I know nothing, I know nothing."

"Then how will you pay your hotel bill?" I cried in consternation. "And what shall you do afterwards?"

He looked at me vaguely, but it was clear that he had not understood – perhaps had not even heard – my questions. Then I tried to get him to speak of Polina and the children, but he only returned brief answers of "Yes, yes," and again started to maunder about the Prince, and the likelihood of the latter marrying Mlle. Blanche. "What on earth am I to do?" he concluded. "What on earth am I to do? Is this not ingratitude? Is it not sheer ingratitude?" And he burst into tears.

Nothing could be done with such a man. Yet to leave him alone was dangerous, for something might happen to him. I withdrew from his rooms for a little while, but warned the nursemaid to keep an eye upon him, as well as exchanged a word with the corridor lacquey (a very talkative fellow), who likewise promised to remain on the look-out.

Hardly had I left the General, when Potapitch approached me with a summons from the Grandmother. It was now eight o'clock, and she had returned from the Casino after finally losing all that she possessed. I found her sitting in her chair – much distressed and evidently fatigued. Presently Martha brought her up a cup of tea and forced her to drink it; yet, even then I could detect in the old lady's tone and manner a great change.

"Good evening, Alexis Ivanovitch," she said slowly, with her head drooping. "Pardon me for disturbing you again. Yes, you must pardon an old, old woman like myself, for I have left behind me all that I possess – nearly a hundred thousand roubles! You did quite right in declining to come with me this evening. Now I am without money – without a single groat. But I must not delay a moment; I must leave by the 9:30 train. I have sent for that English friend of yours, and am going to beg of him three thousand francs for a week. Please try and persuade him to think nothing of it, nor yet to refuse me, for I am still a rich woman who possesses three villages and a couple of mansions. Yes, the money shall be found, for I have not yet squandered *everything*. I tell you this in order that he may have no doubts about – Ah, but here he is! Clearly he is a good fellow."

True enough, Astley had come hot-foot on receiving the Grandmother's appeal. Scarcely stopping even to reflect, and with scarcely a word, he counted out the three thousand francs under a note of hand which she duly signed. Then, his business done, he bowed, and lost no time in taking his departure.

"You too leave me, Alexis Ivanovitch," said the Grandmother. "All my bones are aching, and I still have an hour in which to rest. Do not be hard upon me, old fool that I am. Never again shall I blame young people for being frivolous. I should think it wrong even to blame that unhappy General of yours. Nevertheless, I do not mean to let him have any of my money (which is all that he desires), for the reason that I look upon him as a perfect blockhead, and consider myself, simpleton though I be, at least wiser than *he* is. How surely does God visit old age, and punish it for its presumption! Well, good-bye. Martha, come and lift me up."

However, I had a mind to see the old lady off; and, moreover, I was in an expectant frame of mind – somehow I kept thinking that *something* was going to happen; wherefore, I could not rest quietly in my room, but stepped out into the corridor, and then into the Chestnut Avenue for a few minutes' stroll. My letter to Polina had been clear and firm, and in the present crisis, I felt sure, would prove final. I had heard of De Griers' departure, and, however much Polina might reject me as a *friend*, she might not reject me altogether as a *servant*. She would need me to fetch and carry for her, and I was ready to do so. How could it have been otherwise?

Towards the hour of the train's departure I hastened to the station, and put the Grandmother into her compartment – she and her party occupying a reserved family saloon.

"Thanks for your disinterested assistance," she said at parting. "Oh, and please remind Prascovia of what I said to her last night. I expect soon to see her."

Then I returned home. As I was passing the door of the General's suite, I met the nursemaid, and inquired after her master. "There is nothing new to report, sir," she replied quietly. Nevertheless I decided to enter, and was just doing so when I halted thunderstruck on the threshold. For before me I beheld the General and Mlle. Blanche – laughing gaily at one another! – while beside them, on the sofa, there was seated her mother. Clearly the General was almost out of his mind with joy, for he was talking all sorts of nonsense, and bubbling over with a long-drawn, nervous laugh – a laugh which twisted his face into innumerable wrinkles, and caused his eyes almost to disappear.

Afterwards I learnt from Mlle. Blanche herself that, after dismissing the Prince and hearing of the General's tears, she bethought her of going to comfort the old man, and had just arrived for the purpose when I entered. Fortunately, the poor General did not know that his fate had been decided – that Mlle. had long ago packed her trunks in readiness for the first morning train to Paris!

Hesitating a moment on the threshold I changed my mind as to entering, and departed unnoticed. Ascending to my own room, and opening the door, I perceived in the semi-darkness a figure seated on a chair in the corner by the window. The figure did not rise when I entered, so I approached it swiftly, peered at it closely, and felt my heart almost stop beating. The figure was Polina!

CHAPTER FOURTEEN

THE SHOCK MADE ME utter an exclamation.

"What is the matter? What is the matter?" she asked in a strange voice. She was looking pale, and her eyes were dim.

"What is the matter?" I re-echoed. "Why, the fact that you are *here!*"

"If I am here, I have come with all that I have to bring," she said. "Such has always been my way, as you shall presently see. Please light a candle."

I did so; whereupon she rose, approached the table, and laid upon it an open letter.

"Read it," she added.

"It is De Griers' handwriting!" I cried as I seized the document. My hands were so tremulous that the lines on the pages danced before my eyes. Although, at this distance of time, I have forgotten the exact phraseology of the missive, I append, if not the precise words, at all events the general sense.

"Mademoiselle," the document ran, "certain untoward circumstances compel me to depart in haste. Of course, you have of yourself remarked that hitherto I have always refrained from having any final explanation with you, for the reason that I could not well state the whole circumstances; and now to my difficulties the advent of the aged Grandmother, coupled with her subsequent proceedings, has put the final touch. Also, the involved state of my affairs forbids me to write with any finality concerning those hopes of ultimate bliss upon which, for a long while past, I have permitted myself to feed. I regret the past, but at the same time hope that in my conduct you have never been able to detect anything that was unworthy of a gentleman and a man of honour. Having lost, however, almost the whole of my money in debts incurred by your stepfather, I find myself driven to the necessity of saving the remainder; wherefore, I have instructed certain friends of mine in St. Petersburg to arrange for the sale of all the property which has been mortgaged to myself. At the same time, knowing that, in addition, your frivolous stepfather has squandered money which is exclusively yours, I have decided to absolve him from a certain moiety of the mortgages on his property, in order that you may be in a position to recover of him what you have lost, by suing him in legal fashion. I trust, therefore, that, as matters now stand, this action of mine may bring you some advantage. I trust also that this same action leaves me in the position of having fulfilled every obligation which is incumbent upon a man of honour and refinement. Rest assured that your memory will for ever remain graven in my heart."

"All this is clear enough," I commented. "Surely you did not expect aught else from him?" Somehow I was feeling annoyed.

"I expected nothing at all from him," she replied – quietly enough, to all outward seeming, yet with a note of irritation in her tone. "Long ago I made up my mind on the subject, for I could read his thoughts, and knew what he was thinking. He thought that possibly I should sue him – that one day I might become a nuisance." Here Polina halted for a moment, and stood biting her lips. "So of set purpose I redoubled my contemptuous treatment of him, and waited to see what he would do. If a telegram to say that we had become legatees had arrived from, St. Petersburg, I should have flung at him a quittance for my foolish stepfather's debts, and then dismissed him. For a long time I have hated him. Even in earlier days he was not a man; and now! – Oh, how gladly I could throw those fifty thousand roubles in his face, and spit in it, and then rub the spittle in!"

"But the document returning the fifty-thousand rouble mortgage – has the General got it? If so, possess yourself of it, and send it to De Griers."

"No, no; the General has not got it."

"Just as I expected! Well, what is the General going to do?" Then an idea suddenly occurred to me. "What about the Grandmother?" I asked.

Polina looked at me with impatience and bewilderment.

"What makes you speak of *her?*" was her irritable inquiry. "I cannot go and live with her. Nor," she added hotly, "will I go down upon my knees to *any one*."

"Why should you?" I cried. "Yet to think that you should have loved De Griers! The villain, the villain! But I will kill him in a duel. Where is he now?"

"In Frankfort, where he will be staying for the next three days."

"Well, bid me do so, and I will go to him by the first train tomorrow," I exclaimed with enthusiasm.

She smiled.

"If you were to do that," she said, "he would merely tell you to be so good as first to return him the fifty thousand francs. What, then, would be the use of having a quarrel with him? You talk sheer nonsense."

I ground my teeth.

"The question," I went on, "is how to raise the fifty thousand francs. We cannot expect to find them lying about on the floor. Listen. What of Mr. Astley?" Even as I spoke a new and strange idea formed itself in my brain.

Her eyes flashed fire.

"What? *you yourself* wish me to leave you for him?" she cried with a scornful look and a proud smile. Never before had she addressed me thus.

Then her head must have turned dizzy with emotion, for suddenly she seated herself upon the sofa, as though she were powerless any longer to stand.

A flash of lightning seemed to strike me as I stood there. I could scarcely believe my eyes or my ears. She *did* love me, then! It *was* to me, and not to Mr. Astley, that she had turned! Although she, an unprotected girl, had come to me in my room – in an hotel room – and had probably compromised herself thereby, I had not understood!

Then a second mad idea flashed into my brain.

"Polina," I said, "give me but an hour. Wait here just one hour until I return. Yes, you MUST do so. Do you not see what I mean? Just stay here for that time."

And I rushed from the room without so much as answering her look of inquiry. She called something after me, but I did not return.

Sometimes it happens that the most insane thought, the most impossible conception, will become so fixed in one's head that at length one believes the thought or the conception to be reality. Moreover, if with the thought or the conception there is combined a strong, a passionate, desire, one will come to look upon the said thought or conception as something fated, inevitable, and foreordained – something bound to happen. Whether by this there is connoted something in the nature of a combination of presentiments, or a great effort of will, or a self-annulment of one's true expectations, and so on, I do not know; but, at all events that night saw happen to me (a night which I shall never forget) something in the nature of the miraculous. Although the occurrence can easily be explained by arithmetic, I still believe it to have been a miracle. Yet why did this conviction take such a hold upon me at the time, and remain with me ever since? Previously, I had thought of the idea, not as an occurrence which was ever likely to come about, but as something which *never* could come about.

The time was a quarter past eleven o'clock when I entered the Casino in such a state of hope (though, at the same time, of agitation) as I had never before experienced. In the gaming-rooms there were still a large number of people, but not half as many as had been present in the morning.

At eleven o'clock there usually remained behind only the real, the desperate gamblers – persons for whom, at spas, there existed nothing beyond roulette, and who went thither for that alone. These gamesters took little note of what was going on around them, and were interested in none of the appurtenances of the season, but played from morning till night, and would have been ready to play through the night until dawn had that been possible. As it was, they used to disperse unwillingly when, at midnight, roulette came to an end. Likewise, as soon as ever roulette was drawing to a close and the head croupier had called "Les trois derniers coups," most of them were ready to stake on the last three rounds all that they had in their pockets – and, for the most part, lost it. For my own part I proceeded towards the table at which the Grandmother had lately sat; and, since the crowd around it was not very large, I soon obtained standing room among the ring of gamblers, while directly in front of me, on the green cloth, I saw marked the word "Passe."

"Passe" was a row of numbers from 19 to 36 inclusive; while a row of numbers from 1 to 18 inclusive was known as "Manque." But what had that to do with me? I had not noticed – I had not so much as heard the numbers upon which the previous coup had fallen, and so took no bearings when I began to play, as, in my place, any *systematic* gambler would have done. No, I merely extended my stock of twenty ten-gülden pieces, and threw them down upon the space "Passe" which happened to be confronting me.

"Vingt-deux!" called the croupier.

I had won! I staked upon the same again – both my original stake and my winnings.

"Trente-et-un!" called the croupier.

Again I had won, and was now in possession of eighty ten-gülden pieces. Next, I moved the whole eighty on to twelve middle numbers (a stake which, if successful, would bring me in a triple profit, but also involved a risk of two chances to one). The wheel revolved, and stopped at twenty-four. Upon this I was paid out notes and gold until I had by my side a total sum of two thousand gülden.

It was as in a fever that I moved the pile, en bloc, on to the red. Then suddenly I came to myself (though that was the only time during the evening's play when fear cast its cold spell over me, and showed itself in a trembling of the hands and knees). For with horror I had realised that I *must* win, and that upon that stake there depended all my life.

"Rouge!" called the croupier. I drew a long breath, and hot shivers went coursing over my body. I was paid out my winnings in bank-notes – amounting, of course, to a total of four thousand florins, eight hundred gülden (I could still calculate the amounts).

After that, I remember, I again staked two thousand florins upon twelve middle numbers, and lost. Again I staked the whole of my gold, with eight hundred gülden, in notes, and lost. Then madness seemed to come upon me, and seizing my last two thousand florins, I staked them upon twelve of the first numbers – wholly by chance, and at random, and without any sort of reckoning. Upon my doing so there followed a moment of suspense only comparable to that which Madame Blanchard must have experienced when, in Paris, she was descending earthwards from a balloon.

"Quatre!" called the croupier.

Once more, with the addition of my original stake, I was in possession of six thousand florins! Once more I looked around me like a conqueror – once more I feared nothing as I threw down four thousand of these florins upon the black. The croupiers glanced around them, and exchanged a few words; the bystanders murmured expectantly.

The black turned up. After that I do not exactly remember either my calculations or the order of my stakings. I only remember that, as in a dream, I won in one round sixteen thousand florins; that in the three following rounds, I lost twelve thousand; that I moved the remainder (four thousand) on to "Passe" (though quite unconscious of what I was doing – I was merely waiting, as it were, mechanically, and without reflection, for something) and won; and that, finally, four times in succession I lost. Yes, I can remember raking in money by thousands – but most frequently on the twelve, middle numbers, to which I constantly adhered, and which kept appearing in a sort of regular order – first, three or four times running, and then, after an interval of a couple of rounds, in another break of three or four appearances. Sometimes, this astonishing regularity manifested itself in patches; a thing to upset all the calculations of note - taking gamblers who play with a pencil and a memorandum-book in their hands Fortune perpetrates some terrible jests at roulette!

Since my entry not more than half an hour could have elapsed. Suddenly a croupier informed me that I had, won thirty thousand florins, as well as that, since the latter was the limit for which, at any one time, the bank could make itself responsible, roulette at that table must close for the night. Accordingly, I caught up my pile of gold, stuffed it into my pocket, and, grasping my sheaf of bank-notes, moved to the table in an adjoining salon where a second game of roulette was in progress. The crowd followed me in a body, and cleared a place for me at the table; after which, I proceeded to stake as before – that is to say, at random and without calculating. What saved me from ruin I do not know.

Of course there were times when fragmentary reckonings *did* come flashing into my brain. For instance, there were times when I attached myself for a while to certain figures and coups – though always leaving them, again before long, without knowing what I was doing.

In fact, I cannot have been in possession of all my faculties, for I can remember the croupiers correcting my play more than once, owing to my having made mistakes of the gravest order. My brows were damp with sweat, and my hands were shaking. Also, Poles came around me to proffer their services, but I heeded none of them. Nor did my luck fail me now. Suddenly, there arose around me a loud din of talking and laughter. "Bravo, bravo!" was the general shout, and some people even clapped their hands. I had raked in thirty thousand florins, and again the bank had had to close for the night!

"Go away now, go away now," a voice whispered to me on my right. The person who had spoken to me was a certain Jew of Frankfurt – a man who had been standing beside me the whole while, and occasionally helping me in my play.

"Yes, for God's sake go," whispered a second voice in my left ear. Glancing around, I perceived that the second voice had come from a modestly, plainly dressed lady of rather less than thirty – a woman whose face, though pale and sickly-looking, bore also very evident traces of former beauty. At the moment, I was stuffing the crumpled bank-notes into my pockets and collecting all the gold that was left on the table. Seizing up my last note for five hundred gülden, I contrived to insinuate it, unperceived, into the hand of the pale lady. An overpowering impulse had made me do so, and I remember how her thin little fingers pressed mine in token of her lively gratitude. The whole affair was the work of a moment.

Then, collecting my belongings, I crossed to where trente et quarante was being played – a game which could boast of a more aristocratic public, and was played with cards instead of with a wheel. At this diversion the bank made itself responsible for a hundred thousand thalers as the limit, but the highest stake allowable was, as in roulette, four thousand florins. Although I knew nothing of the game – and I scarcely knew the stakes, except those on black and red – I joined the ring of players, while the rest of the crowd massed itself around me. At this distance of time I cannot remember whether I ever gave a thought to Polina; I seemed only to be conscious of a vague pleasure in seizing and raking in the bank-notes which kept massing themselves in a pile before me.

But, as ever, fortune seemed to be at my back. As though of set purpose, there came to my aid a circumstance which not infrequently repeats itself in gaming. The circumstance is that not infrequently luck attaches itself to, say, the red, and does not leave it for a space of say, ten, or even fifteen, rounds in succession. Three days ago I had heard that, during the previous week there had been a run of twenty-two coups on the red – an occurrence never before known at roulette – so that men spoke of it with astonishment. Naturally enough, many deserted the red after a dozen rounds, and practically no one could now be found to stake upon it. Yet upon the black also – the antithesis of the red – no experienced gambler would stake anything, for the reason that every practised player knows the meaning of "capricious fortune." That is to say, after the sixteenth (or so) success of the red, one would think that the seventeenth coup would inevitably fall upon the black; wherefore, novices would be apt to back the latter in the seventeenth round, and even to double or treble their stakes upon it – only, in the end, to lose.

Yet some whim or other led me, on remarking that the red had come up consecutively for seven times, to attach myself to that colour. Probably this was mostly due to self-conceit, for I wanted to astonish the bystanders with the riskiness of my play. Also, I remember that – oh, strange sensation! – I suddenly, and without any challenge from my own presumption, became obsessed with a *desire* to take risks. If the spirit has passed through a great many sensations, possibly it can no longer be sated with them, but grows more excited, and demands more sensations, and stronger and stronger ones, until at length it falls exhausted. Certainly, if the rules of the game had permitted even of my staking fifty thousand florins at a time, I should have staked them. All of a sudden I heard exclamations arising that the whole thing was a marvel, since the red was turning up for the fourteenth time!

"Monsieur a gagné cent mille florins," a voice exclaimed beside me.

I awoke to my senses. What? I had won a hundred thousand florins? If so, what more did I need to win? I grasped the banknotes, stuffed them into my pockets, raked in the gold without counting it, and started to leave the Casino. As I passed through the salons people smiled to see my bulging pockets and unsteady gait, for the weight which I was carrying must have amounted to half a pood! Several hands I saw stretched out in my direction, and as I passed I filled them with all the money that I could grasp in my own. At length two Jews stopped me near the exit.

"You are a bold young fellow," one said, "but mind you depart early tomorrow – as early as you can – for if you do not you will lose everything that you have won."

But I did not heed them. The Avenue was so dark that it was barely possible to distinguish one's hand before one's face, while the distance to the hotel was half a verst or so; but I feared neither pickpockets nor highwaymen. Indeed, never since my boyhood have I done that. Also, I cannot remember what I thought about on the way. I only felt a sort of fearful pleasure – the pleasure of success, of conquest, of power (how can I best express it?). Likewise, before me there flitted the image of Polina; and I kept remembering, and reminding myself, that it was to *her* I was going, that it was in *her* presence I should soon be standing, that it was *she* to whom I should soon be able to relate and show everything. Scarcely once did I recall what she had lately said to me, or the reason why I had left her, or all those varied sensations which I had been experiencing a bare hour and a half ago. No, those sensations seemed to be things of the past, to be things which had righted themselves and grown old, to be things concerning which we needed to trouble ourselves no longer, since, for us, life was about to begin anew. Yet I had just reached the end of the Avenue when there *did* come upon me a fear of being robbed or murdered. With each step the fear increased until, in my terror, I almost started to run. Suddenly, as I issued from the Avenue, there burst upon me the lights of the hotel, sparkling with a myriad lamps! Yes, thanks be to God, I had reached home!

Running up to my room, I flung open the door of it. Polina was still on the sofa, with a lighted candle in front of her, and her hands clasped. As I entered she stared at me in astonishment (for, at the moment, I must have presented a strange spectacle). All I did, however, was to halt before her, and fling upon the table my burden of wealth.

CHAPTER FIFTEEN

I REMEMBER, too, how, without moving from her place, or changing her attitude, she gazed into my face.

"I have won two hundred thousand francs!" cried I as I pulled out my last sheaf of bank-notes. The pile of paper currency occupied the whole table. I could not withdraw my eyes from it. Consequently, for a moment or two Polina escaped my mind. Then I set myself to arrange the pile in order, and to sort the notes, and to mass the gold in a separate heap. That done, I left everything where it lay, and proceeded to pace the room with rapid strides as I lost myself in thought. Then I darted to the table once more, and began to recount the money; until all of a sudden, as though I had remembered something, I rushed to the door, and closed and double-locked it. Finally I came to a meditative halt before my little trunk.

"Shall I put the money there until tomorrow?" I asked, turning sharply round to Polina as the recollection of her returned to me.

She was still in her old place – still making not a sound. Yet her eyes had followed every one of my movements. Somehow in her face there was a strange expression – an expression which I did not like. I think that I shall not be wrong if I say that it indicated sheer hatred.

Impulsively I approached her.

"Polina," I said, "here are twenty-five thousand florins – fifty thousand francs, or more. Take them, and tomorrow throw them in De Griers' face."

She returned no answer.

"Or, if you should prefer," I continued, "let me take them to him myself tomorrow – yes, early tomorrow morning. Shall I?"

Then all at once she burst out laughing, and laughed for a long while. With astonishment and a feeling of offence I gazed at her. Her laughter was too like the derisive merriment which she had so often indulged in of late – merriment which had broken forth always at the time of my most passionate explanations. At length she ceased, and frowned at me from under her eyebrows.

"I am *not* going to take your money," she said contemptuously.

"Why not?" I cried. "Why not, Polina?"

"Because I am not in the habit of receiving money for nothing."

"But I am offering it to you as a *friend*. In the same way I would offer you my very life."

Upon this she threw me a long, questioning glance, as though she were seeking to probe me to the depths.

"You are giving too much for me," she remarked with a smile. "The beloved of De Griers is not worth fifty thousand francs."

"Oh Polina, how can you speak so?" I exclaimed reproachfully. "Am *I* De Griers?"

"You?" she cried with her eyes suddenly flashing. "Why, I *hate* you! Yes, yes, I *hate* you! I love you no more than I do De Griers."

Then she buried her face in her hands, and relapsed into hysterics. I darted to her side. Somehow I had an intuition of something having happened to her which had nothing to do with myself. She was like a person temporarily insane.

"Buy me, would you, would you? Would you buy me for fifty thousand francs as De Griers did?" she gasped between her convulsive sobs.

I clasped her in my arms, kissed her hands and feet, and fell upon my knees before her.

Presently the hysterical fit passed away, and, laying her hands upon my shoulders, she gazed for a while into my face, as though trying to read it – something I said to her, but it was clear that she did not hear it. Her face looked so dark and despondent that I began to fear for her reason. At length she drew me towards herself – a trustful smile playing over her features; and then, as suddenly, she pushed me away again as she eyed me dimly.

Finally she threw herself upon me in an embrace.

"You love me?" she said. "*Do* you? – you who were willing even to quarrel with the Baron at my bidding?"

Then she laughed – laughed as though something dear, but laughable, had recurred to her memory. Yes, she laughed and wept at the same time. What was I to do? I was like a man in a fever. I remember that she began to say something to me – though *what* I do not know, since she spoke with a feverish lisp, as though she were trying to tell me something very quickly. At intervals, too, she would break off into the smile which I was beginning to dread. "No, no!" she kept repeating. "*You* are my dear one; *you* are the man I trust." Again she laid her hands upon my shoulders, and again she gazed at me as she reiterated: "You love me, you love me? Will you *always* love me?" I could not take my eyes off her. Never before had I seen her in this mood of humility and affection. True, the mood was the outcome of hysteria; but – ! All of a sudden she noticed my ardent gaze, and smiled slightly. The next moment, for no apparent reason, she began to talk of Astley.

She continued talking and talking about him, but I could not make out all she said – more particularly when she was endeavouring to tell me of something or other which had happened recently. On the whole, she appeared to be laughing at Astley, for she kept repeating that he was waiting for her, and did I know whether, even at that moment, he was not standing beneath the window? "Yes, yes, he is there," she said. "Open the window, and see if he is not." She pushed me in that direction; yet, no sooner did I make a movement to obey her behest than she burst into laughter, and I remained beside her, and she embraced me.

"Shall we go away tomorrow?" presently she asked, as though some disturbing thought had recurred to her recollection. "How would it be if we were to try and overtake Grandmamma? I think we should do so at Berlin. And what think you she would have to say to us when we caught her up, and her eyes first lit upon us? What, too, about Mr. Astley? *He* would not leap from the Shlangenberg for my sake! No! Of that I am very sure!" – and she laughed. "Do you know where he is going next year? He says he intends to go to the North Pole for scientific investigations, and has invited me to go with him! Ha, ha, ha! He also says that we Russians know nothing, can do nothing, without European help. But he is a good fellow all the same. For instance, he does not blame the General in the matter, but declares that Mlle. Blanche – that love – But no; I do not know, I do not know." She stopped suddenly, as though she had said her say, and was feeling bewildered. "What poor creatures these people are. How sorry I am for them, and for Grandmamma! But when are you going to kill De Griers? Surely you do not intend actually to murder him? You fool! Do you suppose that I should *allow* you to fight De Griers? Nor shall you kill the Baron." Here she burst out laughing. "How absurd you looked when you were talking to the Burmergelms! I was watching you all the time – watching you from where I was sitting. And how unwilling you were to go when I sent you! Oh, how I laughed and laughed!"

Then she kissed and embraced me again; again she pressed her face to mine with tender passion. Yet I neither saw nor heard her, for my head was in a whirl....

It must have been about seven o'clock in the morning when I awoke. Daylight had come, and Polina was sitting by my side – a strange expression on her face, as though she had seen a vision and was unable to collect her thoughts. She too had just awoken, and was now staring at the money on the table. My head ached; it felt heavy. I attempted to take Polina's hand, but she pushed me from her, and leapt from the sofa. The dawn was full of mist, for rain had fallen, yet she moved to the window, opened it, and, leaning her elbows upon the window-sill, thrust out her head and shoulders to take the air. In this position did she remain for several minutes, without ever looking round at me, or listening to what I was saying. Into my head there came the uneasy thought: What is to happen now? How is it all to end? Suddenly Polina rose from the window, approached the table, and, looking at me with an expression of infinite aversion, said with lips which quivered with anger:

"Well? Are you going to hand me over my fifty thousand francs?"

"Polina, you say that *again, again?*" I exclaimed.

"You have changed your mind, then? Ha, ha, ha! You are sorry you ever promised them?"

On the table where, the previous night, I had counted the money there still was lying the packet of twenty five thousand florins. I handed it to her.

"The francs are mine, then, are they? They are mine?" she inquired viciously as she balanced the money in her hands.

"Yes; they have *always* been yours," I said.

"Then *take* your fifty thousand francs!" and she hurled them full in my face. The packet burst as she did so, and the floor became strewed with bank-notes. The instant that the deed was done she rushed from the room.

At that moment she cannot have been in her right mind; yet, what was the cause of her temporary aberration I cannot say. For a month past she had been unwell. Yet what had brought about this *present* condition of mind, above all things, this outburst? Had it come of wounded pride? Had it come of despair over her decision to come to me? Had it come of the fact that, presuming too much on my good fortune, I had seemed to be intending to desert her (even as De Griers had done) when once I had given her the fifty thousand francs? But, on my honour, I had never cherished any such intention. What was at fault, I think, was her own pride, which kept urging her not to trust me, but, rather, to insult me – even though she had not realised the fact. In her eyes I corresponded to De Griers, and therefore had been condemned for a fault not wholly my own. Her mood of late had been a sort of delirium, a sort of light-headedness – that I knew full well; yet, never had I sufficiently taken it into consideration. Perhaps she would not pardon me now? Ah, but this was *the present*. What about the future? Her delirium and sickness were not likely to make her forget what she had done in bringing me De Griers' letter. No, she must have known what she was doing when she brought it.

Somehow I contrived to stuff the pile of notes and gold under the bed, to cover them over, and then to leave the room some ten minutes after Polina. I felt sure that she had returned to her own room; wherefore, I intended quietly to follow her, and to ask the nursemaid aid who opened the door how her mistress was. Judge, therefore, of my surprise when, meeting the domestic on the stairs, she informed me that Polina had not yet returned, and that she (the domestic) was at that moment on her way to my room in quest of her!

"Mlle. left me but ten minutes ago," I said. "What can have become of her?" The nursemaid looked at me reproachfully.

Already sundry rumours were flying about the hotel. Both in the office of the commissionaire and in that of the landlord it was whispered that, at seven o'clock that morning, the Fräulein had left the hotel, and set off, despite the rain, in the direction of the Hôtel d'Angleterre. From words and hints let fall I could see that the fact of Polina having spent the night in my room was now public property. Also, sundry rumours were circulating concerning the General's family affairs. It was known that last night he had gone out of his mind, and paraded the hotel in tears; also, that the old lady who had arrived was his mother, and that she had come from Russia on purpose to forbid her son's marriage with Mlle. de Cominges, as well as to cut him out of her will if he should disobey her; also that, because he had disobeyed her, she had squandered all her money at roulette, in order to have nothing more to leave to him. "Oh, these Russians!" exclaimed the landlord, with an angry toss of the head, while the bystanders laughed and the clerk betook himself to his accounts. Also, every one had learnt about my winnings; Karl, the corridor lacquey, was the first to congratulate me. But with these folk I had nothing to do. My business was to set off at full speed to the Hôtel d'Angleterre.

As yet it was early for Mr. Astley to receive visitors; but, as soon as he learnt that it was *I* who had arrived, he came out into the corridor to meet me, and stood looking at me in silence with his steel-grey eyes as he waited to hear what I had to say. I inquired after Polina.

"She is ill," he replied, still looking at me with his direct, unwavering glance.

"And she is in your rooms."

"Yes, she is in my rooms."

"Then you are minded to keep her there?"

"Yes, I am minded to keep her there."

"But, Mr. Astley, that will raise a scandal. It ought not to be allowed. Besides, she is very ill. Perhaps you had not remarked that?"

"Yes, I have. It was I who told you about it. Had she not been ill, she would not have gone and spent the night with you."

"Then you know all about it?"

"Yes; for last night she was to have accompanied me to the house of a relative of mine. Unfortunately, being ill, she made a mistake, and went to your rooms instead."

"Indeed? Then I wish you joy, Mr. Astley. Apropos, you have reminded me of something. Were you beneath my window last night? Every moment Mlle. Polina kept telling me to open the window and see if you were there; after which she always smiled."

"Indeed? No, I was not there; but I was waiting in the corridor, and walking about the hotel."

"She ought to see a doctor, you know, Mr. Astley."

"Yes, she ought. I have sent for one, and, if she dies, I shall hold you responsible."

This surprised me.

"Pardon me," I replied, "but what do you mean?"

"Never mind. Tell me if it is true that, last night, you won two hundred thousand thalers?"

"No; I won a hundred thousand florins."

"Good heavens! Then I suppose you will be off to Paris this morning?"

"Why?"

"Because all Russians who have grown rich go to Paris," explained Astley, as though he had read the fact in a book.

"But what could I do in Paris in summer time? – I *love* her, Mr. Astley! Surely you know that?"

"Indeed? I am sure that you do *not*. Moreover, if you were to stay here, you would lose everything that you possess, and have nothing left with which to pay your expenses in Paris. Well, good-bye now. I feel sure that today will see you gone from here."

"Good-bye. But I am *not* going to Paris. Likewise – pardon me – what is to become of this family? I mean that the affair of the General and Mlle. Polina will soon be all over the town."

"I daresay; yet, I hardly suppose that that will break the General's heart. Moreover, Mlle. Polina has a perfect right to live where she chooses. In short, we may say that, as a family, this family has ceased to exist."

I departed, and found myself smiling at the Englishman's strange assurance that I should soon be leaving for Paris. "I suppose he means to shoot me in a duel, should Polina die. Yes, that is what he intends to do." Now, although I was honestly sorry for Polina, it is a fact that, from the moment when, the previous night, I had approached the gaming-table, and begun to rake in the packets of bank-notes, my love for her had entered upon a new plane. Yes, I can say that now; although, at the time, I was barely conscious of it. Was I, then, at heart a gambler? Did I, after all, love Polina not so *very* much? No, no! As God is my witness, I loved her! Even when I was returning home from Mr. Astley's my suffering was genuine, and my self-reproach sincere. But presently I was to go through an exceedingly strange and ugly experience.

I was proceeding to the General's rooms when I heard a door near me open, and a voice call me by name. It was Mlle.'s mother, the Widow de Cominges who was inviting me, in her daughter's name, to enter.

I did so; whereupon, I heard a laugh and a little cry proceed from the bedroom (the pair occupied a suite of two apartments), where Mlle. Blanche was just arising.

"Ah, c'est lui! Viens, donc, bête! Is it true that you have won a mountain of gold and silver? J'aimerais mieux l'or."

"Yes," I replied with a smile.

"How much?"

"A hundred thousand florins."

"Bibi, comme tu es bête! Come in here, for I can't hear you where you are now. Nous ferons bombance, n'est-ce pas?"

Entering her room, I found her lolling under a pink satin coverlet, and revealing a pair of swarthy, wonderfully healthy shoulders – shoulders such as one sees in dreams – shoulders covered over with a white cambric nightgown which, trimmed with lace, stood out, in striking relief, against the darkness of her skin.

"Mon fils, as-tu du cœur?" she cried when she saw me, and then giggled. Her laugh had always been a very cheerful one, and at times it even sounded sincere.

"Tout autre – " I began, paraphrasing Corneille.

"See here," she prattled on. "Please search for my stockings, and help me to dress. Aussi, si tu n'es pas trop bête je te prends à Paris. I am just off, let me tell you."

"This moment?"

"In half an hour."

True enough, everything stood ready-packed – trunks, portmanteaux, and all. Coffee had long been served.

"Eh bien, tu verras Paris. Dis donc, qu'est-ce que c'est qu'un 'utchitel'? Tu étais bien bête quand tu étais 'utchitel.' Where are my stockings? Please help me to dress."

And she lifted up a really ravishing foot – small, swarthy, and not misshapen like the majority of feet which look dainty only in bottines. I laughed, and started to draw on to the foot a silk stocking, while Mlle. Blanche sat on the edge of the bed and chattered.

"Eh bien, que feras-tu si je te prends avec moi? First of all I must have fifty thousand francs, and you shall give them to me at Frankfurt. Then we will go on to Paris, where we will live together, et je te ferai voir des étoiles en plein jour. Yes, you shall see such women as your eyes have never lit upon."

"Stop a moment. If I were to give you those fifty thousand francs, what should I have left for myself?"

"Another hundred thousand francs, please to remember. Besides, I could live with you in your rooms for a month, or even for two; or even for longer. But it would not take us more than two months to get through fifty thousand francs; for, look you, je suis bonne enfante, et tu verras des étoiles, you may be sure."

"What? You mean to say that we should spend the whole in two months?"

"Certainly. Does that surprise you very much? Ah, vil esclave! Why, one month of that life would be better than all your previous existence. One month – et après, le déluge! Mais tu ne peux comprendre. Va! Away, away! You are not worth it. – Ah, que fais-tu?"

For, while drawing on the other stocking, I had felt constrained to kiss her. Immediately she shrunk back, kicked me in the face with her toes, and turned me neck and crop out of the room.

"Eh bien, mon 'utchitel,'" she called after me, "je t'attends, si tu veux. I start in a quarter of an hour's time."

I returned to my own room with my head in a whirl. It was not my fault that Polina had thrown a packet in my face, and preferred Mr. Astley to myself. A few bank-notes were still fluttering about the floor, and I picked them up. At that moment the door opened, and the landlord appeared – a person who, until now, had never bestowed upon me so much as a glance. He had come to know if I would prefer to move to a lower floor – to a suite which had just been tenanted by Count V.

For a moment I reflected.

"No!" I shouted. "My account, please, for in ten minutes I shall be gone."

"To Paris, to Paris!" I added to myself. "Every man of birth must make her acquaintance."

Within a quarter of an hour all three of us were seated in a family compartment – Mlle. Blanche, the Widow de Cominges, and myself. Mlle. kept laughing hysterically as she looked at me, and Madame re-echoed her; but *I* did not feel so cheerful. My life had broken in two, and yesterday had infected me with a habit of staking my all upon a card. Although it might be that I had failed to win my stake, that I had lost my senses, that I desired nothing better, I felt that the scene was to be changed only *for a time*. "Within a month from now," I kept thinking to myself, "I shall be back again in Roulettenberg; and *then* I mean to have it out with you, Mr. Astley!" Yes, as now I look back at things, I remember that I felt greatly depressed, despite the absurd gigglings of the egregious Blanche.

"What is the matter with you? How dull you are!" she cried at length as she interrupted her laughter to take me seriously to task.

"Come, come! We are going to spend your two hundred thousand francs for you, et tu seras heureux comme un petit roi. I myself will tie your tie for you, and introduce you to Hortense. And when we have spent your money you shall return here, and break the bank again. What did those two Jews tell you? – that the thing most needed is daring, and that you possess it? Consequently, this is not the first time that you will be hurrying to Paris with money in your pocket. Quant à moi, je veux cinquante mille francs de rente, et alors – – "

"But what about the General?" I interrupted.

"The General? You know well enough that at about this hour every day he goes to buy me a bouquet. On this occasion, I took care to tell him that he must hunt for the choicest of flowers; and when he returns home, the poor fellow will find the bird flown. Possibly he may take wing in pursuit – ha, ha, ha! And if so, I shall not be sorry, for he could be useful to me in Paris, and Mr. Astley will pay his debts here."

In this manner did I depart for the Gay City.

CHAPTER SIXTEEN

Of Paris what am I to say? The whole proceeding was a delirium, a madness. I spent a little over three weeks there, and, during that time, saw my hundred thousand francs come to an end. I speak only of the *one* hundred thousand francs, for the other hundred thousand I gave to Mlle. Blanche in pure cash. That is to say, I handed her fifty thousand francs at Frankfurt, and, three days later (in Paris), advanced her another fifty thousand on note of hand. Nevertheless, a week had not elapsed ere she came to me for more money. "Et les cent mille francs qui nous restent," she added, "tu les mangeras avec moi, mon utchitel." Yes, she always called me her "utchitel." A person more economical, grasping, and mean than Mlle. Blanche one could not imagine. But this was only as regards *her own* money. *My* hundred thousand francs (as she explained to me later) she needed to set up her establishment in Paris, "so that once and for all I may be on a decent footing, and proof against any stones which may be thrown at me – at all events for a long time to come." Nevertheless, I saw nothing of those hundred thousand francs, for my own purse (which she inspected daily) never managed to amass in it more than a hundred francs at a time; and, generally the sum did not reach even that figure.

"What do *you* want with money?" she would say to me with air of absolute simplicity; and I never disputed the point. Nevertheless, though she fitted out her flat very badly with the money, the fact did not prevent her from saying when, later, she was showing me over the rooms of her new abode: "See what care and taste can do with the most wretched of means!" However, her "wretchedness" had cost fifty thousand francs, while with the remaining fifty thousand she purchased a carriage and horses.

Also, we gave a couple of balls – evening parties attended by Hortense and Lisette and Cléopatre, who were women remarkable both for the number of their liaisons and (though only in some cases) for their good looks. At these reunions I had to play the part of host – to meet and entertain fat mercantile parvenus who were impossible by reason of their rudeness and braggadocio, colonels of various kinds, hungry authors, and journalistic hacks – all of whom disported themselves in fashionable tailcoats and pale yellow gloves, and displayed such an aggregate of conceit and gasconade as would be unthinkable even in St. Petersburg – which is saying a great deal! They used to try to make fun of me, but I would console myself by drinking champagne and then lolling in a retiring-room. Nevertheless, I found it deadly work. "C'est un utchitel," Blanche would say of me, "qui a gagné deux cent mille francs, and but for me, would have had not a notion how to spend them. Presently he will have to return to his tutoring. Does any one know of a vacant post? You know, one must do something for him."

I had the more frequent recourse to champagne in that I constantly felt depressed and bored, owing to the fact that I was living in the most bourgeois commercial milieu imaginable – a milieu wherein every sou was counted and grudged. Indeed, two weeks had not elapsed before I perceived that Blanche had no real affection for me, even though she dressed me in elegant clothes, and herself tied my tie each day. In short, she utterly despised me. But that caused me no concern. Blasé and inert, I spent my evenings generally at the Château des Fleurs, where I would get fuddled and then dance the cancan (which, in that establishment, was a very indecent performance) with éclat. At length, the time came when Blanche had drained my purse dry. She had conceived an idea that, during the term of our residence together, it would be well if I were always to walk behind her with a paper and pencil, in order to jot down exactly what she spent, what she had saved, what she was paying out, and what she was laying by. Well, of course I could not fail to be aware that this would entail a battle over every ten francs; so, although for every possible objection that I might make she had prepared a suitable answer, she soon saw that I made no objections, and therefore, had to start disputes herself. That is to say, she would burst out into tirades which were met only with silence as I lolled on a sofa and stared fixedly at the ceiling. This greatly surprised her. At first she imagined that it was due merely to the fact that I was a fool, "un utchitel"; wherefore she would break off her harangue in the belief that, being too stupid to understand, I was a hopeless case. Then she would leave the room, but return ten minutes later to resume the contest. This continued throughout her squandering of my money – a squandering altogether out of proportion to our means. An example is the way in which she changed her first pair of horses for a pair which cost sixteen thousand francs.

"Bibi," she said on the latter occasion as she approached me, "surely you are not angry?"

"No-o-o: I am merely tired," was my reply as I pushed her from me. This seemed to her so curious that straightway she seated herself by my side.

"You see," she went on, "I decided to spend so much upon these horses only because I can easily sell them again. They would go at any time for *twenty* thousand francs."

"Yes, yes. They are splendid horses, and you have got a splendid turn-out. I am quite content. Let me hear no more of the matter."

"Then you are not angry?"

"No. Why should I be? You are wise to provide yourself with what you need, for it will all come in handy in the future. Yes, I quite see the necessity of your establishing yourself on a good basis, for without it you will never earn your million. My hundred thousand francs I look upon merely as a beginning – as a mere drop in the bucket."

Blanche, who had by no means expected such declarations from me, but, rather, an uproar and protests, was rather taken aback.

"Well, well, what a man you are!" she exclaimed. "Mais tu as l'esprit pour comprendre. Sais-tu, mon garçon, although you are a tutor, you ought to have been born a prince. Are you not sorry that your money should be going so quickly?"

"No. The quicker it goes the better."

"Mais – sais-tu – mais dis donc, are you *really* rich? Mais sais-tu, you have too much contempt for money. Qu'est-ce que tu feras après, dis donc?"

"Après I shall go to Homburg, and win another hundred thousand francs."

"Oui, oui, c'est ça, c'est magnifique! Ah, I know you will win them, and bring them to me when you have done so. Dis donc – you will end by making me love you. Since you are what you are, I mean to love you all the time, and never to be unfaithful to you. You see, I have not loved you before parce que je croyais que tu n'es qu'un utchitel (quelque chose comme un lacquais, n'est-ce pas?) Yet all the time I have been true to you, parce que je suis bonne fille."

"You lie!" I interrupted. "Did I not see you, the other day, with Albert – with that black-jowled officer?"

"Oh, oh! Mais tu es – "

"Yes, you are lying right enough. But what makes you suppose that I should be angry? Rubbish! Il faut que jeunesse se passe. Even if that officer were here now, I should refrain from putting him out of the room if I thought you really cared for him. Only, mind you, do not give him any of my money. You hear?"

"You say, do you, that you would not be angry? Mais tu es un vrai philosophe, sais-tu? Oui, un vrai philosophe! Eh bien, je t'aimerai, je t'aimerai. Tu verras-tu seras content."

True enough, from that time onward she seemed to attach herself only to me, and in this manner we spent our last ten days together. The promised "étoiles" I did not see, but in other respects she, to a certain extent, kept her word. Moreover, she introduced me to Hortense, who was a remarkable woman in her way, and known among us as Thérèse Philosophe.

But I need not enlarge further, for to do so would require a story to itself, and entail a colouring which I am loth to impart to the present narrative. The point is that with all my faculties I desired the episode to come to an end as speedily as possible. Unfortunately, our hundred thousand francs lasted us, as I have said, for very nearly a month – which greatly surprised me. At all events, Blanche bought herself articles to the tune of eighty thousand francs, and the rest sufficed just to meet our expenses of living. Towards the close of the affair, Blanche grew almost frank with me (at least, she scarcely lied to me at all) – declaring, amongst other things, that none of the debts which she had been obliged to incur were going to fall upon my head. "I have purposely refrained from making you responsible for my bills or borrowings," she said, "for the reason that I am sorry for you. Any other woman in my place would have done so, and have let you go to prison. See, then, how much I love you, and how good-hearted I am! Think, too, what this accursed marriage with the General is going to cost me!"

True enough, the marriage took place. It did so at the close of our month together, and I am bound to suppose that it was upon the ceremony that the last remnants of my money were spent. With it the episode – that is to say, my sojourn with the Frenchwoman – came to an end, and I formally retired from the scene.

It happened thus: A week after we had taken up our abode in Paris there arrived thither the General. He came straight to see us, and thenceforward lived with us practically as our guest, though he had a flat of his own as well. Blanche met him with merry badinage and laughter, and even threw her arms around him. In fact, she managed it so that he had to follow everywhere in her train – whether when promenading on the Boulevards, or when driving, or when going to the theatre, or when paying calls; and this use which she made of him quite satisfied the General. Still of imposing appearance and presence, as well as of fair height, he had a dyed moustache and whiskers (he had formerly been in the cuirassiers), and a handsome, though a somewhat wrinkled, face. Also, his manners were excellent, and he could carry a frockcoat well – the more so since, in Paris, he took to wearing his orders. To promenade the Boulevards with such a man was not only a thing possible, but also, so to speak, a thing advisable, and with this programme the good but foolish General had not a fault to find. The truth is that he had never counted upon this programme when he came to Paris to seek us out. On that occasion he had made his appearance nearly shaking with terror, for he had supposed that Blanche would at once raise an outcry, and have him put from the door; wherefore, he was the more enraptured at the turn that things had taken, and spent the month in a state of senseless ecstasy. Already I had learnt that, after our unexpected departure from Roulettenberg, he had had a sort of a fit – that he had fallen into a swoon, and spent a week in a species of garrulous delirium. Doctors had been summoned to him, but he had broken away from them, and suddenly taken a train to Paris. Of course Blanche's reception of him had acted as the best of all possible cures, but for long enough he carried the marks of his affliction, despite his present condition of rapture and delight. To think clearly, or even to engage in any serious conversation, had now become impossible for him; he could only ejaculate after each word "Hm!" and then nod his head in confirmation. Sometimes, also, he would laugh, but only in a nervous, hysterical sort of a fashion; while at other times he would sit for hours looking as black as night, with his heavy eyebrows knitted. Of much that went on he remained wholly oblivious, for he grew extremely absent-minded, and took to talking to himself. Only Blanche could awake him to any semblance of life. His fits of depression and moodiness in corners always meant either that he had not seen her for some while, or that she had gone out without taking him with her, or that she had omitted to caress him before departing. When in this condition, he would refuse to say what he wanted – nor had he the least idea that he was thus sulking and moping. Next, after remaining in this condition for an hour or two (this I remarked on two occasions when Blanche had gone out for the day – probably to see Albert), he would begin to look about him, and to grow uneasy, and to hurry about with an air as though he had suddenly remembered something, and must try and find it; after which, not perceiving the object of his search, nor succeeding in recalling what that object had been, he would as suddenly relapse into oblivion, and continue so until the reappearance of Blanche – merry, wanton, half-dressed, and laughing her strident laugh as she approached to pet him, and even to kiss him (though the latter reward he seldom received). Once, he was so overjoyed at her doing so that he burst into tears. Even I myself was surprised.

From the first moment of his arrival in Paris, Blanche set herself to plead with me on his behalf; and at such times she even rose to heights of eloquence – saying that it was for *me* she had abandoned him, though she had almost become his betrothed and promised to become so; that it was for *her* sake he had deserted his family; that, having been in his service, I ought to remember the fact, and to feel ashamed. To all this I would say nothing, however much she chattered on; until at length I would burst out laughing, and the incident would come to an end (at first, as I have said, she had thought me a fool, but since she had come to deem me a man of sense and sensibility). In short, I had the happiness of calling her better nature into play; for though, at first, I had not deemed her so, she was, in reality, a kind-hearted woman after her own fashion. "You are good and clever," she said to me towards the finish, "and my one regret is that you are also so wrong-headed. You will *her* be a rich man!"

"Un vrai Russe – un Kalmuk" she usually called me.

Several times she sent me to give the General an airing in the streets, even as she might have done with a lacquey and her spaniel; but, I preferred to take him to the theatre, to the Bal Mabille, and to restaurants. For this purpose she usually allowed me some money, though the General had a little of his own, and enjoyed taking out his purse before strangers. Once I had to use actual force to prevent him from buying a phaeton at a price of seven hundred francs, after a vehicle had caught his fancy in the Palais Royal as seeming to be a desirable present for Blanche. What could *she* have done with a seven-hundred-franc phaeton? – and the General possessed in the world but a thousand francs! The origin even of those francs I could never determine, but imagined them to have emanated from Mr. Astley – the more so since the latter had paid the family's hotel bill. As for what view the General took of myself, I think that he never divined the footing on which I stood with Blanche. True, he had heard, in a dim sort of way, that I had won a good deal of money; but more probably he supposed me to be acting as secretary – or even as a kind of servant – to his inamorata. At all events, he continued to address me, in his old haughty style, as my superior. At times he even took it upon himself to scold me. One morning in particular, he started to sneer at me over our matutinal coffee. Though not a man prone to take offence, he suddenly, and for some reason of which to this day I am ignorant, fell out with me. Of course even he himself did not know the reason. To put things shortly, he began a speech which had neither beginning nor ending, and cried out, à bâtons rompus, that I was a boy whom he would soon put to rights – and so forth, and so forth. Yet no one could understand what he was saying, and at length Blanche exploded in a burst of laughter. Finally something appeased him, and he was taken out for his walk. More than once, however, I noticed that his depression was growing upon him; that he seemed to be feeling the want of somebody or something; that, despite Blanche's presence, he was missing some person in particular. Twice, on these occasions, did he plunge into a conversation with me, though he could not make himself intelligible, and only went on rambling about the service, his late wife, his home, and his property. Every now and then, also, some particular word would please him; whereupon he would repeat it a hundred times in the day – even though the word happened to express neither his thoughts nor his feelings. Again, I would try to get him to talk about his children, but always he cut me short in his old snappish way, and passed to another subject. "Yes, yes – my children," was all that I could extract from him. "Yes, you are right in what you have said about them." Only once did he disclose his real feelings. That was when we were taking him to the theatre, and suddenly he exclaimed: "My unfortunate children! Yes, sir, they *are* unfortunate children." Once, too, when I chanced to mention Polina, he grew quite bitter against her. "She is an ungrateful woman!" he exclaimed. "She is a bad and ungrateful woman! She has broken up a family. If there were laws here, I would have her impaled. Yes, I would." As for De Griers, the General would not have his name mentioned. "He has ruined me," he would say. "He has robbed me, and cut my throat. For two years he was a perfect nightmare to me. For months at a time he never left me in my dreams. Do not speak of him again."

It was now clear to me that Blanche and he were on the point of coming to terms; yet, true to my usual custom, I said nothing. At length, Blanche took the initiative in explaining matters. She did so a week before we parted.

"Il a de la chance," she prattled, "for the Grandmother is now *really* ill, and therefore, bound to die. Mr. Astley has just sent a telegram to say so, and you will agree with me that the General is likely to be her heir. Even if he should not be so, he will not come amiss, since, in the first place, he has his pension, and, in the second place, he will be content to live in a back room; whereas *I* shall be Madame General, and get into a good circle of society" (she was always thinking of this) "and become a Russian châtelaine. Yes, I shall have a mansion of my own, and peasants, and a million of money at my back."

"But, suppose he should prove jealous? He might demand all sorts of things, you know. Do you follow me?"

"Oh, dear no! How ridiculous that would be of him! Besides, I have taken measures to prevent it. You need not be alarmed. That is to say, I have induced him to sign notes of hand in Albert's name. Consequently, at any time I could get him punished. Isn't he ridiculous?"

"Very well, then. Marry him."

And, in truth, she did so – though the marriage was a family one only, and involved no pomp or ceremony. In fact, she invited to the nuptials none but Albert and a few other friends. Hortense, Cléopatre, and the rest she kept firmly at a distance. As for the bridegroom, he took a great interest in his new position. Blanche herself tied his tie, and Blanche herself pomaded him – with the result that, in his frockcoat and white waistcoat, he looked quite comme il faut.

"Il est, pourtant, *très* comme il faut," Blanche remarked when she issued from his room, as though the idea that he was "*très* comme il faut" had impressed even her. For myself, I had so little knowledge of the minor details of the affair, and took part in it so much as a supine spectator, that I have forgotten most of what passed on this occasion. I only remember that Blanche and the Widow figured at it, not as "de Cominges," but as "du Placet." Why they had hitherto been "de Cominges" I do not know – I only know that this entirely satisfied the General, that he liked the name "du Placet" even better than he had liked the name "de Cominges." On the morning of the wedding, he paced the salon in his gala attire and kept repeating to himself with an air of great gravity and importance: "Mlle. Blanche du Placet! Mlle. Blanche du Placet, du Placet!" He beamed with satisfaction as he did so. Both in the church and at the wedding breakfast he remained not only pleased and contented, but even proud. She too underwent a change, for now she assumed an air of added dignity.

"I must behave altogether differently," she confided to me with a serious air. "Yet, mark you, there is a tiresome circumstance of which I had never before thought – which is, how best to pronounce my new family name. Zagorianski, Zagozianski, Madame la Générale de Sago, Madame la Générale de Fourteen Consonants – oh these infernal Russian names! The *last* of them would be the best to use, don't you think?"

At length the time had come for us to part, and Blanche, the egregious Blanche, shed real tears as she took her leave of me. "Tu étais bon enfant" she said with a sob. "Je te croyais bête et tu en avais l'air, but it suited you." Then, having given me a final handshake, she exclaimed, "Attends!"; whereafter, running into her boudoir, she brought me thence two thousand-franc notes. I could scarcely believe my eyes! "They may come in handy for you," she explained, "for, though you are a very learned tutor, you are a very stupid man. More than two thousand francs, however, I am not going to give you, for the reason that, if I did so, you would gamble them all away. Now good-bye. Nous serons toujours bons amis, and if you win again, do not fail to come to me, et tu seras heureux."

I myself had still five hundred francs left, as well as a watch worth a thousand francs, a few diamond studs, and so on. Consequently, I could subsist for quite a length of time without particularly bestirring myself. Purposely I have taken up my abode where I am now partly to pull myself together, and partly to wait for Mr. Astley, who, I have learnt, will soon be here for a day or so on business. Yes, I know that, and then – and then I shall go to Homburg. But to Roulettenberg I shall not go until next year, for they say it is bad to try one's luck twice in succession at a table. Moreover, Homburg is where the best play is carried on.

CHAPTER SEVENTEEN

It is a year and eight months since I last looked at these notes of mine. I do so now only because, being overwhelmed with depression, I wish to distract my mind by reading them through at random. I left them off at the point where I was just going to Homburg. My God, with what a light heart (comparatively speaking) did I write the concluding lines! – though it may be not so much with a light heart, as with a measure of self-confidence and unquenchable hope. At that time had I any doubts of myself? Yet behold me now. Scarcely a year and a half have passed, yet I am in a worse position than the meanest beggar. But what is a beggar? A fig for beggary! I have ruined myself – that is all. Nor is there anything with which I can compare myself; there is no moral which it would be of any use for you to read to me. At the present moment nothing could well be more incongruous than a moral. Oh, you self-satisfied persons who, in your unctuous pride, are forever ready to mouth your maxims – if only you knew how fully I myself comprehend the sordidness of my present state, you would not trouble to wag your tongues at me! What could you say to me that I do not already know? Well, wherein lies my difficulty? It lies in the fact that by a single turn of a roulette wheel everything for me, has become changed. Yet, had things befallen otherwise, these moralists would have been among the first (yes, I feel persuaded of it) to approach me with friendly jests and congratulations. Yes, they would never have turned from me as they are doing now! A fig for all of them! What am I? I am zero – nothing. What shall I be tomorrow? I may be risen from the dead, and have begun life anew. For still, I may discover the man in myself, if only my manhood has not become utterly shattered.

I went, I say, to Homburg, but afterwards went also to Roulettenberg, as well as to Spa and Baden; in which latter place, for a time, I acted as valet to a certain rascal of a Privy Councillor, by name Heintze, who until lately was also my master here. Yes, for five months I lived my life with lacqueys! That was just after I had come out of Roulettenberg prison, where I had lain for a small debt which I owed. Out of that prison I was bailed by – by whom? By Mr. Astley? By Polina? I do not know. At all events, the debt was paid to the tune of two hundred thalers, and I sallied forth a free man. But what was I to do with myself? In my dilemma I had recourse to this Heintze, who was a young scapegrace, and the sort of man who could speak and write three languages. At first I acted as his secretary, at a salary of thirty gülden a month, but afterwards I became his lacquey, for the reason that he could not afford to keep a secretary – only an unpaid servant. I had nothing else to turn to, so I remained with him, and allowed myself to become his flunkey. But by stinting myself in meat and drink I saved, during my five months of service, some seventy gülden; and one evening, when we were at Baden, I told him that I wished to resign my post, and then hastened to betake myself to roulette.

Oh, how my heart beat as I did so! No, it was not the money that I valued – what I wanted was to make all this mob of Heintzes, hotel proprietors, and fine ladies of Baden talk about me, recount my story, wonder at me, extol my doings, and worship my winnings. True, these were childish fancies and aspirations, but who knows but that I might meet Polina, and be able to tell her everything, and see her look of surprise at the fact that I had overcome so many adverse strokes of fortune. No, I had no desire for money for its own sake, for I was perfectly well aware that I should only squander it upon some new Blanche, and spend another three weeks in Paris after buying a pair of horses which had cost sixteen thousand francs. No, I never believed myself to be a hoarder; in fact, I knew only too well that I was a spendthrift. And already, with a sort of fear, a sort of sinking in my heart, I could hear the cries of the croupiers – "Trente et un, rouge, impair et passe," "Quarte, noir, pair et manque." How greedily I gazed upon the gaming-table, with its scattered louis d'or, ten-gülden pieces, and thalers; upon the streams of gold as they issued from the croupier's hands, and piled themselves up into heaps of gold scintillating as fire; upon the ell – long rolls of silver lying around the croupier. Even at a distance of two rooms I could hear the chink of that money – so much so that I nearly fell into convulsions.

Ah, the evening when I took those seventy gülden to the gaming table was a memorable one for me. I began by staking ten gülden upon passe. For passe I had always had a sort of predilection, yet I lost my stake upon it. This left me with sixty gülden in silver. After a moment's thought I selected zero – beginning by staking five gülden at a time. Twice I lost, but the third round suddenly brought up the desired coup. I could almost have died with joy as I received my one hundred and seventy-five gülden. Indeed, I have been less pleased when, in former times, I have won a hundred thousand gülden. Losing no time, I staked another hundred gülden upon the red, and won; two hundred upon the red, and won; four hundred upon the black, and won; eight hundred upon manque, and won. Thus, with the addition of the remainder of my original capital, I found myself possessed, within five minutes, of seventeen hundred gülden. Ah, at such moments one forgets both oneself and one's former failures! This I had gained by risking my very life. I had dared so to risk, and behold, again I was a member of mankind!

I went and hired a room, I shut myself up in it, and sat counting my money until three o'clock in the morning. To think that when I awoke on the morrow, I was no lacquey! I decided to leave at once for Homburg. There I should neither have to serve as a footman nor to lie in prison. Half an hour before starting, I went and ventured a couple of stakes – no more; with the result that, in all, I lost fifteen hundred florins. Nevertheless, I proceeded to Homburg, and have now been there for a month.

Of course, I am living in constant trepidation, playing for the smallest of stakes, and always looking out for something – calculating, standing whole days by the gaming-tables to watch the play – even seeing that play in my dreams – yet seeming, the while, to be in some way stiffening, to be growing caked, as it were, in mire. But I must conclude my notes, which I finish under the impression of a recent encounter with Mr. Astley. I had not seen him since we parted at Roulettenberg, and now we met quite by accident. At the time I was walking in the public gardens, and meditating upon the fact that not only had I still some fifty gülden in my possession, but also I had fully paid up my hotel bill three days ago. Consequently, I was in a position to try my luck again at roulette; and if I won anything I should be able to continue my play, whereas, if I lost what I now possessed, I should once more have to accept a lacquey's place, provided that, in the alternative, I failed to discover a Russian family which stood in need of a tutor. Plunged in these reflections, I started on my daily walk through the Park and forest towards a neighbouring principality. Sometimes, on such occasions, I spent four hours on the way, and would return to Homburg tired and hungry; but, on this particular occasion, I had scarcely left the gardens for the Park when I caught sight of Astley seated on a bench. As soon as he perceived me, he called me by name, and I went and sat down beside him; but, on noticing that he seemed a little stiff in his manner, I hastened to moderate the expression of joy which the sight of him had called forth.

"*You* here?" he said. "Well, I had an idea that I should meet you. Do not trouble to tell me anything, for I know all – yes, all. In fact, your whole life during the past twenty months lies within my knowledge."

"How closely you watch the doings of your old friends!" I replied. "That does you infinite credit. But stop a moment. You have reminded me of something. Was it you who bailed me out of Roulettenberg prison when I was lying there for a debt of two hundred gülden? *someone* did so."

"Oh dear no! – though I knew all the time that you were lying there."

"Perhaps you could tell me who *did* bail me out?"

"No; I am afraid I could not."

"What a strange thing! For I know no Russians at all here, so it cannot have been a Russian who befriended me. In Russia we Orthodox folk *do* go bail for one another, but in this case I thought it must have been done by some English stranger who was not conversant with the ways of the country."

Mr. Astley seemed to listen to me with a sort of surprise. Evidently he had expected to see me looking more crushed and broken than I was.

"Well," he said – not very pleasantly, "I am none the less glad to find that you retain your old independence of spirit, as well as your buoyancy."

"Which means that you are vexed at not having found me more abased and humiliated than I am?" I retorted with a smile.

Astley was not quick to understand this, but presently did so and laughed.

"Your remarks please me as they always did," he continued. "In those words I see the clever, triumphant, and, above all things, cynical friend of former days. Only Russians have the faculty of combining within themselves so many opposite qualities. Yes, most men love to see their best friend in abasement; for generally it is on such abasement that friendship is founded. All thinking persons know that ancient truth. Yet, on the present occasion, I assure you, I am sincerely glad to see that you are *not* cast down. Tell me, are you never going to give up gambling?"

"Damn the gambling! Yes, I should certainly have given it up, were it not that – "

"That you are losing? I thought so. You need not tell me any more. I know how things stand, for you have said that last in despair, and therefore, truthfully. Have you no other employment than gambling?"

"No; none whatever."

Astley gave me a searching glance. At that time it was ages since I had last looked at a paper or turned the pages of a book.

"You are growing blasé," he said. "You have not only renounced life, with its interests and social ties, but the duties of a citizen and a man; you have not only renounced the friends whom I know you to have had, and every aim in life but that of winning money; but you have also renounced your memory. Though I can remember you in the strong, ardent period of your life, I feel persuaded that you have now forgotten every better feeling of that period – that your present dreams and aspirations of subsistence do not rise above pair, impair rouge, noir, the twelve middle numbers, and so forth."

"Enough, Mr. Astley!" I cried with some irritation – almost in anger. "Kindly do not recall to me any more recollections, for I can remember things for myself. Only for a time have I put them out of my head. Only until I shall have rehabilitated myself, am I keeping my memory dulled. When that hour shall come, you will see me arise from the dead."

"Then you will have to be here another ten years," he replied. "Should I then be alive, I will remind you – here, on this very bench – of what I have just said. In fact, I will bet you a wager that I shall do so."

"Say no more," I interrupted impatiently. "And to show you that I have not wholly forgotten the past, may I enquire where Mlle. Polina is? If it was not you who bailed me out of prison, it must have been she. Yet never have I heard a word concerning her."

"No, I do not think it was she. At the present moment she is in Switzerland, and you will do me a favour by ceasing to ask me these questions about her." Astley said this with a firm, and even an angry, air.

"Which means that she has dealt you a serious wound?" I burst out with an involuntary sneer.

"Mlle. Polina," he continued, "Is the best of all possible living beings; but, I repeat, that I shall thank you to cease questioning me about her. You never really knew her, and her name on your lips is an offence to my moral feeling."

"Indeed? On what subject, then, have I a better right to speak to you than on this? With it are bound up all your recollections and mine. However, do not be alarmed: I have no wish to probe too far into your private, your secret affairs. My interest in Mlle. Polina does not extend beyond her outward circumstances and surroundings. About them you could tell me in two words."

"Well, on condition that the matter shall end there, I will tell you that for a long time Mlle. Polina was ill, and still is so. My mother and sister entertained her for a while at their home in the north of England, and thereafter Mlle. Polina's grandmother (you remember the mad old woman?) died, and left Mlle. Polina a personal legacy of seven thousand pounds sterling. That was about six months ago, and now Mlle. is travelling with my sister's family – my sister having since married. Mlle.'s little brother and sister also benefited by the Grandmother's will, and are now being educated in London. As for the General, he died in Paris last month, of a stroke. Mlle. Blanche did well by him, for she succeeded in having transferred to herself all that he received from the Grandmother. That, I think, concludes all that I have to tell."

"And De Griers? Is he too travelling in Switzerland?"

"No; nor do I know where he is. Also I warn you once more that you had better avoid such hints and ignoble suppositions; otherwise you will assuredly have to reckon with me."

"What? In spite of our old friendship?"

"Yes, in spite of our old friendship."

"Then I beg your pardon a thousand times, Mr. Astley. I meant nothing offensive to Mlle. Polina, for I have nothing of which to accuse her. Moreover, the question of there being anything between this Frenchman and this Russian lady is not one which you and I need discuss, nor even attempt to understand."

"If," replied Astley, "you do not care to hear their names coupled together, may I ask you what you mean by the expressions 'this Frenchman,' 'this Russian lady,' and 'there being anything between them'? Why do you call them so particularly a 'Frenchman' and a 'Russian lady'?"

"Ah, I see you are interested, Mr. Astley. But it is a long, long story, and calls for a lengthy preface. At the same time, the question is an important one, however ridiculous it may seem at the first glance. A Frenchman, Mr. Astley, is merely a fine figure of a man. With this you, as a Britisher, may not agree. With it I also, as a Russian, may not agree – out of envy. Yet possibly our good ladies are of another opinion. For instance, one may look upon Racine as a broken-down, hobbledehoy, perfumed individual – one may even be unable to read him; and I too may think him the same, as well as, in some respects, a subject for ridicule. Yet about him, Mr. Astley, there is a certain charm, and, above all things, he is a great poet – though one might like to deny it. Yes, the Frenchman, the Parisian, as a national figure, was in process of developing into a figure of elegance before we Russians had even ceased to be bears. The Revolution bequeathed to the French nobility its heritage, and now every whipper-snapper of a Parisian may possess manners, methods of expression, and even thoughts that are above reproach in form, while all the time he himself may share in that form neither in initiative nor in intellect nor in soul – his manners, and the rest, having come to him through inheritance. Yes, taken by himself, the Frenchman is frequently a fool of fools and a villain of villains. Per contra, there is no one in the world more worthy of confidence and respect than this young Russian lady. De Griers might so mask his face and play a part as easily to overcome her heart, for he has an imposing figure, Mr. Astley, and this young lady might easily take that figure for his real self – for the natural form of his heart and soul – instead of the mere cloak with which heredity has dowered him. And even though it may offend you, I feel bound to say that the majority also of English people are uncouth and unrefined, whereas we Russian folk can recognise beauty wherever we see it, and are always eager to cultivate the same. But to distinguish beauty of soul and personal originality there is needed far more independence and freedom than is possessed by our women, especially by our younger ladies. At all events, they need more *experience*. For instance, this Mlle. Polina – pardon me, but the name has passed my lips, and I cannot well recall it – is taking a very long time to make up her mind to prefer you to Monsieur de Griers. She may respect you, she may become your friend, she may open out her heart to you; yet over that heart there will be reigning that loathsome villain, that mean and petty usurer, De Griers. This will be due to obstinacy and self-love – to the fact that De Griers once appeared to her in the transfigured guise of a marquis, of a disenchanted and ruined liberal who was doing his best to help her family and the frivolous old General; and, although these transactions of his have since been exposed, you will find that the exposure has made no impression upon her mind. Only give her the De Griers of former days, and she will ask of you no more. The more she may detest the present De Griers, the more will she lament the De Griers of the past – even though the latter never existed but in her own imagination. You are a sugar refiner, Mr. Astley, are you not?"

"Yes, I belong to the well-known firm of Lovell and Co."

"Then see here. On the one hand, you are a sugar refiner, while, on the other hand, you are an Apollo Belvedere. But the two characters do not mix with one another. I, again, am not even a sugar refiner; I am a mere roulette gambler who has also served as a lacquey. Of this fact Mlle. Polina is probably well aware, since she appears to have an excellent force of police at her disposal."

"You are saying this because you are feeling bitter," said Astley with cold indifference. "Yet there is not the least originality in your words."

"I agree. But therein lies the horror of it all – that, how trepidation, playing ever mean and farcical my accusations may be, they are none the less *true*. But I am only wasting words."

"Yes, you are, for you are only talking nonsense!" exclaimed my companion – his voice now trembling and his eyes flashing fire. "Are you aware," he continued, "that wretched, ignoble, petty, unfortunate man though you are, it was at *her* request I came to Homburg, in order to see you, and to have a long, serious talk with you, and to report to her your feelings and thoughts and hopes – yes, and your recollections of her, too?"

"Indeed? Is that really so?" I cried – the tears beginning to well from my eyes. Never before had this happened.

"Yes, poor unfortunate," continued Astley. "She *did* love you; and I may tell you this now for the reason that now you are utterly lost. Even if I were also to tell you that she still loves you, you would none the less have to remain where you are. Yes, you have ruined yourself beyond redemption. Once upon a time you had a certain amount of talent, and you were of a lively disposition, and your good looks were not to be despised. You might even have been useful to your country, which needs men like you. Yet you remained here, and your life is now over. I am not blaming you for this – in my view all Russians resemble you, or are inclined to do so. If it is not roulette, then it is something else. The exceptions are very rare. Nor are you the first to learn what a taskmaster is yours. For roulette is not exclusively a Russian game. Hitherto, you have honourably preferred to serve as a lacquey rather than to act as a thief; but what the future may have in store for you I tremble to think. Now good-bye. You are in want of money, I suppose? Then take these ten louis d'or. More I shall not give you, for you would only gamble it away. Take care of these coins, and farewell. Once more, *take care* of them."

"No, Mr. Astley. After all that has been said I – "

"*Take care* of them!" repeated my friend. "I am certain you are still a gentleman, and therefore I give you the money as one gentleman may give money to another. Also, if I could be certain that you would leave both Homburg and the gaming-tables, and return to your own country, I would give you a thousand pounds down to start life afresh; but, I give you ten louis d'or instead of a thousand pounds for the reason that at the present time a thousand pounds and ten louis d'or will be all the same to you – you will lose the one as readily as you will the other. Take the money, therefore, and good-bye."

"Yes, I *will* take it if at the same time you will embrace me."

"With pleasure."

So we parted – on terms of sincere affection.

But he was wrong. If *I* was hard and undiscerning as regards Polina and De Griers, *he* was hard and undiscerning as regards Russian people generally. Of myself I say nothing. Yet – yet words are only words. I need to *act*. Above all things I need to think of Switzerland. Tomorrow, tomorrow – Ah, but if only I could set things right tomorrow, and be born again, and rise again from the dead! But no – I cannot. Yet I must show her what I can do. Even if she should do no more than learn that I can still play the man, it would be worth it. Today it is too late, but *tomorrow*. Yet I have a presentiment that things can never be otherwise. I have got fifteen louis d'or in my possession, although I began with fifteen gülden. If I were to play carefully at the start – But no, no! Surely I am not such a fool as that? Yet *why* should I not rise from the dead? I should require at first but to go cautiously and patiently and the rest would follow. I should require but to put a check upon my nature for one hour, and my fortunes would be changed entirely. Yes, my nature is my weak point. I have only to remember what happened to me some months ago at Roulettenberg, before my final ruin. What a notable instance that was of my capacity for resolution! On the occasion in question I had lost everything – everything; yet, just as I was leaving the Casino, I heard another gülden give a rattle in my pocket! "Perhaps I shall need it for a meal," I thought to myself; but a hundred paces further on, I changed my mind, and returned. That gülden I staked upon manque – and there *is* something in the feeling that, though one is alone, and in a foreign land, and far from one's own home and friends, and ignorant of whence one's next meal is to come, one is nevertheless staking one's very last coin! Well, I won the stake, and in twenty minutes had left the Casino with a hundred and seventy gülden in my pocket! That is a fact, and it shows what a last remaining gülden can do.... But what if my heart had failed me, or I had shrunk from making up my mind? ...

No; tomorrow all shall be ended!

READ THE MOST POPULAR ROYAL CLASSICS

20,000 Leagues Under the Sea BY JULES VERNE
A Christmas Carol BY CHARLES DICKENS
A Tale of Two Cities BY CHARLES DICKENS
Aesop's Fables BY AESOP
Alice in Wonderland BY LEWIS CARROLL
Anna Karenina BY LEO TOLSTOY
Anne of Green Gables BY LUCY MAUD MONTGOMERY
Around the World in 80 Days BY JULES VERNE
Black Beauty BY ANNA SEWELL
Candide BY VOLTAIRE
Common Sense BY THOMAS PAINE
Crime and Punishment BY FYODOR DOSTOEVSKY
Don Quixote BY MIGUEL DE CERVANTES
Dracula BY BRAM STOKER
Dubliners BY JAMES JOYCE
Emma BY JANE AUSTEN
Frankenstein BY MARY SHELLEY
Great Expectations BY CHARLES DICKENS
Grimm's Fairy Tales BY JAKOB AND WILHELM GRIMM
Gulliver's Travels BY JONATHAN SWIFT
Hamlet BY WILLIAM SHAKESPEARE
Heart of Darkness BY JOSEPH CONRAD
Jane Eyre BY CHARLOTTE BRONTË
Journey to the Center of the Earth BY JULES VERNE
Les Misérables BY VICTOR HUGO
Macbeth BY WILLIAM SHAKESPEARE
Meditations BY MARCUS AURELIUS
Middlemarch BY GEORGE ELIOT
Moby Dick BY HERMAN MELVILLE
Nicomachean Ethics BY ARISTOTLE
North and South BY ELIZABETH GASKELL
Northanger Abbey BY JANE AUSTEN
Notes from the Underground BY FYODOR DOSTOYEVSKY
Oliver Twist BY CHARLES DICKENS
On War BY CARL VON CLAUSEWITZ
Plato: Five Dialogues BY PLATO
Politics BY ARISTOTLE
Pride & Prejudice BY JANE AUSTEN
Robinson Crusoe BY DANIEL DEFOE
Sense & Sensibility BY JANE AUSTEN
Sons and Lovers BY D. H. LAWRENCE

ROYAL CLASSICS

Tarzan of the Apes by Edgar Rice Burroughs
Tess of the d'Urbervilles by Thomas Hardy
The Adventures of Huckleberry Finn by Mark Twain
The Adventures of Sherlock Holmes by A. Conan Doyle
The Adventures of Tom Sawyer by Mark Twain
The Art of War by Sun Tzu
The Brothers Karamazov by Fyodor Dostoevsky
The Call of the Wild by Jack London
The Count of Monte Cristo by Alexandre Dumas
The Hound of the Baskervilles by Arthur Conan Doyle
The Iliad by Homer
The Importance of Being Earnest by Oscar Wilde
The Jungle Book by Rudyard Kipling
The Last of the Mohicans by James Fenimore Cooper
The Lost World by Arthur Conan Doyle
The Metamorphosis by Franz Kafka
The Murder on the Links by Agatha Christie
The Mysterious Affair at Styles by Agatha Christie
The Odyssey by Homer
The Origin of Species by Charles Darwin
The Picture of Dorian Gray by Oscar Wilde
The Portrait of a Lady by Henry James
The Prince by Niccolò Machiavelli
The Prince and the Pauper by Mark Twain
The Prophet by Kahlil Gibran
The Republic by Plato
The Scarlet Letter by Nathaniel Hawthorne
The Secret Garden by Frances Hodgson Burnett
The Strange Case of Dr. Jekyll & Mr. Hyde by Robert Louis Stevenson
The Swiss Family Robinson by Johann David Wyss
The Tale of Peter Rabbit by Beatrix Potter
The Tenant of Wildfell Hall by Anne Brontë
The Three Musketeers by Alexandre Dumas
The Time Machine by H. G. Wells
The Wealth of Nations by Adam Smith
The Wind in the Willows by Kenneth Grahame
The Wizard of Oz by L. Frank Baum
This Side of Paradise by F. Scott Fitzgerald
Treasure Island by Robert Louis Stevenson
Ulysses by James Joyce
Vanity Fair by William Makepeace Thackeray
War and Peace by Leo Tolstoy
Wuthering Heights by Emily Brontë

www.ingramcontent.com/pod-product-compliance
Lightning Source LLC
Chambersburg PA
CBHW020913310726
48980CB00011B/861/J